Chapter

Springtime 2012

At first, when I found myself locked in Howard Carter's house for the night, I thought it must be an elaborate prank. A little later, when I smashed one of his pictures, I stopped seeing the funny side. Spending my holiday incarcerated in an Egyptian prison wasn't what I had in mind when I decided to spend a chunk of redundancy money on this trip.

Surely the place must be security wired or alarmed, have a night patrol, or a sensor, or something. Perhaps it did - on the outside - to stop intruders getting in. But I was already in; well and truly bolted in. And banging on the door roused only my own temper.

Ok, so tourist numbers were down in these post revolutionary days. But surely that was no reason to leave a prime - well, prime-ish - site unguarded. Admittedly Luxor has a lot of contenders for the epithet.

But these considerations were slow to dawn. I spent the first hour or so of solitude, in the darkening golden twilight, enjoying the place to myself in the sanguine certainty of being set free any moment. I pictured a gap-toothed Egyptian unlatching the door, wearing galabeya and turban. He'd be called Mohammed, or Ahmed - they all seem to be. He'd bow me out of the house, lovingly caressing the massive tip he'd earned for his part in the ruse; hard to blame him with visitors so far down. Dan would be there, grinning like an idiot. We'd all laugh. I'd be a gracious victim. A taxi would be waiting. Within half-an-hour I'd be in the bar of the Jolie Ville hotel, sipping a glass of Obelisk wine, happily conceding there was a moment back there I'd thought I was trapped for the night.

Dan, my other half, thinks himself a great practical joker. He's done everything from replacing toffee apples with toffee onions at Halloween, to buying Christmas cards with a repeatable sound loop, tearing off the activated sound device and hiding it inside his sister's curtain pole. Apparently the sound of sleigh bells jing-a-linging at 3am was enough to turn her off Christmas for life.

It's hard now to explain my initial certainty Dan was playing a trick on me. It seems totally illogical, when he'd spent the afternoon in a golf club on the East bank at Luxor, while I'd spent it traipsing around random tourist attractions on the West bank - and hadn't shared my tour plan with him in advance. All I can say is, he has form.

It wasn't beyond the bounds of imagining for him actually to have been trailing me all afternoon, with exactly this purpose in mind. Locking me in an empty tomb, say, would be precisely Dan's idea of holiday hilarity. He'd think nothing of forking out a hefty tip to the guard to turn the key.

Carter's Conundrums

by

Fiona Deal

Text copyright © 2012 Fiona Deal
All Rights Reserved

In Dan's eyes it wouldn't be bribery, simply his way of supporting the local economy.

You see, Dan loves a wind-up; I figure this mean's he's either a deeply tortured soul deserving of sympathy, or else he needs a vent for a ridiculously over-active imagination, and practical jokes are the best he can come up with. I'm sure there must be more constructive outlets for his creativity. You'd think with a mind like his he should be at the forefront of technological advancement, an Evangelist for Apple, an Imagineer for Disney or something. Instead he's an accountant, working for KPMG in Canary Wharf. Which perhaps explains everything!

I know he thinks I carry my fascination with Egypt too far. So he'd see shutting me up in Howard Carter's house for a couple of hours a justly punishment for the eons I'd spent jawing away at him about how staggering it all was.

In the spirit of defiance towards the twisted contortions of his psyche, I decided to enjoy it. So I set off on another tour of inspection, determined to make the most of my time alone before my diabolical boyfriend set me free.

I have to say they've done a fantastic job of turning the house into a museum. It's a fitting tribute to the man who lived there and contributed such a thrilling moment to history with the discovery of Tutankhamun's tomb. It's like entering a time capsule. I lost myself in the spine-tingling sensation of stepping back into the past, expecting Howard Carter himself to emerge from a doorway at every turn.

Seeing his grey fedora and panama hats hanging on the wall, as I'd seen then on his head in so many black-and-white photographs and film-clips, raised goose bumps. I pored over copies of his dig notes from the opening of the tomb, as well as manuscript letters and diaries. His writing was a largely indecipherable squiggle, but knowing it was the genuine article sent a shiver up my spine.

The furniture recreated the 1920's with no pretensions to comfort. The dècor might even be called Spartan. A lot of the mementos were Carter's own. I studied his typewriter and field telephone, his suitcases and shaving box, his record player and collection of 78's, even his easel, carefully set up in a corner.

Carter was an accomplished artist, producing beautiful watercolours of Nile flora, fauna and birdlife. According to the signage he originally came to Egypt as an artist, hired in 1891 to paint the artefacts discovered on archaeological digs.

Several of his works adorned the walls. I paused in his study to contemplate a series of watercolours of ducks. There was also a stunning detail of a temple-wall scene from Hatshepsut's temple, Deir el Bahri, showing Queen Ahmes being led to a chamber where she would give birth to Hatshepsut. It was autographed by Carter and dated 1896.

According to the legend beneath it, Carter originally painted the image for the purposes of scientific recording, but subsequently sold images like this to tourists.

I could see why they might want to buy them from him. The painting was exquisite in its simplicity. Just a head and shoulders image, Queen Ahmes was captured in profile, a Mona Lisa-like smile on her lips. A feathered crown encircled her head, protective wings fanning down to her shoulder, a vulture head rising from the centre of her brow. The painting was shaded in the softest pastel greens, blues, yellows, with small details in washed orange.

I moved on and found myself enthralled by the dark room. A tiny room, painted deep red, with black-and white photographs pinned up on a kind of washing line, and tall, dusty chemical bottles lining the shelves. It's where Harry Burton developed the more than 2000 photographs taken inside Tutankhamun's tomb. To my mind they're among the most absorbing pictures ever taken. His camera was there, an enormous box-like contraption on a stand, more like a bedside cabinet than a camera.

The whole experience reminded me of Carter's famous statement about Tutankhamun. "The mystery of his life still eludes us - the shadows move but the dark is never quite uplifted." It expressed perfectly how I felt wandering, in a bit of a dream, around Carter's house. The silence seemed to carry faint echoes of conversations that must once have taken place here; the atmosphere still charged with the excitement of discovery, of history in the making. I felt I could lift a veil on the past, somehow reach out and touch it. But the echoes and atmosphere shifted back to silence and stillness.

It was only when my mind drifted to the fabled story of a cobra sliding into Carter's house and killing his lucky canary, I started to slip towards anxiety. It dawned on me I was hungry. There was only a dribble of water left in the bottle I'd brought with me. I consoled myself with the sight if the toilet in the old-fashioned bathroom. I didn't yet need to test if it was in working condition. But, all things considered, the novelty of being alone here was definitely wearing off.

It was getting dark. And I was starting to worry; a niggling little pinprick voice asking if perhaps my entrapment wasn't a goofy prank after all. Unbelievably, I didn't even have my mobile phone with me. Usually the thing's attached to me like a limpet. But Dan had commandeered our only adaptor plug to charge his laptop last night. So I'd left my phone merrily charging on the bedside table when I left for my West Bank sightseeing trip.

I went back across the domed central chamber, through the entrance corridor, and rattled the door one more time, just to check Dan hadn't come and sneakily unlocked it while I was off on my time travels. Still firmly bolted.

I banged on it a bit more, as much to give myself something to do, as in any real hope of being heard; then slumped onto the bench under a poster board of Carter and his benefactor the Earl of Carnarvon. I stared at them for a while through the gloom. Two men standing stiffly posed for the camera, moustachioed, and in their tweeds, looking dapper, out-dated and vaguely uncomfortable in front of the tomb's enclosing wall.

How was it possible I'd been locked in with them? I wondered if they minded my company for the night; or if their ghosts preferred to reminisce on old times without an uninvited guest. If this wasn't one of Dan's more devious tricks, it dawned on me I was in trouble, and had the prospect of a very uncomfortable night ahead. I couldn't quite see myself bucking up the courage to slip under the covers of Howard Carter's bed, like a modern day Goldilocks, despite the availability of his bedroom.

Swallowing a little surge of panic, I mentally re-ran events leading up to my lock-in. It's fair to say I'd arrived at Carter's house much later than originally planned – although I failed to see how that accounted for my current predicament.

Dan and I had gone our separate ways for the afternoon.

We'd spent the morning lazing on sun-beds by the hotel infinity pool; Dan with his nose firmly stuck in the latest spy thriller; me, gazing across the Nile to the Theban Hills of the West Bank, mentally planning my afternoon's sightseeing. While Luxor is breathlessly hot in the afternoons, the sites are quieter. All the tourists on their pre-booked excursions and off the Nile cruise boats tend to do their visiting in the mornings. While tourist numbers are down, those that are here all seem to be doing their excursions en masse.

Dan and I had done the organised trips on a previous trip to Egypt. They're great as an introduction to the major archaeological and historical sites. But, as with all these things, they're a bit of a route march, with never enough time to just sit and contemplate the sheer immensity of everything - in both scale and the passage of time. And, of course, there's always the inevitable detour by way of the local alabaster factory, papyrus shop or perfume factory.

Dan's not the Egypt-freak I am. Having toured the cultural sites before, he has no real desire to do so again. He did tramp round Karnak with me the other day, craning his neck back to peer up at the forest of sandstone columns towering above us. He likes Karnak. He remembers seeing Roger Moore's James Bond darting around the place toting his gun in The Spy Who Loved Me. But he drew the line at a trip into the desert of the West Bank in temperatures approaching forty degrees to climb in and out of rock-cut tombs and scramble over what he calls, 'piles of rock'. By which he means the crumbled ruins of thousands-of-years-old temples.

I suppose I'm lucky he's here in Egypt with me at all. It wouldn't be his choice. He's more a fly-drive-around-America type. But Egypt's so brilliantly affordable at the moment, with the political situation so unsettled. And, this being my post-redundancy 'time-out' holiday, he gave in with good grace and came along for the chill-out-and-get-a-suntan experience.

His plan for the afternoon was to head to Luxor golf course. How playing golf in the hammering Egyptian heat is preferable to shade hopping at the sites, I can't imagine. But I've found it's best to keep these thoughts to myself. So, armed with a huge bottle of water, straw sun-hat, camera and my guidebook, I'd set off on my own.

Once deposited by the ferry on the West Bank, I'd planned to hire a taxi to take me to the sites. But there was a welcome breeze blowing, and I fancied the feel of the wind on my face. So I hired a scooter.

I make it sound so easy. Actually it was a feat of heated negotiation akin to a stand-up fight. But I've become quite adept at the haggling lark. The scooter-man's opening price was 4000 L.E. This approximates to £470. My starting position was a fiver. Twenty minutes of fun-and-games later, I handed over my 220 L.E. (about £25), and he handed me a broken crash helmet and a rusty scooter key. I'm not sure which of us came out of the bargain better. I'd been accused of taking the food from his family's mouths, and the roof from over their heads. But by the time we shook hands, he was calling me 'my queen', and telling me I looked like Nefertiti. This is patently untrue. So I gather I must have over-paid him.

It took me a little while to get the hang of the scooter, which kept stalling. Sand in the engine, I suppose. It gets everywhere. But soon enough I was chugging and backfiring my way towards the ticket office where I stopped to buy my ticket for Howard Carter's House. Then I turned right to take the road along the foothills of the buff-coloured Theban cliffs, deciding to visit the Valley of the Kings first.

It took about fifteen minutes of noisy, dusty scootering to get there. I paid the entrance fee, relinquished my camera, ran the gauntlet of the street vendors, and took potluck on which tombs were open.

I spent a happy time exploring the tombs of Horemheb, Merenptah and Ramses III; caught up in the romance and intrigue of their stories: Horemheb, the fiction writer's favourite candidate as murderer of Tutankhamun; Merenptah, thirteenth son of Ramses II, succeeding only because his father lived into his nineties; and Ramses III, alleged murder victim of a harem conspiracy.

I know it might sound strange to be fascinated by people who've been dead for thousands of years. But something about Pharaonic Egypt has me captivated. I have no interest in learning to read hieroglyphics, or knowing more than the popular mythology about the Egyptian Pantheon of gods and goddesses. But ever since my first trip, when I gazed wide-eyed at the Tutankhamun treasure in the Cairo museum, I've read just about everything I can lay my hands on about the golden age of the pharaohs.

So, it was with my head full of the personalities of this golden empire that I reclaimed my camera, sliced a determined path through the inevitable market traders and turned the scooter back towards the Nile.

The sun was already sinking behind me in a blaze of hothouse colours as I sputtered towards Howard Carter's house. I was much later than planned, delayed I guess by the decision to opt for the scooter over a taxi, and my complete absorption in the tombs. I glanced at my watch; glad to see I still had time to visit, despite the approach of closing time.

The staff member on entry-duty was distracted from my arrival by two taxi-drivers jabbering in Arabic at the top of their lungs and gesticulating wildly just outside the doorway. I'm not sure what the problem was, but it was causing consternation to all concerned. There was only one taxi in the car park, and both drivers were stabbing their fingers towards it, the volume of their shouting rising to fever pitch. So I guess there was some dispute over passengers, or fares, or rental, or something similar. Barely breaking off to take the entrance ticket from me, tear off the perforated edge and hand it back, the poor harassed attendant hardly acknowledged me as I stepped over the threshold. He was remonstrating with the pair, gesticulating for them to leave almost as wildly as they were waving their arms around at each other.

I have to say I was rather pleased about this at the time. Sometimes in these places the attendants latch onto you and accompany your every footstep; then hold out their hand for the ubiquitous baksheesh. I wanted to be free to wander round unhindered and soak up the atmosphere.

Reluctantly, I decided this meant I couldn't ask him to switch on the hologram presentation of Howard Carter describing his discovery of Tutankhamun's tomb. The Trip Advisor reviews said it was very good. But glancing again at my watch, and knowing it lasted about twenty minutes, I knew I was running too short on time anyway.

I smiled a greeting a couple of tourists leaving as I entered, exchanging raised eyebrows at the noise of the thunderous argument going on outside. Then I paused to study the photographs and information boards about Howard Carter and Lord Carnarvon in the entrance hallway.

Emerging from the hallway, I entered the dome-ceilinged centre of the house. Rooms branched off in all directions. The cool breezes blowing through were wonderful, after the melting heat of outside, although it wasn't clear where they were coming from, as most of the windows and shutters were closed. There was no one else there.

I enjoyed wandering around on my own, minutely observing the photographs and the collection of writings on the desk in Carter's study. I wandered into the 1920's style kitchen and wondered how on earth people really cooked on those original gas stoves, and kept things cold in the odd little box-like refrigerator. And I stood for a long time at the shuttered window in Carter's bedroom, squinting through the slats at the dying glow of sunset behind the Valley of the Kings. I imagined Carter himself standing in exactly the same spot, and felt myself go all goose-bumpy.

A glance at my watch told me it was already past closing time. The light was fading beyond radiant sunset into deep golden twilight. I was alone in Howard Carter's house and it was getting dark. It was time to go.

And that's when I'd discovered I was trapped.

I couldn't believe they'd locked up and left without doing a last tour of inspection to check all visitors had gone. I know the attendant was distracted when I arrived, but surely he hadn't failed to clock me altogether. Crazily, it seemed so. Only one other explanation presented itself as I mentally trawled through the possibilities with darkness settling all around me. Perhaps, on his tour of inspection, he'd poked his head into Carter's bedroom at the precise moment I'd ducked under the bed; so failed to spot me.

This seemed to be stretching incredulity to the limit. I remembered I'd pulled my camera from my bag to take a snap of Carter's shaving box, and my bangle caught on the strap. It slipped off my wrist, dropped to the floor and rolled under the bed. I'd scrambled under to retrieve it. It wasn't a very big bed. And I doubt I was on my hands and knees on the floor more than a few seconds. But other than that, I'd surely been in plain sight the whole time, had anyone come looking.

But whatever the explanation, the simple fact was the attendant had locked up and left, and I was trapped inside.

The certainty it was a goofy hoax was gone. The scooter-man was no doubt hopping up and down thinking I'd robbed him of the useless piece of junk. Dan was probably itching for a lager, and cursing my lateness. But give it another hour or so and he'd have no choice but to conclude something had happened to me. Assuming I really was incarcerated for the night, I'd have some serious explaining to do when they came to unbolt the place in the morning.

It got very dark for a while. I sat with my knees drawn up on the bench, resting my head forward on my folded arms, feeling a bit pathetic. Then I noticed a shaft of pale light across the floor. The moon was up. It sent silver darts through the slatted windows, piercing the shadows with pale monochrome light; easily bright enough to see by, with eyes already accustomed to the inky blackness of night time.

I did another slow tour of the house, testing all the windows. In Carter's study, I was rewarded. The latch lifted and the tall window swung open towards me. My heart skipped a beat. But the ray of hope died quickly. The wooden shutters were well and truly bolted. I could see the bolt, up at picture-rail height, beyond my reach in these high-ceilinged rooms.

I pulled a chair over to the window. Admittedly, it looked a little fragile. I guess it was almost antique after all. I tested it, then gingerly stepped up on it. It held. I tugged on the bolt. Nothing. So I tugged harder. Surely they must open the damn things sometimes, even if only for cleaning. It refused to budge. So I shifted my position, put all my strength into it, and shoved. Easy, with the benefit of hindsight, isn't it, to see the inevitable outcome?

The chair splintered beneath me. I grabbed at the opened window frame, swung backwards, suspended momentarily, then crashed downwards, slamming into the desk, before hitting the floor. The desk skidded across the floor and ploughed into the wall. There was a frozen moment of silence, then the ear-splitting, heart-wrenching explosion of shattering glass, as the lamp bounced off the desk, and one of the wall mounted pictures splintered and smashed to the tiled floor.

17

Winded, I lay motionless a moment. Horror descended. I heaved myself up to survey the damage, feeling sick and shaky, and testing for bruises. Goddammit, not only was I locked up in this mausoleum, I was hell-bent on wrecking the joint.

I collected up the chair fragments; then righted the desk, pushing it back to an approximation of its original position, straightening the bits and pieces on top with nerveless fingers. Cold sweat broke out all over me. I pictured myself, handcuffed and head-bowed, my image satellite-beamed into homes across the planet, accused of defiling this historically significant place.

The lampstand was relatively unscathed, although it's glass shade was in smithereens. But what really knocked the breath from me was picking up the broken picture frame, shards of glass sticking out at all angles, turning it over, and seeing Carter's beautiful watercolour of Queen Ahmes staring up at me.

I sank onto the floor, knees too weak to hold me up. Before, I'd just had some explaining to do. Now I potentially faced charges of criminal damage.

I think I may have sat there like that for quite a long time. I have no idea really. Just that, eventually, my muscles started to cramp. I dragged myself out of the terrified torpor I'd dropped into, and set myself to completing the task of clearing up.

I used my canvas bag to sweep the broken glass into a neat pile under the open window; then turned my attention to the painting.

The frame was a goner. Totally fractured, the wood split apart, glass falling out all over. So I carefully eased the picture from the frame, holding my breath, working at snail's pace in case the paper caught on a sliver of glass and tore. Eventually it was free. I rested it on my open palms a moment, admiring it in the moonlight. I had no idea if it was the original. But it was a moment of reverence, none the less. I might actually be holding in my hands an authentic Carter artwork. Something he'd touched, created, autographed, more than a century ago.

It was as I went to lay it carefully on the desktop I realised it wasn't a single sheet, but a longer roll of paper, folded in half along the top edge. This became apparent as a smaller piece of paper fluttered out from between the folds.

I rescued it from the floor, and carried it towards the window to see it better in the moonlight. It felt a teensy bit brittle, and looked vaguely yellowed around the edges - hard to tell without proper light. There was a squiggly line of writing across the top. It looked familiar, the same indecipherable scrawl I'd been studying earlier. I'm no graphologist, but it looked like Carter's handwriting to me. There were four words in ink. I couldn't make them out in the darkness, although the third word might have been 'equal'.

The rest of the page was covered in what looked like columns of drawings. It didn't need a degree in Egyptology to deduce these were hieroglyphics; scratchy looking birds, feathers, snakes and suchlike. But I'm no Champollion; so decoding them was beyond me.

Staring, somewhat bemused and transfixed, at this strange find, a car horn honked outside. I jumped violently. Headlight beams sliced across the ceiling. This was followed by the sound of slamming doors, raised voices and torchlight bouncing down the pathway outside.

Don't ask me what flight of madness, or instinct, or guilty conscience made me shove the slip of paper into my pocket. I've not been able to adequately justify it to myself. The closest thing I can compare it to is that moment you've got your hand in the sweetie jar and the door opens, bathing you in harsh caught-in-the-act-ness. The urge to hide the evidence was just too overwhelming to deny.

Casting one last look at the havoc I'd wrought in Carter's study - there really was no way to hide it - I made my way, on rather wobbly legs, across the domed vestibule towards the entrance door.

A key crunched in the lock, and the door swung open. Four men stood staring at me through the gloom. I recognised three of them; the one wearing the sweat-stained galabeya - owner of the runaway scooter; the Nubian-looking one who'd earlier absent-mindedly taken my ticket from me at this very doorway; and the one in Chinos and the Ralph Lauren shirt, with the rather forbidding frown, who was my boyfriend.

'Bloody Hell Meredith.' The clue to Dan's mood wasn't so much in the expletive, as in his use of my name. He calls me Merry, or more usually Pinkie. He fondly imagines it's rather cute. 'What in God's name do you think you're playing at? I've been going out of my mind!'

I don't know if the other three minded the reference to God. They were studying me much as I imagine a mongoose might study a snake, as if unsure who had the upper hand.

The fourth man stepped forward. He was clearly the one in authority here. If the uniform and black beret didn't give it away, the gun swinging from the belt holding in his ample stomach was clue enough. Tourist police, I gathered. He spoke in heavily accented English, 'Meezder Fledger, dis eez Meez Peenk?'

'It is,' Dan snapped.

Everyone started talking at once; me included. I, of course, was defending myself hotly in the face of Dan's bad temper. 'For God's sake, woman! I thought you'd been kidnapped, or worse! They've been holding tourists for ransom at roadblocks on the Sinai Peninsular on and off for weeks. There's been a revolution, you know! Or has it somehow escaped your attention? You need to pull that head of yours out of bloody la-la pharaoh-land and start noticing what's going on around you in the twenty-first century. And another thing! You waltzed off for your afternoon's sightseeing without even taking your mobile phone with you! Just how stupid are you? Anything could have happened!'

This while, to judge from their raised voices and urgent gesticulations, a similar cat-and-mouse exchange was going on between the police officer and house attendant. While I didn't understand a word of what was being said as their heated exchange was conducted in rapid Arabic, the officer was clearly firing accusations and the attendant was vehemently denying everything, all the while casting me suspicious and hostile glances; as if I might have somehow sneaked in when his back was turned, just to get him in trouble.

'I didn't mean to get locked in!' I shouted, wondering just how I'd turned from the victim to the villain of the piece within a heartbeat of being set free. 'I thought you were playing one of your blasted tricks on me! Let's face it; this wouldn't be the first time on holiday I've fallen victim to the bizarre workings of your brain! What about that time in Tanzania when you paid the ranger to pretend we'd run out of petrol – remember? We were sitting in an open sided jeep in the middle of a pride of lions! And it was only last year, on that cruise, you arranged for the taxi driver to drop us at the wrong dock after an excursion and managed to convince me the cruise ship had left port without us!' It did nothing for my self-esteem to recall that both times I fell for his shenanigans hook, line and two weighted sinkers.

'Don't be ridiculous,' Dan snapped. 'This isn't the same thing at all. On both those occasions, I was with you. I fail to see how you can accuse me of locking you in here when I was at a golf course on the other side of the river!'

It was the scooter man who cut into the furious crossfire to tug at my sleeve, peer into my face and say, 'You okaay, my queen?' So, to give full credit where it's due, it seemed he might be genuinely concerned for my welfare, not just his noisy rust-bucket of a scooter. I told you I'd overpaid him.

The volume subsided a bit, but everyone kept talking, mostly in English now - some of it rather faulty - but clearly enough so I could piece together the evening's events.

Dan summarised the essential points, his voice pitched thankfully a few decibels lower than before. 'This shopkeeper chappie raised the alarm with the authorities when you didn't return with his scooter.' He nodded at the scooter-man, who bowed and grinned a broken-toothed acknowledgement of his part in instigating my rescue. 'I reported you missing at about the same time. The officer here deduced your description fitted both scenarios.' I glanced at the large, rotund figure of the policeman, and he, too, nodded and flashed his dark eyes to confirm Dan's story. 'So we all joined forces and started scouring the tourist sites of the West bank searching for the scooter, or perhaps you, lying by the roadside.'

I wondered what it was about that pitiful excuse for a bike that aroused such manly zeal, not really appreciating Dan's dry attempt at humour. Unfortunately it seemed they'd worked south-to-north, fruitlessly scouting out the temple of Medinet Habu, the ancient worker's village of Deir el Medina, the Valley of the Queens, the crumbled Ramesseum, Hatshepsut's mortuary temple and that of Seti I before stopping by Howard Carter's house en route to the Valley of the Kings. So I guess I could see how they'd worked themselves into a stew.

'We were just about to turn along the road to the Valley when the officer here spotted the scooter parked by the grassy verge,' Dan confirmed.

'So you darted off to rouse the house attendant here from his getting-ready-for-bed routine, so you could return brandishing a key!' I deduced, flashing a glance at the attendant, still glaring at me with a brooding menace I found a bit hard to take.

'Yes,' Dan said. 'Exactly that.'

'Why the hell didn't you knock on the door or a window to let me know you'd found me?' I demanded curtly. 'It might have saved me my attempt to demolish the study! Honestly! Men!' I knew I had to own up to it sooner or later, and trying to turn the tables on them to apportion a bit of the blame seemed as good a way as any to do it.

Four pairs of eyes narrowed on my face with varying degrees of alarm.

'Ok Meredith; what have you done?'

I didn't feel quite so defiant as I led them towards Howard Carter's study. Shame-faced would be more like it. I was also fighting down nauseating embarrassment, forcibly confronted with a mortifying example of my own stupidity when the officer stepped past me into the hallway, reached for a switch and snapped on the overhead light, flooding the space with harsh electric brightness. In all the hours I'd been incarcerated, it never once occurred to me to look for a light switch! What a numskull!

We entered the study. Predictably, the house attendant took one look, and threw up his hands in horror. Casting me an evil glance that put his others in the shade, he started up a racket of wailing, protesting his defence more volubly than ever.

The officer took it all in at a glance, barked for silence, and sent the poor excitable man off to conduct an impromptu inventory to ensure I hadn't destroyed anything else. I submitted to the ignominy of turning out the contents of my canvas bag onto the desk.

But other than these precautionary measures, the situation was accepted at face value. After a bit more back-biting between me and Dan – he felt an irrepressible need to castigate me loudly and, in my view, unfairly, for not sitting demurely waiting to be rescued - the fingers of blame were set aside. The obvious conclusion was the one reached. I had inadvertently been shut up in Howard Carter's house by the whimsy of chance, bad luck and worse timing. It seems I really must have ducked under the bed to retrieve my bangle at the precise moment the attendant checked the bedroom. He apparently failed to spot the scooter in the car park because I'd parked it behind a convenient bush.

I gave my contact details to the police officer and reassured him I would, of course, pay for the damage. Dan dispensed generous amounts of baksheesh all round. The scooter-man - Mohammed it turned out - grinned his way outside to the car park, treated me to a flamboyant bow fitting for his queen, hoisted the skirts of his galabeya around his knees and, accepting the rusty key and broken crash helmet from me, leapt onto the scooter and zipped away. I was just opening my mouth to protest the suspicious lack of engine noise, when the scooter backfired mightily from the gate. I cannot tell you how much better this made me feel.

The house attendant - Mohammed it turned out - mollified by the quantity of notes in his hand, muttered one last half-hearted and unintelligible imprecation in my direction, and trudged off. I gathered from this he lived somewhere close by.

Ahmed, the police officer, now all smiles and flashing dark eyes at the prospect of the great story he had to tell, waved us towards his car and gave us a lift back to our hotel.

Dan ticked me off the whole way. This was a bit of moral high ground too good to step down from quickly. I concentrated on the thought of the omelette I planned to order from room service, and kidded myself I hadn't half-inched the slip of paper now burning a hole in my pocket.

Chapter 2

Discretion definitely being the better part of valour, next day I decided not to provoke Dan's ire, and reconciled myself to a day without sightseeing. In fairness, this was no great sacrifice. The Jolie Ville is a fantastic place to wile away a few holiday hours.

We'd done the inevitable post mortem the night before. Dan was in no frame of mind to see the funny side, or concede my reasoning for initially suspecting him of skulduggery. It seemed my disappearing act really had scared him. And he wasn't that happy about the amount he'd shelled out in baksheesh either.

But things settled back into their normal perspective in the soft, warm light of a new day. Other than needing to fork out a few quid for a new 1920's lampshade and a picture frame to restore Queen Ahmes to her rightful place on the wall, no real harm was done. So we made friends, and I accepted the penance of keeping my head in the twenty-first century for the day. Although, quite how I'd ended up cast as the guilty party in all this, I'm not sure. The left-behind mobile phone I daresay. I admit it was dumb.

We had a leisurely breakfast outside on the terrace overlooking the dark, shifting waters of the Nile, absently watching kingfishers darting in and out of the reeds; and feeding titbits of croissant to the visiting heron stalking between the tables.

The Jolie Ville has a small on-site zoo, and we'd promised ourselves a visit. So mid-morning we wandered through the grounds and waved at Mohammed, one of the zookeepers, as we arrived. We'd already met Mohammed. He had the daily task of leading Ramses the camel around the hotel grounds to entice guests for rides. We'd already succumbed to the novelty, not to say indignity of this. We'd both clambered onto Ramses' back, (one at a time, I hasten to add, not wanting to over burden the poor creature - Dan weighs nearly fifteen stone after all), clinging on to the pommel for dear life while he lurched us violently backwards and forwards in the threat-to-life-and-limb-act of getting to his feet. Once up, it's relatively plain sailing - easy to see why camels earned the tag ships of the desert. The rolling motion takes a bit of getting used to, and it's further off the ground than it looks, but it's tremendous fun.

We spent a pleasant hour in the zoo. It's really a children's petting zoo, with donkeys, a pen with sheep and goats mixed together, a huge family of floppy-eared rabbits, a bunch of tortoises, a couple of banana-snatching monkeys, and two truly evil-looking red-eyed pelicans. I don't imagine children are encouraged to do too much petting of them! Ramses the camel, tethered sans saddle, was taking a break from giving rides, shading himself under a wide

29

canopy. We treated him to a couple of oranges pilfered from breakfast, and posed for a couple of holiday snaps.

But already I could feel myself growing restless. I'd folded the scrap of paper inside my passport, secreted inside the safe in our room. There'd been no time to study it properly. While Dan was in the shower I'd frowned over the short line of squiggly writing. I was pretty sure it read, 'Find my equal here'. But the ink was faded, and Howard Carter's handwriting - if Howard Carter's handwriting it was - was not the easiest in the world to read. As for the hieroglyphics, I'd barely had time to give them more than a cursory glance, enough only to admire the skilled way they were drawn.

The temperature was hitting the forties again. So we wandered back to our room and donned our swimming gear. The lure of the swimming pool was too strong to resist. We had a choice of three pools. There's an adults only pool where they pipe classical music at sunset – all very civilised. And a huge new infinity pool near the recently developed part of the hotel. But the newly planted palm trees haven't reached maturity yet, and the glare of the sun is ferocious. So we preferred the original infinity pool, with its spectacular view across to the Theban hills, and plenty of shade - even though it meant a trek to the far side of the island. I may not have mentioned the Jolie Ville's situated on an island, and oasis of tranquillity away from the hustle and bustle of Luxor. The walk to the further off pool is really no trouble, as the hotel gardens are beautiful, maintained by a veritable army of gardeners.

We spent a happy time generally being holidaymakers on holiday, splashing about and hanging onto the infinity edge, gazing across the river, watching the Nile cruise boats glide by.

Dan was back to his usual carefree self. But I was finding it increasingly hard to relax. We flopped onto sun-loungers, pulling them deep into the shade of one of the wicker umbrellas surrounding the pool. Dan lost himself in his spy novel straight away. I lay there all fidgety, watching a hawk riding the shimmering heat haze against the densely blue sky. He looked for all the world like the falcon-God Horus surveying his kingdom.

I was itching to take a proper look at the scrap of paper I'd misappropriated. One moment I was swamped with a fiery flush of shame for walking off with it so brazenly. I couldn't imagine what had come over me. I'm not usually given to kleptomania. The next I was burning with curiosity about how and why an antique-looking scrap of paper covered with hieroglyphic squiggles should end up hidden between the folds of a painting. It was a hot business all round.

A gentle snore alerted me Dan had fallen asleep. Once out, he's usually comatose for ages. It pretty much takes a klaxon to wake him. You should hear the god-awful noise his alarm clock makes. I wouldn't wish it as a punishment on my worst enemy. There are lots of very sound reasons why Dan and I maintain our separate homes, despite being together ten years. His alarm clock is definitely towards the top of the list.

The Jolie Ville's not known for its klaxons. I watched him a moment; then gently poked him in the ribs. He snorted appealingly, but didn't wake up.

It didn't take me too long to nip back to our room and extract the small sheet of paper from the safe. I smoothed it out and stared long and hard at it. It offered up no secrets. So I pulled my laptop from the drawer, powered it up and Googled "howard carter handwriting". I struck gold at the first search. A few clicks of the mouse later I was consulting scanned copies of Carter's diaries and excavation journals. I compared them with the scrap of paper beside me. While a lot of this scratchy early twentieth century writing looks much the same to me, pretty much regardless of author, I was fairly sure I was looking at the same hand.

I'd been reasonably certain of it in the moonlight back in Carter's study, having spent so long poring over the extracts of his notes and letters displayed there. Now I was close to definite. But no closer to knowing what it meant.

I allowed myself the diversion of reading through the transcripts from the 1922 season of excavation on the website. It was stirring stuff. Carter arrived in Luxor on

Friday 27 October 1922. His notes for Wednesday 1 November say, 'Commenced operations in the Valley of the Kings.' He goes on in a short paragraph to describe clearing ancient stone huts of the necropolis workmen from around the entrance to the tomb of Ramses VI.

A breath-taking three days later, on Saturday 4 November, his diary reads simply, 'First steps of tomb found.' The next day, his entry is a masterpiece of understated brevity, 'Discovered tomb under tomb of Ramses VI. Investigated same & found seals intact'.

Wow! Can you imagine the buzz he must have felt? His scanty one-line journal entries definitely don't convey it. But in a separate ring-binder titled 'Notes, Diary, and Articles, Referring to the Theban Royal Necropolis and the Tomb of Tutankhamun' - and probably written a little later - Carter made extended records, also written in ink in his own hand. These were also scanned and transcribed on the website.

I skim-read the entry for the same date, Sunday 5 November 1922 - fireworks night, appropriately enough. I'll bet he felt like letting off a few fireworks of his own that night.

He described how towards sunset they'd cleared down to the level of the twelfth step. This was enough to expose a large part of the upper portion of a plastered and sealed doorway. Carter concluded this was evidence enough to show it really was an entrance to a tomb. From the outward appearance of the seals, he considered it to be intact. At that stage, he had no idea whose tomb he'd found, although he deduced from the seal impressions it was somebody important.

He recorded how he noticed some cement-like plaster had fallen away at the top of the doorway. So, to check it out he made a small hole, shone a torch through, and saw the passage beyond was completely filled, floor to ceiling, with stones and rubble.

Again, this looked like good news, evidence of something deserving of some effort to seal it up. He wrote, "It was a thrilling moment for an excavator, quite alone save his native staff of workmen, to suddenly find himself, after so many years of toilsome work, on the verge of what looked like a magnificent discovery - an untouched tomb." I'll bet!

But despite his excitement, the smallness of the entrance puzzled him. It didn't measure up to other royal tombs in the Valley. He debated whether he'd found the tomb of a noble, buried there by royal consent, or perhaps royal cache. He stated, "As far as my investigations had gone there was absolutely nothing to tell me."

Had he dug on a few more inches, he'd have found the seal impressions showing Tutankhamun's insignia distinctly. But it was getting late, night had fallen, the full moon had risen high in the eastern sky, so he refilled the excavation for protection and returned home to cable to Lord Carnarvon (then in England) the following message:-

"At last have made wonderful discovery in Valley; a magnificent tomb with seals intact; re-covered same for your arrival; congratulations "

Something about this cable made me pause and reflect.

Two words bothered me, 'wonderful' and 'magnificent'. I could certainly see how it must have been wonderful to discover anything at all in the Valley, especially as I knew he'd spent long years searching. But with everything he'd already stated about his doubts re what he'd found - the puzzling issue of the smallness of the entrance, the possibility it was a cache - how did he dare be so confident as to describe it as 'a magnificent tomb'?

The possibility he'd written the whole thing up later, including both his conjecture about what he might be about to find, with his certain knowledge of what he found in reality - a magnificent tomb by anyone's reckoning - couldn't apply to the cable. The date he sent it was fixed to 5 November, weeks before the tomb was opened.

Magnificent. It's an adjective of towering proportions. Why did he need to apply an epithet at all? Surely describing it simply as a tomb - or even an excavated doorway - with seals intact was enough to have Carnarvon rushing to book passage on the next steamer from England

35

to Egypt. Especially since a doorway and blocked entrance passage were, in reality, all he'd unearthed so far. It seemed a risky business to over-egg the find at this early stage, incurring the distinct possibility the egg would end up all over him.

I puzzled over it a bit more, then gave up, accepting the clairvoyance of his prediction would forever remain one of life's unanswerable mysteries. It was totally irrelevant now anyway. The simple fact is Carter did discover a magnificent tomb. He's always been one of my heroes because of it.

Now I'd established to my reasonable satisfaction the handwriting on the scrap of paper I'd nicked was probably Carter's, I turned my attention to the hieroglyphics.

There was what appeared to be six densely packed columns of the picture language squeezed onto the page, under Carter's four-word header. He certainly was a man given to paucity of words.

I Googled hieroglyphics, which led to a few more minutes' diversion, while I happily converted my name and Dan's into the picture language through a nifty online device known as the alphabet translator.

I'd been aware hieroglyphics suffered a lack of vowels. My name has rather a lot of them. So I was a bit miffed when the e's and i's in Meredith Pink returned a surfeit of reeds. Dan Fletcher was slightly less abundant; as it appears only e's and i's have been given, confusingly, the same reed emblem.

I downloaded a copy of the alphabet; then turned back to the crowded pictograms on the page beside me. Several frustrating moments later, I conceded the translation of hieroglyphics would not be the work of moments. Very little on the typewriter alphabet resembled the sophisticated complexity of the inked images in front of me. They were in columns, for one thing, not nice neat lines I could follow.

I took my hat off to Jean-Francois Champollion. How the hell he made sense of hieroglyphics in the first place, with only the Rosetta stone to help him, was beyond my comprehension. Some people have genius. It's as simple - and as awesome - as that.

I glanced at my watch, and realised I'd been mucking about on the computer for nearly an hour. The Internet must surely be the best time wasting device of the early twenty-first century. It's possible to lose hours, weeks, days, of your life surfing away. These are hours, weeks and days we can never get back to turn to anything more productive. But I'm not complaining. Some of the most productive times of my life have been spent happily zipping about the web - particularly if you're willing to suspend disbelief and view my thirst for most things Egyptian as productive. I suspect Dan would say I was stretching it a bit.

I plugged my laptop in to charge and wondered what to do next. I was determined to make some sense of the hieroglyphics. So I copied the first column onto the helpfully provided hotel notepad. When I say 'copied', please allow me some artistic license. I'm no artist. Presuming Howard Carter fashioned the originals, he most certainly was.

I locked up the scrap of paper in the safe again, and took a stroll to the small parade of gift shops in the reception building of the Jolie Ville. There were two books on Egyptian hieroglyphics to choose from. So I selected the one looking least like the 'for dummies' version - Carter was certainly not that - and headed back to the sun lounger and my slumbering boyfriend.

The first chapter of my newly purchased book was enough to further embed my admiration for Champollion. I've never been much good at languages. My Dad's always joked I speak only two: English and Rubbish! Unbelievably, I have an A'level in French. But this was a total cheat. A hefty part of it was made up, not of spoken, written, or translated French, but of writing essays on French literature. How bizarre is that? I guess they seriously thought they were teaching us something. But all I did was read English translations of Jean-Paul Sartre's' 'Les Jeux Sont Faits' and Henri Queffélec's 'Un Recteur de l'île de Sein', then write about them in English for the exam. For a girl who would go on to spend fifteen years of her career taking information from others and writing about it as a PR and Communications officer, this was no great challenge. But did it teach me so speak French? No.

I'd brought the Jolie Ville notepaper with me, with my abominably copied apologies for hieroglyphics on it. So I set about trying to match up anything I'd copied with anything I could find flipping the pages in the book.

I was gnawing my pencil and frowning over a particularly impenetrable combination of a circle, a squiggle and a bird, when a familiar voice near my elbow interrupted my concentration to ask, 'Pinkie, what are you doing?'

I decided a statement of the bloomin' obvious was probably my safest response. 'I'm trying to learn to read hieroglyphics.'

Dan has a wonderful repertoire of facial expressions. The one he treated me to now was a study in pained patience. 'Forgive me for asking, but why?'

This didn't present quite such an easy response. So I shrugged. This was meant to convey a kind of seemed-like-a-good-idea-at the time nonchalance.

'Yes, well judging by the frown on your face, you're not enjoying it much. You know, Pink; you're supposed to have fun on holiday. If you can't just kick back and read a trashy novel or something, your time might be better spent planning your next career move. I'm not sure I see how studying a language that's been dead for millennia is going to stand you in good stead for getting a new job.'

I wasn't too sure I liked the hectoring tone of this. 'I am having fun,' I protested. 'And besides, I don't have to make a decision right away. If I choose to spend a few hours trying to read hieroglyphics rather than the latest blockbuster, who are you to argue?'

He sidestepped this neatly by reaching across from his sun-lounger to mine for the scrap of Jolie Ville notepaper. He frowned at it. 'Are you teaching yourself to write them too? If so, I don't recommend you take it up as the new day job. You're not very good, are you?'

I poked my tongue out at him, and he grinned. As I said, he loves winding me up. He studied my appallingly transcribed stick drawings again, 'What's it supposed to say anyway?'

'I don't know. That's what I'm trying to figure out.'

His expression this time told me the workings of my tiny mind were so remote from his comprehension as to be beyond strange, probably somewhere closer to alien, and of some weird subspecies, come to that.

'Pinkie, the things you like doing in the name of escapism are completely beyond me.' Proof my interpretation of his facial contortions was spot on.

Refusing to dignify this with a response, I stuck the pencil back in my mouth and chewed on it some more, flipping forward another few pages in the book.

'So if you're using that book to translate them, where'd you copy them from in the first place?'

'Why the sudden interest?' I parried. 'You're not usually bothered with anything Egyptian beyond the certainty of good weather.'

'I was just having second thoughts about your career options. If you're seriously into all this ancient relic stuff, maybe you should go to college and study it properly. You could work in a museum, or for a publishing company writing travel guides or something. There must be other odd-balls like you out there who'll pay good money to read up on this dead stuff.'

You see; Dan really can be awfully sweet. And the trouble with that was it made me want to confide in him.

So I put the book down and twisted round to face him. 'If I tell you why I'm trying to translate those hieroglyphics,' I nodded at the notepaper still in his hand, do you promise not to over react?'

His expression promised nothing. Was suddenly quite forbidding, in fact. Certainly wary, and a bit resigned to hearing something he'd probably prefer not to. But it was too late now. So I told him there was more to the smashed picture of Queen Ahmes than just the broken glass. It was

41

always going to be just a matter of time before I admitted all to him. I tell Dan everything. Generally whether he wants to hear it or not.

'So, let me get this straight,' he said when I'd finished telling the story. 'You walked out of Howard Carter's house last night with a bit of paper in your pocket that may or may not contain Carter's handwriting, that may or may not have been put in the picture frame by Carter himself, that may or may not be of historical significance; but which was definitely not yours to take. And you did this right under the nose of a local police officer. Oh, and at a time of political and military unrest, when tourists should really just keep their heads down and enjoy the sunshine, not risk calling the wrath of the authorities down on top of them.'

I had to accept this was a reasonably accurate summary of events, so nodded.

'Are you mad?'

'I just wasn't thinking straight. The car horn made me jump. I felt guilty about trashing the place. I was pretty stressed out about being locked in there at all. I just acted on instinct. And once it was in my pocket the time never seemed right to pull it out again,'

'What, not even when the policeman - what was his name? Mohammed?'

'Ahmed.'

'Yes, well, Mohammed, Ahmed, whatever - not even when he asked you to turn your bag out onto the desk?'

'Especially not then.'

'And what about in the cold - well hot - light of day today?'

'No; not really; I can't see a way of returning it now without admitting how I accidentally left with it in the first place.'

'Meredith, you stole it!'

'Yes, well, it's not as if it was premeditated or anything. I didn't mean to get shut up in Howard Carter's house. Breaking the picture was an accident. How was I to know there was some mysterious piece of paper hidden there? It's probably nothing anyway.'

'Yes, but you don't know that. You're intrigued enough to be sitting there trying to cram a PHD's-worth of learning into an afternoon.'

'True, but that's because it is intriguing. Even you must be able to see that?'

'Perhaps. But Pinkie it's not your mystery to solve. Whether these hieroglyphics turn out to be meaningless doodles drawn to amuse himself while waiting for the kettle to boil, which ended up in the picture frame quite by chance; or whether they contain some deep, dark secret to be hidden away, and were deliberately put there, the fact remains they belong to the Egyptian Antiquities service, not you.'

'I didn't know you'd heard of the Egyptian Antiquities Service!'

'Don't sidestep the issue. You've quite clearly taken leave of your senses. And I'm not going to join you by taking leave of mine. We should head over to the police station right now, and give your precious scrap of paper to - what was his name? Mohammed?'

'Ahmed.'

'To Ahmed, with profuse apologies.'

'You don't mean that.'

'I do - unless you're prepared to do the only other sensible thing and destroy it. If it really has been shut up inside a picture frame for nearly a century, I don't suppose anyone's going to miss it.'

'But then I'd never find out if it says anything important.'

He cast me a look of long suffering. 'Pinkie, how do you seriously think you're going to figure out that message - if it is a message - without taking a degree in ancient languages? Even I can see you're not going to achieve it by looking at that book. And from what you tell me this is only one small section of the total hieroglyphics on that sheet.'

I didn't have an answer to this, so remained obstinately silent.

He swung his legs over the side of the sun lounger and leaned towards me. There was a bit more sympathy in his expression now, but it was the kind you might show a very small child when attempting to explain a big, grown up concept. In other words, he was looking at me as if I was a half-wit, but not unkindly. 'Ok, let's play it your way. Say you do find some miraculous way of reading it - maybe you find some helpful idiot who knows how to translate hieroglyphics but conveniently fails to ask you where you came across them. And say it does turn out to be important, and the same convenient idiot somehow tells you what it says without realising the significance himself. Then what?'

'Then, I don't know. I haven't thought that far. I hadn't really thought as far as the deep, dark secret bit. You're a few steps ahead of me, and I've only just told you about it! I just thought it was a bit of a puzzle and wanted to figure it out.'

'So, I'll tell you. Then you find yourself in possession of an Egyptological find that should be on display in the Cairo Museum, or handed over to an archaeologist, or something. How are you going to explain how it came into your hands then?'

I shrugged, 'I could say I found it, or picked it up in a curio shop?'

He gave a snort of disgust. 'Honestly Pinkie, you get worse!' But he was still calling me Pinkie, so all was not lost.

'Look Dan,' I appealed to him, 'I didn't mean to steal it, but I can't deny I did. You're absolutely right, I don't read hieroglyphics, and I don't know anyone who does. So my chances of reading the inscriptions are probably zilch. But can't I just keep it as a kind of special souvenir of a weird and wonderful experience? I mean, not many people can say they've been trapped inside Howard Carter's house for the night, can they? Can't we just call it my little secret, or my moment of madness, and leave it at that?'

'You are the absolute limit,' he said. But I knew this meant he'd given in. I imagine, in truth, he didn't much relish the prospect of re-acquaintance with Ahmed. Two nights running is probably a bit much in anyone's book for a brush with the law. And this time we'd - well I - would be on the wrong side of it.

I thought that was the end of the subject. But while we were getting showered and dressed for dinner, Dan asked to see the original scrap of paper.

I took it out of the safe and showed it to him. He studied it in silence, then handed it back without comment, so I locked it away again.

But later, over dinner at the Lantern restaurant, a short taxi-ride away in Luxor, he enquired, 'So who was this Queen ... Ahmed, did you say she was called?'

'Ahmes. She was the great royal wife of Thutmosis I. He was one of the first great warrior pharaohs of the 18th Dynasty, somewhere around 1500 BC; so about three-and-a-half-thousand years ago. They were the parents of Queen Hatshepsut.'

'I feel like I've heard of her. Sounds like hot chicken soup. Have you told me about her before?'

'We visited her mortuary temple on the West bank when we were here last time,' I reminded him. 'It's the one that rises on terraces against the cliffs. You know, where those German tourists were killed in the terrorist attack of '97.'

'Yes, it vaguely rings a bell. She set herself up as Pharaoh or something, right?'

After ten years, Dan still has the ability to surprise me. 'Well remembered, I'm impressed.'

'Tell me about the painting again.'

So I described Carter's watercolour of Queen Ahmes, the appealing simplicity and soft pastel colours of the portrait.

'And it was drawn from a relief on one of the walls of the temple, did you say?'

'Yes, that's what it said on the legend under the picture in Carter's study.'

'And the scrawl at the top of the page you pilfered reads, "find my equal here"?'

'I think so. You saw yourself, the ink's a bit faded, and the handwriting's pretty indecipherable.'

'Well it seems to me maybe you need to go and look at the original image. Surely that's what he means by her equal - always assuming it's Queen Ahmes he's referring to.

47

"Find my equal here" must mean the wall carving he copied. Maybe you'll find he copied the hieroglyphics from there too. The walls of the temples out here seem to be covered with them. And then perhaps you can get someone to help you decipher them, without having to admit to the scrap of paper.'

You see, I told you Dan can be a sweetheart!

Chapter 3

But Dan wasn't such a sweetheart as to come with me to visit Hatshepsut's temple. So the following afternoon while he took himself back to the golf course, I returned to the West Bank for more sightseeing. Fingers crossed this repeat of our separate excursions from two days before wouldn't prove a bad omen! I had my fully charged mobile phone with me, so hopefully not.

I didn't reprise the ferry or scooter experiences, but asked Reception to call me a taxi from the line-up outside the hotel. The driver - Saleh, such a welcome change from Mohammed - drove me across Luxor bridge, then turned right to skirt the West bank of the Nile. The road was lined with fields of sugarcane and okra. I was treated to glimpses of farmers toiling in the dusty green fields, their long galabeya's hooked up into loose, white, knee-length cotton underpants. We passed laden donkey carts and decrepit-looking tractors, a bizarre blend of semi-ancient and vaguely modern, all equally weighed down with mountains of harvested sugarcane.

As we approached modern Gurna, the agricultural fields gave way to inhabited, but roofless, mud brick houses, with metal construction poles sticking up into the air. Apparently people only have to pay tax on completed buildings. No prizes for guessing, then, why the vast majority are unfinished. Goats, dogs, chicken and countless grubby children scampered around in the dust. Men sat outside their houses smoking water pipes. Women, completely enveloped in long black Moslem robes, walked along the roadside with huge wicker baskets on their heads, presumably off to do the daily grocery shop. The great thing about Egypt is nobody appears to go hungry. There's poverty, yes, but no shortage of food.

Leaving the modern village behind us, we turned towards the Theban hills, a low-lying mountain range of creased, tawny gold cliffs rising from the cultivated land about a mile inland from the riverbank. Back on my first visit to Egypt with my parents as a teenager, the foothills were covered in the tumbledown dwellings of the old village of Gurna. Now the shacks, huts and mud-brick homes have been swept away, the people relocated to New Gurna, the village we'd just passed through, hugging the West Bank of the Nile near the ferry landing. Excavators have cleared away the debris of the old settlement to reveal hills riddled with holes like a mountainous Swiss cheese made of mellow gold rock. These are the tombs of the nobles, dating back millennia, and there are several thousand of them.

As I always did when confronted with these pockmarked hills, I mused on how strange it was to think people built their homes on top of the ancient necropolis, using centuries-old tombs as storerooms, sometimes even living in them. Perhaps it goes some way towards explaining the thriving industry in tomb robbing which sprang up in the nineteenth century as Victorian explorers started taking an interest in the place.

The taxi driver dropped me off in the temple car park. I was accosted the moment I arrived by the usual swarm of boys selling concertina postcard packs and dodgy replica artefacts. These typically range from 6-inch-high obelisks and pyramids, to similar-sized busts of Tutankhamun and Nefertiti, via the whole Pantheon of animal-headed Gods and Goddesses. Made of some sort of resin, I guess, they're mostly pretty crude, but some have a certain charm. I bet most visitors to Egypt have a souvenir scarab or such-like lurking in a cupboard somewhere, or gathering dust on a shelf.

I think the expression 'in-your-face' must have been coined in Egypt. The curio sellers have no awareness of the concept of personal space. Or, if they do, they blithely invade it regardless, shoving their wares in your face. It can be intensely wearisome, like constantly swatting flies. But I've never found it threatening or intimidating. I've become adept at issuing a firm 'no thank you' or better, the Arabic 'laa shokran', which means the same thing.

I took pity on a tiny, raggedy little girl no more than seven or eight, with bare feet, wearing a filthy pink dress. I

51

gave her a couple of coins in exchange for a papyrus bookmark. Actually, I don't suppose for a moment it was genuine papyrus, probably banana skin. But she had such a pretty face, with huge Bambi eyes, and she hung back while the others did their lions-stalking-wildebeest routine; only coming to tug at my cotton trousers and bleat up at me when I'd cut a decisive swathe through the pack.

After that I was left relatively undisturbed to buy my ticket and pass through the security gate, I stood by the low stone wall and took time to savour the panorama stretching before of me.

A long causeway led in a straight line from where I was standing near the ticket office to the foot of dramatic limestone cliffs rising steeply behind the expansive desert plain in a wide semi-circle, under the vaulting blue sky. Without the causeway to direct the gaze, you could be forgiven for not immediately noticing the low, wide monument set against the rock. But there it was, Hatshepsut's perfectly proportioned memorial temple, rising in low terraces, connected by a central ramp, to meet the jagged cliff-face. The monument and bay of cliffs worked together in total harmony, a perfect example of a man-made structure blending beautifully with its natural surroundings.

According to my guidebook, Hatshepsut's architect created this stunning work of art by "divining that only long horizontal lines could live in the presence of the overwhelming vertical lines of the background."

I squinted through my sunglasses, and tried to wish away the modern eyesores; the small knots of tourists in their baseball caps and t-shirts, the rest house selling cold drinks and snacks, the gaudy post-card and curio kiosks, and the long electric trolley buses snaking up and down the causeway transporting visitors from the ticket office to the temple forecourt.

The heat rippled across the desert plain, visible as a shimmering haze rising off the dust. I'd read somewhere that Deir el-Bahri holds a record as one of the hottest places on earth. Standing sweltering under an unrelenting sun, I could well believe it. But I eschewed the trolley bus, preferring instead to stroll slowly along the causeway towards the temple. As I approached it, I imagined myself part of an ancient religious procession, walking in the footsteps of Hatshepsut herself. Although, thinking about it, I doubt she was expected to walk; was more probably carried on a litter, hoisted high on the shoulders of her serving men, while others walked alongside waving ostrich feather fans above her head to shade her from the sun.

There's something larger than life about ancient Egyptian royalty. Perhaps unsurprising, since pharaohs were worshipped as gods. Their names reach across the centuries to stir our modern senses, full of romance, power

53

and mystery. So maybe they achieved immortality after all, an afterlife they couldn't have imagined, despite the lifetimes they spent preparing for it. Eternal life was not so much in the fields of Amenti, or the imperishable stars, but in having their stories unveiled millennia after their bodies were wrapped in linen, sealed inside their sarcophagus and buried in their tombs.

Hatshepsut reigned nearly three-and-a-half thousand years ago. It's a mind-numbing passage of time by anyone's standards. Her claim to fame is the remarkable act of having herself declared Pharaoh while she was acting as regent for the child king who would later grow up to be the great warrior pharaoh Thutmosis III. It seems she ruled as a man, even to the extent of having herself depicted in the male regalia of nemes headdress and false beard.

I was so caught up in my imaginings about her I nearly leapt out of my skin when a hand lightly touched my shoulder and a male voice said, 'Hello again.'

I crashed back into the twenty-first century and found myself staring at a vaguely familiar face. It has to be said, it was quite a good-looking face, attached to a rather fit body dressed in sand-coloured chinos and a loose-fitting white cotton shirt, open at the throat, with the sleeves rolled back to reveal tanned forearms.

'You don't remember me, do you?' The softly chiding tone was really quite appealing, as if my faulty memory was a pinprick to a rapidly deflating ego.

I racked my brains and finally placed him. 'Yes. Luxor Museum. Last week.'

Funnily enough, it was admiring a masterful sculpture of Thutmosis III. Life-sized, exquisitely modelled, and in near perfect condition, it was one of the museum's most prized possessions. From what I could recall, we'd had one of those polite stranger-to-stranger conversations finding ourselves shoulder-to-shoulder staring at the same museum exhibit. I think I may have started it, commenting inanely, 'Remarkable, isn't it?'

'Yes, those ancient Egyptian artisans were certainly master craftsmen.'

'He looks very purposeful, striding forward like that.'

'Well, I suppose he must have had some strength of character. He was Egypt's finest warrior pharaoh. Apparently he never lost a battle. And he's said to have fought something like fourteen of them!'

I must have stared in surprise at him, because he laughed. 'Sorry, I have a bad habit of sounding like a walking guidebook.'

And with that, he'd smiled apologetically, and wandered off in the opposite direction from my chosen route around the museum.

Now he smiled again, revealing even white teeth in a tanned face. 'I can bore you rigid with some guidebook regalia about this place too, if you let me.'

I found myself liking him. There was a nice self-deprecating charm emerging from behind the designer sunglasses.

'I was doing a pretty good job of that for myself,' I smiled back at him. 'Hatshepsut's one of my favourite characters from the ancient Egyptian cast of heroes and villains. In fact you startled me out of a daydream. I was imagining myself nearly three-and-a-half thousand years in the past, trying to picture what this temple must have looked like then.'

'Pretty awesome, I should think. It's hard to imagine how they got trees to grow this far from the Nile. But look, there are still planting holes here.' We gazed down at the blackened roots of an ancient myrrh tree. According to the small label stuck into the ground alongside it, was a rare species brought back from the African land of Punt, believed to be modern day Somalia, and planted during Hatshepsut's reign. 'Apparently the avenue you've just walked along was once lined with gardens, filled with tamarisk, sycamore fig and persea trees. Not easy to visualise it now, is it?'

We both shaded our eyes against the glare of the sun, and stared at the stark, barren landscape. Probably best described as a dust bowl, it stretched away from the curve of bronzed cliffs for miles before reaching the distant strip of dull green bordering the Nile.

'So, you've been here before?' he asked after a moment's pause.

'This is my fourth trip to Egypt,' I confirmed, 'and I've visited this temple on all the previous ones.'

'Are you here on your own?' He immediately cringed, and sent me a sheepish grin. 'Sorry, that sounded like a bad chat-up line. I didn't mean it that way. Just wondering if you'd mind some company while you're here? It'd be nice to spend some time with someone who clearly loves it here.'

'My boyfriend's playing golf. He likes Egypt for its suntan potential. But he's not hooked on the historical side. I am, so we tend to do our own thing during the day. I can see the same Egyptian bug bit you as it did me. So, sure, why not?'

He held out his hand, 'Adam Tennyson. Good to meet you - a fellow Egypt fan.'

'Freak,' I said.

'I beg your pardon?'

'It's Egypt freak, not fan. According to my boyfriend it goes beyond being a fan into something altogether more fanatical. But I guess the cap fits. So I accept it.'

He laughed. 'In which case, I've just found myself a new label, too.'

'Meredith Pink,' I said, and shook his hand, which, embarrassingly, I'd been holding during this exchange. 'But please call me Merry. Everyone else does.'

He smiled at me, and we walked towards the temple, gazing up at its terraces. 'So, which do you think Hatshepsut was?' he asked. 'Heroine or villainess?'

'For the sake of female solidarity, I'll say I admire her as the first feminist. She must have been pretty brave to assert her right to rule.'

'Ah, but she claimed divine birth right.'

'Yes, something about the God Amun taking on the form of her father the pharaoh and impregnating her mother?' I'd read up on it since Dan pronounced I should search for Queen Ahmes' equal here.

He looked suitably impressed. 'The scenes depicting her divine conception are carved on the walls here. Theological proof she was entitled to ascend the throne as king, if you're prepared to believe her own propaganda.'

And with this announcement, I'd struck gold; my principle reason for this afternoon's visit being to seek them out. 'Do you know where they are?'

He tilted his head sideways as if consulting an inner site plan. 'Middle colonnade, if I remember rightly. Do you want to take a look?'

'Definitely. I don't remember the guide pointing them out last time I was here.'

'Well they're pretty hard to see. They were deliberately defaced after Hatshepsut died. I'm not sure Thutmosis III appreciated being ousted by her for so many years. I think chiselling out her images was his way of getting even.'

We started up the ramp to the middle colonnade, me climbing the shallow steps, Adam on the stone slope. He led me to the right hand side of the temple, behind two rows of pillars. My first reaction was sharp disappointment. For a start, rope barriers stopped us getting close to the wall reliefs. Secondly the shadowed dimness behind the portico, shaded from the blinding sunlight beyond, made the faint carvings near invisible. Although I suspect even well lit they'd be hard to see, the carving shallow and, as Adam said, badly damaged.

Adam pointed out the first scene showing Queen Ahmes. 'See, there she is sitting on a couch. The figure next to her is Amun-Ra. He's offering her an ankh sign, the hieroglyph for "life". I think it's meant to be a tactful way of showing her being impregnated by the god.'

I squinted at the images he was pointing out, but struggled to make out what he described. 'Is that hieroglyphic text up there?' I pointed at the wall, a faint buzz of excitement returning as I wondered if I'd found Carter's copied text.

'Yes, it describes what happened. I won't remember it exactly; it's a while since I studied the transcripts. But I think

59

the essence of it is something along the following lines...' He straightened up as if about to deliver poetry, hamming it up a bit as if I might laugh at him. "'Then came the glorious god Amun himself, lord of the thrones of both lands. When he had taken the form of her husband, he found her resting in the palace. She awoke at the perfume of the god and, enflamed with love he hastened towards her.'" Adam broke off and gave a small, self-conscious cough, but ploughed on as if determined to finish now he'd started. "'She exulted at the sight of his beauty. His love entered all her limbs; the palace filled with the sweet perfumes of the god. She gladdened him with herself and kissed him.'"

He gave a slight, formal bow as he finished, so I clapped dutifully, really rather impressed, both with his recall of this ancient erotica, and with the somewhat comedic way he'd delivered it. But I had to concede it didn't seem likely these were Carter's mysterious scratchings.

Adam led me further along the wall. My heart gave a little leap in my chest. Here was the model for Carter's watercolour of Queen Ahmes. It was faint, damaged, but discernible.

Adam continued his tour. In this scene, you can just about make out Hatshepsut's mother being led to her birthing chamber by the frog-headed goddess Heket and the ram-headed god Khnum, both associated with childbirth.

That's Amun-Ra up there, standing nearby to affirm he's Hatshepsut's father.'

'What about the texts?' I asked. 'Do you know what these ones say?'

He looked at me a bit quizzically. 'Some stunningly immodest proclamation by Hatshepsut, if memory serves correctly; describing herself as godlike in all her manifestations; her manner, her spirit, basically everything she did.

I stared at him, rather fascinated. 'How do you know all this stuff?'

'Oh, I'm a thwarted Egyptologist,' he said offhandedly.

'What do you mean; thwarted?'

'It's a long story. I won't bore you with the details.'

My silence invited him to go on.

'The headlines are I started studying Egyptology for my degree. My parents brought my brother and me here when we were kids. I was bitten by the Egypt bug, as you said earlier. But events conspired, forcing me to leave university early. I spent years working my way up in banking. I did alright for myself and I have to say the bonus money was, well, a bonus. But I got disillusioned with the whole thing. The banking crisis was the last straw. I couldn't square it with myself any more, working in a sector selling our economy down the river. So I bailed out. My wife left me when she realised our lifestyle was going to take a hit.' He broke off, as if he'd strayed inadvertently into personal territory and was uncomfortable finding himself there. He shrugged, 'So I'm pretty much back where I started, taking time out, studying Egyptology - not university this time - just online distance learning. I'm too old to train to become an archaeologist, I suspect. So I'm trying to figure out if there's a way of making any other sort of career out of the magical and mystical history of this land.'

How old, I wondered? About forty at a guess. I mentally shook away this thought. 'Wow, good for you. Any luck?"

'Not yet. To sign up as a guide on the cruise ships or for the tour operators, you have to be Egyptian Egyptologist. Fair enough, I suppose. It's their country. And I daresay the tourists want authenticity. Not some throw-back of an English public schoolboy come to wax lyrical about a civilisation so far removed from his own.'

'So, are you staying at a hotel while you're out here?' I asked.

'No, I rent a small flat near the Souk. It's not over-endowed with mod cons. But it does have air-conditioning, so I'm not complaining. I decided to immerse myself in modern-Egyptian culture as well as the more ancient civilisation. It feels more authentic. I'd rather rub shoulders with the locals' in the coffee bars and actually try to fit in a bit, than hole up in some luxury tourist hotel, where the facilities may be amazing, but the guests are just passing through, and it's a new bunch of faces every couple of weeks or so.' He paused, and smiled at me a bit apologetically, as if he'd inadvertently implied something offensive about tourists. 'And what about you? You seem to know more about this ancient stuff than the average holidaymaker. Are you an Egyptologist-in-the-making too?'

'Only in my dreams,' I laughed. 'Snap though. My parents brought my brother and me when we were kids, too. I remember of they took us to the Son et Lumière at Giza. There was this booming voice doing the narration. It sounded like Richard Burton, but I have no idea if it was. The quote I remember was, "Man fears time, but time fears the pyramids". It sent a shiver down my spine. It still does, to be honest. All I can tell you is I was hooked. But my interest has been wholly non-academic; just books, television documentaries, and a bit of online surfing here and there. Just about enough to convince my boyfriend it's an unhealthy fixation more than a wholesome hobby.'

He shared a conspiratorial smile with me, 'I know the feeling. So, it's just a holiday?'

I shrugged. 'Yes and no; like you, it's a bit of a 'time-out' break - a chance to take stock, and decide where to go from here. You see I've just been made redundant.'

'Oh, I'm sorry to hear that. I hope I haven't blundered into a painful subject.'

'No, no; nothing like that,' I assured him. 'I took voluntary redundancy rather than being forced out. So it was my decision really. While it's true I didn't see the organisational restructure coming - although perhaps I should have done, given the economic downturn since the credit crunch - I'm hoping I won't live to regret it. I worked for a charity. The sector's been pretty badly hit by the downturn. Everyone's on an efficiency drive these days. It's unit-cost this, and value-indicator that. So charities are streamlining and paring down their back office functions. I was offered the chance to take voluntary redundancy on an enhanced package; so I took the risk, grabbed the chance, whatever you choose to call it. I'd been there fifteen years, so it was a pretty good deal. I don't have a very big mortgage, and I've always been quite good at saving for a rainy day. So, here I am! Unemployed but not exactly destitute; enjoying a bit of a break from the real world before I face up to the future.'

He grinned at me. 'So, snap twice! We're both unemployed and seeking inspiration in the land of the pharaohs. What did you do for your charity?'

'Well, my CV says I was a communications executive. But that's just a fancy way of saying I wrote stuff. I've copy edited more newsletter articles than you can shake a stick at; written press releases too numerous to mention; and designed webpages and Intranet site-maps aplenty.'

'So maybe you could find a way of writing about Egypt?' he suggested. 'A travelogue, or a blog, or something.'

'That would be great, if I could find an angle no-one else has thought of.' Saying this made me wonder if the story of being locked in Howard Carter's house might have any merit. And thinking about my lock-in reminded me of the scrap of paper with its carefully drawn hieroglyphics. Strange, how in the last few minutes I'd forgotten my whole purpose in being here. I decided this needed remedying, and quickly. 'I thought I might try to teach myself hieroglyphics,' I said as we started wandering away from the birthing scenes. 'Do you read them?' I tried to sound simply interested, not as if I had an ulterior motive.

'Only simple stuff,' he said, accepting the change of subject. 'I can generally recognise a pharaoh's name inside a cartouche. But start me on the more complex arrangements, like spells and invocations, and I don't have a prayer. It's the artwork I like most, which is why I love it here. This temple has some of the best pictorial storytelling anywhere in the world. You don't need to be able to read the text to get a sense of what's going on. Take this wall for example.' We'd strolled round the ramp to the southern colonnade. Now he pointed up at the exquisitely rendered raised reliefs, still showing some original colour. 'The Egyptians produced remarkably accurate drawings of animals, and botanical scenes; as well as maritime stuff. Look up here,' he pointed to the upper registers of the wall. 'Look at the detail on that ship. You can almost sense the movement of the rowers pulling the oars through the water.' In his enthusiasm, he shoved his sunglasses up on top of his head. His animation lit his whole face and shone from his eyes; which were very blue, I noticed.

I studied the scenes, noting all the tiny details, minutely rendered nearly three-and-a-half thousand years ago, very aware of Adam alongside me. All these years I'd pursued a solo love affair with Egypt. Here was someone possibly more enraptured than me. I felt the exhilarating joy of recognising a soul mate. 'And this was while people back home were living in wattle and daub huts!' I exclaimed. 'To look at the beautiful carvings and paintings here makes it seem impossible.'

By some unspoken agreement we started moving away from the colonnade and climbed the ramp to the upper terrace. 'You know, it took Howard Carter six years to copy the reliefs from these walls.' Adam said. 'Six whole years; it's not hard to see why.'

My ears pricked up; Howard Carter again. We reached the top of the slope and stood still for a moment, collecting our breath and admiring this most spectacular part of Hatshepsut's temple. Its smooth pillars, some fronted with colossal statues, stood in sharp contrast to the rugged cliffs looming dramatically behind it, under the sweeping blue sky.

'I don't know much about Howard Carter beyond his discovery of Tutankhamun,' I admitted. 'I know he came out to Egypt as a youngster, hired as an artist to record the wall paintings, but that's about it.'

'I wouldn't get me started on Howard Carter if I were you,' he said with a smile that was a bit sad-edged. 'My thesis was going to be about his forty-five year career in Egypt. I never finished it, but I'd done a lot of the research. He's always been a bit of a hero of mine. I think there's a small bit of me that would've liked to be him. What an extraordinary life! Although by all accounts he was an irascible old bugger, stubborn, pig-headed and a bit of a stickler for his correct way of doing things.'

I laughed, 'Well I don't know you well enough to say whether you take after him in character. But I can understand the hero worship. Seriously, I'm interested to find out a bit more about his work here.' Ulterior motive notwithstanding, Adams' evident love of his subject was infectious.

He perched on the low temple wall, gazing about him. So I sat on the hot stone alongside him, and adjusted my hat so my face was in full shade.

'Well, he wasn't an irascible old bugger when he worked here. He was just a kid of about twenty. He worked here from 1894 to 1899 for the Egypt Exploration Society.

They'd embarked on an ambitious project to preserve a lasting record of the ancient monuments. Even then they were decaying at an alarming rate. He'd already proved himself during his first season, aged seventeen, recording a group of Middle Kingdom tombs at a site called Beni Hasan.

'Here at Deir el-Bahri he was given full charge of the recording. This allowed him to make best use of his artist's eye to capture all the subtleties of ancient Egyptian artwork. Carter produced some of his most iconic work here, perhaps the most famous being the sensitive rendering of the head shoulders of Queen Ahmes, from the relief we saw earlier.'

'I've seen the painting.' I interjected, marvelling at the happenstance of running into someone who could blithely throw Howard Carter and now the Queen Ahmes painting into the conversation; since they were the precise reasons for my visit here. In some distant reaches of my imagination I wondered if Adam might perhaps be a bit telepathic. He certainly seemed to have an almost uncanny knack of tuning into my subconscious and speaking my hidden thoughts out loud. 'There's a framed copy in Howard Carter's House. I was there the other day.' But I held back from adding my unique association with said painting and picture frame.

He beamed at me. 'So, you've seen how exquisite his artwork was. It's hard to imagine now, but this temple was a tumbledown ruin in Carter's early days in Egypt, buried under tons of debris. It's undergone pretty much continuous excavation and restoration since then. It's really only since the 1920s it's been clear enough for visitors to appreciate the temple's beauty. I think we have Howard Carter to thank for putting it on the map. When his paintings of its decoration were published at the end of the nineteenth century, Europeans were enthralled. It was barely mentioned in the guidebooks before then. But ever since it's been among the most iconic of Egyptian monuments.'

I gazed about me, trying to imagine the magnificent temple as a tumbledown ruin. 'I've always thought it a curiously modern temple, even though it's one of the oldest,' I mused. 'It's so unique in its design.'

'Not so unique really,' Adam said. 'It was meant to function as a memorial temple, so it has all the standard features. I think what makes this temple so dramatically different is the way it takes advantage of its natural setting.'

'I was thinking the same thing when I arrived. The cliffs provide a jaw-dropping backdrop. They really frame it, don't they?'

'Yes, I'm pretty sure this site must have been chosen at least partly because of the setting. But Hatshepsut may have had other reasons too. It's a staggering fact, but this temple is built on almost exactly the same axial line as the temple of Amun at Karnak.'

'What do you mean?'

'Here, stand up, look...!' He held out his hand and almost lifted me to my feet, then spun me away from the temple so I faced back towards the Nile. He stood close behind me, reaching round to point past my shoulder, so my line of sight travelled down his extended arm and pointing finger. He wore a nice aftershave, I noticed; not one I recognised, but nice. 'See the minaret in the distance, and the crane just off to the left of it?'

I squinted through the heat haze and finally located these distant landmarks.

'Now, just look slightly behind them, and to the left; notice anything?'

I squinted some more. Suddenly I thought I could see what he was getting so excited about. 'Yes, that's the main Pylon at Karnak, isn't it?' It must have been miles away, on the other side of the Nile, barely visible in the heat haze.

'Exactly! Now the awesome fact is, if you extend the principle axis of Hatshepsut's temple, here, where we're standing, due east to Karnak, it runs within a hundred metres of the axis of the temple of Amun-Ra. Considering the special prominence Hatshepsut gave the god, she claimed he was her father after all, I'm betting that's no coincidence! She had her obelisks raised there, equal and opposite to her great mortuary temple here.'

Equal and opposite. I felt a thrill of possibility. Hatshepsut's obelisk. "Find my equal here". Perhaps that's

70

where Carter's tantalising invitation was supposed to lead me.

Chapter 4

'So, is this Adam bloke on the level?' Dan took a swig of his beer and skewered me with a look over the rim of his glass.

We'd opted for a lazy evening at the Jolie Ville, rather than venturing further afield to one of the Luxor restaurants for dinner. We'd enjoyed a rather sumptuous meal at La Fleur, the onsite à la carte restaurant, and were now relaxing in the Ascot bar with our drinks. I'd told him all about meeting Adam of course, bubbling over with glee at finding a kindred spirit.

'Just because he shares my interests, why shouldn't he be on the level?'

'Hm, just keep your wits about you. This is post revolutionary Egypt, and you don't know him from ... well, from Adam.'

I rolled my eyes at him. 'Since you've made it clear none of this historical stuff floats your boat, and seem quite happy to let me explore on my own, I don't see how you can complain when I fall into conversation with someone who feels the same way I do.'

'Yes, well, striking up a conversation with a like-minded chap is one thing. Arranging to meet him at Karnak to inspect the obelisks is another ball game altogether. I'm not sure I should encourage you.'

'So come along,' I invited. 'You can meet him and judge for yourself if he's on the level.'

He grimaced at me, another of his hugely expressive facial contortions. This one eloquently conveyed he'd rather watch paint dry. 'I went to Karnak with you last week. Besides, I don't know why you can't just look up about the obelisks online.'

It was impossible to explain the sense of discovery I'd felt exploring Hatshepsut's temple in Adam's company. He'd brought it to life in the way no guidebook could. On the way out he'd shown me the wall reliefs depicting Hatshepsut's obelisks being transported from the quarry in Aswan and raised at Karnak – a feat modern engineers struggled to comprehend. Three previous guided tours had never sparked the same sense of enlightenment. As if I wasn't just looking at a relic of the past, but could somehow reach back and touch it. As if history was really just a displacement of time.

I didn't voice these thoughts. Dan's not the jealous type. But I guess there are limits.

'Pinkie, we've only got a couple of days left before we go home,' he reminded me.

This was not a welcome prospect. I didn't feel ready yet to face up to pragmatic considerations about getting another job and keeping the wolf from the door. For all that we'd been here nearly two weeks, it felt like we'd only just arrived.

Dan had only paused to take a sip of his beer. 'Wouldn't you rather spend them soaking up the sun instead of getting all hot and dusty tramping round the monuments? It's not as if you haven't seen them before.'

My facial expressions must be as revealing as his. Or he's become equally adept at reading them. Either way, he signed.

'Ok, I guess not. But please go careful. I'm sure this guy's just a harmless boffin, but I know what you fanatical-types are like when you get carried away. I don't relish the prospect of rescuing you from another scrape like getting locked in Howard Carter's house.'

* * *

I looked at Adam's smiling face next morning and bet he'd never in his whole life been described by anyone who'd met him as a harmless boffin. While I'd waxed lyrical to Dan about the joy of encountering a kindred spirit, I may not have mentioned said kindred spirit's good looks.

We met in the huge car park, me emerging from a taxi, him jumping off a scooter at the same time. Negotiating the hordes of curio sellers outside their souvenir kiosks was a far easier task in Adam's company. He called greetings to a couple of them, so I figured he was a familiar figure around the temple. We bought our tickets, strolled through the security gate, and approached the gigantic first pylon of the temple along a short avenue of sphinxes.

'Now, before we go any further, spin round, look across to the other side of the river, into the foothills bang opposite, and tell me what you see.'

I did as instructed, shading my eyes and squinting into the distance. 'Hatshepsut's temple.'

'See? I told you so. Bang opposite, and far easier to see from here than Karnak is in reverse, as you saw for yourself yesterday.'

'I can't believe I've never spotted it before. It really is straight ahead, isn't it?'

'Well, to be fair, I think they've cleared away some of the foliage this side of the river recently, palm trees and whatnot, to give a clearer line of sight.'

We turned back to face the temple.

'So, we're agreed still? We want to look at the Karnak through Hatshepsut's eyes?' he queried. It was the plan we'd made yesterday when I'd asked him if Howard Carter had much to do with Karnak.

'Not especially, as far as I know,' he'd answered. 'It would have been part of his remit when he was Chief Inspector of the Egyptian Antiquities service here. He had

75

that role for about five years from the age of twenty-five to thirty. But Karnak doesn't stand out as significant. I'll give you a for-instance. There was a massive incident at Karnak in 1899, so during Carter's first year in his new job. Some of the columns in the Hypostyle Hall toppled over. Apparently the thunderous crash was heard for miles around. But Carter never mentioned it, as far as I'm aware. So Karnak doesn't seem to have featured high on his priorities list.'

I was disappointed to hear this. I just had a gut feeling the key to understanding Carter's cryptic message-in-the-picture was in a better understanding of his life before Tutankhamun. And, of course, in matching up the hieroglyphics - always assuming he'd copied them, in the same way he'd copied the relief of Queen Ahmes from the walls of Hatshepsut's temple. For the time being, Hatshepsut seemed my best lead. I was intrigued to learn her temple at Deir el-Bahri was built on the same axis as her obelisks in the Temple of Amun. It was a long shot. But it was the only hint of something 'equal' I'd come up with so far.

It also presented another opportunity to visit one of my favourite places on the planet, and with someone who could breathe new life into it. This, of course, was my secondary motive, not my first.

'Yes, let's stick with Hatshepsut,' I confirmed now, in response to Adam's question. 'I never knew that stuff about

76

the axis of the temples aligning. I'm intrigued. And Karnak's almost too big to get your head around. So let's focus on her bits of it.'

'Ok, so you need to ignore pretty much everything around us. It wouldn't have been here in her day. You have to remember she's one of the earliest of the A-list pharaohs. True, some people have heard of Khufu, builder of the great pyramid at Giza. He pre-dated Hatshepsut by a thousand years or so. But I'd defy most people to be able to name the owners of the other two.'

'I can't' I conceded.

'And you know more than most,' he said.

I felt my whole body glow with pride at this unexpected compliment.

He went on, 'Those who subscribe to the Discovery Channel or National Geographic will probably have heard of Thutmosis III, and perhaps Amenhotep III, both great 18th Dynasty kings who followed Hatshepsut.'

I nodded. 'Yup, I could reel out the bare bones if asked.'

'But the stellar pharaohs and their famous sidekicks came later. Most people have heard of Akhenaten, the heretic pharaoh, who set aside the old gods to worship just one, the sun god. He's famous as the first monotheist in history. And everyone knows Nefertiti, his wife, from the exquisite stone bust now on display in Berlin. They ruled a

77

hundred years or so after Hatshepsut, and just before Tutankhamun. Everyone's heard of King Tut, of course. But the other famous names, Ramses II, his great royal wife Nefertari, and Cleopatra were later. In Cleopatra's case, much later, we're talking 1500 years later.'

'So you're telling me the Karnak we see today would be largely unrecognisable to Hatshepsut.'

'Exactly; most of it was built by later pharaohs. Take these sphinxes...'

I peered up at the imposing row of sphinxes on either side of me, set high above the causeway on their massive plinths. They had lion bodies and ram heads, symbols of the god Amun. That was the extent of my knowledge about them.

'... They were carved for Amenhotep III, and later appropriated by Ramses II. He was good at that, carving his name and image on all manner of stuff that didn't belong to him. So, snap your fingers and magic them away. They wouldn't have been here.'

'And the Pylon?' I asked as we approached the immense stone gateway, rising well over a hundred metres on either side of the entrance to the temple. Each stone block, piled one upon the other, was the size of a small car.

'Nope; very young indeed: probably Dynasty 30. Remember, Hatshepsut reigned towards the beginning of the 18th. So, for all that it's served as the formal entrance to the Temple of Amun for the last 2300 years or so, Hatshepsut wouldn't have known it.'

We entered the open court. Adam's eyes moved in a quick circular survey of the broken columns, shrines, statuary and sphinxes, and he shook his head. 'Imagine it all away. It's new.'

We walked through the next stone Pylon, and entered perhaps the most awe inspiring religious structure on earth; the Hypostyle Hall. I'd tried several times to do it justice in photographs, and always failed miserably. It's impossible to convey the size and grandeur of this vast forest of columns - towering above us like enormous stone skyscrapers. I caught my breath, as I always do, and swung my eyes towards Adam for his verdict.

'Now we're getting somewhere,' he confirmed. 'In Hatshepsut's day it's possible these two central rows of columns stood here. They're definitely 18th Dynasty.'

There were six on each side of the central aisle, gigantic tree-trunk-like pillars, but bigger than any tree trunk you can possibly imagine, with open papyrus flower capitals at the top. Taller by some metres than the neighbouring columns spreading out behind them on either side, they loomed above us, grandiose and imposing. 'The rest were added later by Seti I and his son Ramses II.' He nonchalantly waved away the other massive columns - more than a hundred of them. 'In Hatshepsut's day these two rows of columns most likely formed a colonnade, similar to the one you've probably seen in Luxor temple.'

'So, it was an avenue lined with columns, not an immense hall positively packed to the gunnels with them.'

He grinned and nodded. Even so, the sheer scale was overwhelming.

He led me out the other side of the Hypostyle Hall past the rear wall, pausing by the next stone gateway along. 'Now, this she'd definitely have known. We've entered the part of the temple built by her father, Thutmosis I.' We walked into a small open court dominated by the monolithic block of granite pointing up into the dense blue sky.'

'Her father's obelisk?' I asked.

'Yes, he definitely had the idea before she did. Originally he raised two obelisks here, although only this one remains. But Hatshepsut out-did him in scale. Her obelisks dwarfed his by a massive eight metres, and were sheathed in electrum.'

'My goodness, they must have been blinding.' The intensity of the Egyptian sunlight alone was potentially eyesight ruining. I couldn't begin to imagine the brightness of it bouncing back off two huge needles of granite encased in metal.

We strolled past the jumbled rockery of the next Pylon, and there in a maze-like gallery of piled up stone, found Hatshepsut's obelisk.

'It's doesn't seem as grand as the other one, does it? Despite its size?' I mused.

'That's because you can't get a clear line of sight on it the way you can her father's from his open courtyard. After Hatshepsut died, Thutmosis III had her obelisks walled up as part of his campaign to obliterate her memory. Seems a bit bonkers, doesn't it? He only succeeded in protecting them from damage, although one of them got broken up later and scattered about Karnak. All these stone blocks around here were probably part of that original wall. You have to give him some credit, I suppose. They're still doing a pretty good job of obscuring it. We'll have to go out towards the sacred lake and look back to really appreciate it.'

I squinted upwards, shielding my eyes against the sun, very willing to appreciate it from here. I craned my neck back to look up the length of the shaft, trying to see if any of the hieroglyphics in any way resembled those I'd copied onto the sheet of paper in my pocket. 'Do you know what the inscriptions say?'

'Yes, you can get a full transcription on the Internet, if you're interested. But the basic gist of it is Hatshepsut dedicating the obelisk to Amun-Ra, her godly father and claiming it was him who inspired her to raise them, "so their pyramidions might mingle with the sky amid the august pillared hall between the great pylons on Thutmosis."' He assumed the same pose as yesterday when directly quoting the texts, standing straight-backed, chin up, deliberately self-effacing in his mimicry. 'There's also a great bit about her not wanting to be thought boastful - Hatshepsut, not boastful, that's a laugh - but instead for people to remark how like her it is to do this, "she who is truthful to her father."'

'And her mother?' I enquired. 'Does she ever get a mention?'

He looked at me curiously. 'Queen Ahmes? No. You pretty much saw her only claim to fame recorded on Hatshepsut's temple walls yesterday. I don't think you'll find her cropping up elsewhere.'

I felt a small puff of deflation, but wasn't ready to abandon hope. 'Let's go and look at the broken bit of obelisk. It's through there in the open courtyard, isn't it?'

He followed me through the corridor of rock, huge sandstone blocks piled on all sides. We emerged into a shadeless expanse of courtyard approaching the scared lake. Here the top fragment of Hatshepsut's broken obelisk lay on its side like the snapped shaft of a giant arrow.

I walked right round it, minutely observing all the carvings, but could see nothing even vaguely resembling Carter's hieroglyphics.

'Those are coronation scenes,' Adam supplied, standing off to one side observing my slow circuit around the fallen monolith.

I gazed around me. 'Would Hatshepsut have recognised where we are now?'

'Possibly. Some of it. I think this is around the oldest part of the temple. There would have been shrines and suchlike here in her day, and the sacred lake. But not much more actually built by her. The obelisks are the main Hatshepsut event. Oh, and her red chapel in the open-air museum near the entrance. We can take a look at it on the way out, if you want? But right now, I don't know about you, I could kill a cold drink.'

This was a good idea. The water I'd brought from the hotel and had been swigging throughout our visit, had gone from ice cold, to lukewarm, and was now positively radioactive. There was a refreshment stand selling soft drinks and postcards immediately behind us. I subsided onto a chair in the shade, as close as I could get to the wall-mounted fan, and gratefully accepted the new bottle of water Adam presented me from the chiller cabinet.

We sat sipping in companionable silence for a while. Then he smiled at me. 'There's a question I've been meaning to ask you all morning.'

'Oh yes?'

'I had a drink with a mate of mine last night. Chap called Ahmed from the local tourist police.'

I stiffened.

'I got to know him in a coffee bar a few weeks back; playing dominoes, of all things! Great game, dominoes; I hadn't played since I was knee-high-to-a-grasshopper. But it seems to be all the rage out here; hubble-bubble pipes and dominoes, a great way to wile away an evening. He's teaching me Arabic. It's an uphill struggle - for both of us. Anyway, he told me this great story about rescuing a British tourist from Howard Carter's House in the wee small hours a couple of nights or so back. Apparently she got locked in by mistake. He described her as very attractive, with shiny brown hair, a cute smile, and a massive canvas bag. It wasn't you by any chance Merry, was it?'

My canvas bag, dropped on the seat beside me because it was too big to fit neatly under the table, seemed to start glowing. I couldn't say whether I did too, just that the airflow from the fan suddenly did nothing at all to counteract the heat.

'How did you guess?' I asked in a rather strangulated voice.

He shrugged. 'Ahmed told me the attractive Englishwoman didn't sit patiently waiting to be rescued. Instead she tried to escape by forcing open a window.'

'Shutters,' I interrupted him flatly. 'The window was already open. It was the shutters I tried to force.'

He chuckled. 'And in this brave attempt to break free, the lovely Englishwoman nearly trashed Howard Carter's study. She smashed a 1920's glass lampshade, and wrote off a picture frame containing one of Carter's watercolours.'

'These are charges I cannot deny.' I kept my voice strictly neutral, although I'll admit the 'attractives' and the 'lovely' were going to my head a bit.

He laughed out loud this time. 'Oh Merry, I've got this fantastic picture in my head of you skidding across the floor, sending Carter's objet d'art flying in all directions. I wish I'd been there! So anyway, what brought you to mind was when Ahmed told me the broken picture was the one of Queen Ahmes. I remembered your interest in seeing the birthing scenes at Deir el-Bahri.'

A shaft of pure panic pierced me. I was pretty sure there was no way his chum Ahmed could know of my subterfuge in misappropriating the scrap of paper. It must be just my guilty conscience going into overdrive. Nevertheless, I decided it was a good thing it was Adam asking me the questions, not his friend. I'd be banged to rights by now, signing my name to a confession for walking off with stolen property.

'You've shown an interest in her again today,' he went on. 'So I decided the coincidence was too much, and it had to be you.'

'Spot on,' I congratulated him, trying to keep up the light-hearted nonchalance. 'You should join your mate in the police force - you'd make a good detective.'

He grinned at me. 'Ahmed's a laugh, and quite a storyteller. He'll be dining out on the tale for weeks.'

I was starting to feel a bit sick. 'I'm glad to have been a source of entertainment,' I said weakly.

'So what is it specifically about Queen Ahmes that's sparked your interest?'

Instinctively I wanted to trust him. But I didn't dare. It suddenly occurred to me I didn't know Adam from, well, you know... Yes, I'm aware Dan had pointed this out to me already. I realised to take him into my confidence would be rash, impetuous and downright stupid. Dan has always said I abandon any vestiges of sense where anything Egyptological is concerned. If I recalled it correctly, he'd also said what he thought about my chances of finding a helpful idiot to help me translate the hieroglyphics. Adam was certainly no idiot. He didn't read hieroglyphs, but as a thwarted Egyptologist, he was probably my best bet of finding someone who could. I found myself liking him more and more, sensing a kindred spirit. But if I told him the truth, and he went running back to his police buddy with the news, I'd no doubt fine myself on the receiving end of a police interrogation faster than you could say Tutankhamun.

So I found myself cobbling together some claptrap about wanting to see the original wall relief before I went home. It didn't sound very convincing, even to my own ears. But I knew the truth. All I could do was hope, in his ignorance of the whole story; he'd swallow the guff I was giving him.

He went quiet for a moment when I stopped dissembling, sipping the last of his water. 'When do you go?' he asked finally. I couldn't see his eyes clearly behind his sunglasses, but the way he said it sounded like he was trying hard to sound casual.

'The day after tomorrow.'

He let the silence draw out for a few moments more. He gazed out under the awning towards the sacred lake for a bit, then looked back at me and said simply, 'I'll miss you.'

I must have looked a bit quizzical, because he went on, 'I know it probably sounds crazy, when we've only just met. But I can't tell you what a breath of fresh air you are, Merry. I've been traipsing round these dusty sites for weeks, boning up on my history and asking myself if this Egyptology lark is really for me. To be honest, I've been having a few second thoughts. What seemed a great idea when I was dreaming about it from the security of a job I loathed was getting a bit scary up close, with just myself for company most days. But yesterday and today, hooking up with you… well, it's been great. No one else has ever looked at this stuff the same way I do.' He indicated our surroundings with an expansive gesture I knew was meant to convey the whole of ancient Egypt, not just the temple we were sitting in now. 'Nobody outside academia, anyway. But you do. Your enthusiasm is infectious. You've shown an interest in every single thing I've said, without your eyes glazing over, without yawning, and without once looking at your watch.'

This so closely mirrored my feelings in reverse, I beamed at him. He'd mentioned an ex-wife, and I had first-hand experience of Dan's reaction to the slightest sign of Egyptological fervour in me; so I figured he was speaking from experience. 'I've hung on your every word,' I said lightly, only slightly teasing.

He smiled. 'And without wishing to sound as if I'm on some massive ego trip, I've loved every second. The story about you getting trapped in Howard Carter's house is like icing on the cake. Tell me if this sounds ridiculous, but I feel like I've been living my life in slow motion black and white; and now, since meeting you, everything's speeded up and burst into glorious Technicolor.' He shook his head at me, and laughed self-consciously. 'On second thoughts, please don't say a word. I heard myself say that out loud, and it was beyond ridiculous.'

But incredibly endearing, I thought. All the really good-looking men I'd known up until now exhibited a kind of arrogant machismo, no matter how unconsciously. Adam's rather self-deprecating, rather poetic, and very slightly insecure manner made a pleasant change. There was a rather charming shop-soiled quality about him, a kind of beaten-up-but-trying-not-to-let-it-show aura. It made me want to take him home and polish him up.

But home for me was back in England. He was staying here in Egypt. And I found myself rather wistfully wishing I could too.

Chapter 5

'Dan, I've decided I'm not coming back to England with you,' I announced. It was late evening on the same day. We'd had dinner at a great restaurant in Luxor called Puddleduck, run by a lovely English couple who'd made Egypt their home. I'd been silently fretting throughout. Now, just as our coffee was served, I made up my mind.

'I beg your pardon?'

'I said I'm not coming back home with you. I'm staying here for a while.'

'Please tell me you're joking.' He delivered this with a kind of exaggerated patience, as if it was one of my odd little whims and would swiftly pass.

'I'm not joking. I've been mulling it over all afternoon.'

'Ok, so you're trying to get me back for all those practical jokes I've played on you. You're going to string me along, get me all wound up, then miraculously appear at the airport just as the last call for the Gatwick flight comes over the tannoy.'

'It's not a wind-up Dan. I'm staying. At least for another couple of weeks.'

'Then you've finally taken leave of your senses!'

'I have not!'

He put down his coffee cup with an air of deliberation. 'Pinkie, I know I have to keep reminding you of this, as you don't seem to give it a moment's serious thought ... but this is post revolutionary Egypt. Things are unpredictable at best. I can't possibly agree to you staying here on your own. Anything could happen to you!'

'It hasn't bothered you to let me go sightseeing on my own!'

'Yes, well, call me naïve, but I don't imagine there's a whole lot that can happen to you in popular tourist sites in broad daylight. Terrorism to one side - it seems that can catch you unawares anywhere in the world these days - you're not likely to get accosted by some chancer while you've got your nose stuffed in a guidebook.' Then he rolled his eyes, 'Forgive me, I was forgetting, you've already been accosted by a chancer...'

'Adam is not a chancer!'

'You can't possibly know that. And besides, you've proved you're not capable of looking after yourself. Look at the whole Howard Carter debacle.'

'That could have happened to anyone. I was just unlucky, that's all.'

'Mm, but it wasn't anyone. It was you. And you scared me half to death. So, if you won't come home for your own sake, come home for mine. I went through all kinds of agonies imagining what I'd say to your mother if you didn't turn up; or, more accurately, imagining what she'd say to me. This takes it to a whole new level. She's going to make mincemeat of me if I leave you here. And, believe me, getting on the wrong side of Puff the Magic Dragon was not what I had in mind when I agreed to this trip!'

'I'll call her. I'll explain. She knows I'm at a crossroads as well as you do.' I decided to appeal to his better nature. He does have one, I think, somewhere deep down. 'Look, Dan, I've never been this free. I don't have a job to go back to. I have a few quid in the bank. The mortgage is covered. I know it can't last forever. There's a deadline looming and then I have to make decisions about where I go from here. But I don't have to make those decisions right now.'

'But Pinkie...'

'But Pinkie nothing! Why don't you stay too?'

'You know I can't do that!'

'Why not? It's only your job you're going back to. You could afford to take a couple of weeks unpaid if you wanted to.'

'Exactly, if I wanted to. I don't. Don't get me wrong; this is a great place for a chill-out break. But it doesn't hold the same appeal for me as it does you. It's too bloody hot for a start. I'm ready to go home.'

'Ok, but I'm not.'

'So, what's this about really Pinkie? Is it the unique freedom, or is it something to do with that scrap of paper you found ... or this Adam bloke you've suddenly hooked up with?'

I decided another hot, defiant retort would do me no credit. That was the pathway to an out-and-out row, sure as God made little green apples.

The truth was I wasn't entirely sure what it was all about, not really. Adam had talked about his life bursting into Technicolor. It wasn't a description I'd have come up with myself. But it expressed perfectly how I was feeling. The answer to Dan's question was yes. It was something to do with the scrap of paper. And yes again, it was something to do with Adam. But I wasn't sure I could explain exactly what; not even to myself. I think maybe it was a sense of stepping out of my everyday humdrum little life.

I'd probably started the ball rolling myself when I applied for voluntary redundancy, just for the hell of it really, and without another job to go to. I'd realised after fifteen years I yearned for something different, but couldn't say precisely what. Perhaps it was as simple as taking a risk for the first time in my life, doing something unexpected, something without a predictable outcome. I'd always been the kind of girl to paint within the lines, play by the rules, never rock the boat. Life was pleasant, cosy and dull, dull, dull.

Perhaps I was yearning for excitement, a big adventure. Maybe it was about being brave enough to use some shock tactics, ruffle some feathers, rattle some cages, and all those other expressions about mixing things up a bit. My life felt a bit like I'd stepped onto the kiddie ride in a theme park, and wished I'd been brave enough to join those screaming their heads off on the rollercoaster, emerging with such exhilaration on their faces.

Going home and getting back on the treadmill was undoubtedly the sensible thing to do. But I didn't want sensible, or responsible, or safe. I wanted the rollercoaster. Adam said his life felt like it had speeded up in the last couple of days. So did mine. And I wasn't ready to slow back down again. Sure, I wanted to be strapped in for the ride; I wasn't about to throw all caution to the winds; but I didn't want to get off. From the moment of my lock-in in Howard Carter's house, my life had taken an unexpected turn. I had no idea where it might lead, but I wanted to find out.

I sighed and opted to level with Dan. 'I think it might be a mix of all the above. I still want to see if I can find a way to decode the hieroglyphics. I'm sure they're probably nothing. But something in me wants to find out one way or the other. I'll admit, Adam's a bit of a walking encyclopaedia on ancient Egypt. It's a bit like having the best tour guide you can imagine, and not having to pay for the privilege. So, yes, I'm a bit star-struck. I don't know anyone else who shares my love of Egypt. Let's face it; you switch off at the mere mention of a pharaoh. And, for possibly the only time in my whole life, I have an opportunity to step outside my normal mundane existence and do something different, even if it's only for a couple more weeks. Won't you allow me that?'

'It's not a question of allowing you. I'm not your keeper. But I want what's best for you Pinkie, and I'm not sure this is it. You seem hell-bent on the pursuit of some pipe dream. I'm not sure what you think those hieroglyphics contain. But I can't help thinking you'll end up disappointed. I can empathise with your yearning for romance. God knows I do know what I look like in the mirror. And I'll admit this fantasy of ancient Egypt you hold in your head leaves me cold. But I'm not sure I can support you in recklessly chasing some whimsy that might expose you to risk.'

You see? Dan's lovely.

* * *

We argued about it for the rest of the evening, but I'd made up my mind and dug in my heels. Next day, it didn't take long to make the arrangements with hotel reception to extend my stay. The receptionist asked if I'd be willing to move to one of the smaller rooms. This was no hardship, as they're nearer my preferred infinity pool. So I signed on the dotted line, and that was it. I was staying.

I spent the whole of the day with Dan by the pool. It was the least I could do. But my mind kept drifting to the next momentous decision I had to make; which was all about what to tell Adam.

Dan had asked me if he was on the level. I felt sure he must be. But confiding in him had felt like a bridge too far at Karnak, and I'd held back. Stepping out of my everyday humdrum little life was one thing. But if it was straight into police custody, that would be a bit of a come down. So I had to tread warily. Trust me to strike up a friendship with the one person whose chumminess with the local police – Ahmed, my rescuer, in particular - pre-dated me, and almost certainly outranked me! Even without the police connection, there were probably thousands of reasons not to take a complete stranger into my confidence about the hieroglyphics.

But this good sound logic was at war with my female intuition. The simple, instinctive truth was I wanted to trust him. But whether this was good judgement of character on my part or more about falling under the spell of a pair of bewitching blue eyes and a poetic soul was the matter for debate.

There was probably also a hefty bit of wishful thinking in the mix. I needed to find a way of translating the hieroglyphics and, cue stage left, into my life walks the next best thing to a fully qualified Egyptologist. Surely this had to be fate lending a helping hand. I hadn't asked to be locked in Howard Carter's house, but I had been. And I hadn't gone looking for Adam, but he'd turned up at a fortuitous moment. This seemed like a happy coincidence, and my mother always taught me not to look a gift horse in the mouth.

And, let's face it. I was predisposed to be biased in his favour. Here was someone whose fascination with ancient Egypt surpassed even my own. I knew a soul mate when I saw one. Ok, I'll qualify that by saying I've never encountered a soul mate before. But it didn't mean I couldn't recognise him as such now.

But it was all so much subjective judgement. What finally tipped the balance was finding him online. A trawl of Facebook failed to turn him up. But I hit the jackpot with LinkedIn. It was a rather out-dated profile, dating back over a year. But there he was, with a rather dodgy photograph of him with much shorter hair, and a brief profile describing him as a fund manager. The bit that snagged my glance, and quieted my doubts was seeing the small reference to Egyptology at the Oriental Institute, Oxford University. It was nothing to do with his banking career, but it was as if he couldn't resist mentioning it, even though honesty compelled him to record his degree as unfinished.

I wondered about that a bit. I sensed a mystery. So, really it all boiled down to getting to know Adam better.

We'd said a rather wistful farewell at Karnak. I think we'd both felt a sense of thwarted destiny, however melodramatic it might sound. As if we weren't supposed to walk into each other's lives, only to turn around and walk straight back out again.

We'd exchanged mobile numbers and email addresses. But I sensed a certainty in both of us we were going through the motions and had no real intention of using them. I simply couldn't envisage myself calling him up from England for a chat about the latest Discovery Channel documentary, or becoming email pen pals, sending each other hyperlinks to the latest bits of Internet Egyptology. Whilst I couldn't tell you precisely what the nature of our relationship was, I could tell you what it wasn't. And it wasn't about keeping in touch through the miracles of modern technology, texts or tweets, satellites or Skype, computers or cyberspace.

All of which was not to say these modern miracles didn't have their place, or their uses. I pressed one of them into service that evening, selecting Adam's number from the contacts list in my mobile phone. He answered on the third ring.

'Hi Adam, it's Merry. Look, are you doing anything the day after tomorrow?'

* * *

I helped Dan to pack, shifting my stuff to my new room at the other end of the hotel complex at the same time.

'I still can't believe you're doing this,' he said, as he hefted his suitcase from the bed onto the floor.

'Please, Dan. We've been over and over it. I'm not changing my mind now. I've squared it with my Mum. She's not happy, but she concedes I'm a grown adult capable of thinking and acting for myself.' The eloquence of his raised eyebrow in response to this was rather devastating to my view of myself as a mature, independent person. I pretended I hadn't seen it. 'Dan, let's be friends. I want you to support me in this. It's really just an extended holiday, and in the place I love most in the whole world.'

'I'm still your friend, you little idiot,' he growled. 'I just don't want you coming a cropper. But you know my feelings, and you're determined to go ahead anyway. So let's drop it. Just promise to call me, or at least text me every day.'

I gave him a huge hug, knowing this was his way of giving in with good grace.

I went with him in the taxi to the airport and waved him through the security check; then jumped back in the taxi for the return trip to the Jolie Ville. I admit it did feel a bit weird walking through the hotel grounds to a different room knowing I was on my own now. It was a strangely self-conscious experience, like I was watching myself from the outside.

I took my Kindle into the buffet restaurant with me, and clicked through a few pages of a novel I'd downloaded while I ate my solo evening meal. But it didn't grab me, so I really just used it as a prop and to avoid making eye contact with anyone.

I wasn't brave enough to face the bar as a singleton. So I took a half-bottle of wine from the restaurant back to my room. My initial thought was to sit out on the patio, but I soon twigged I was fast becoming a feast for mosquitoes, so I headed inside. Propped on the pillows, I powered my laptop and Googled Queen Ahmes. But there was virtually no mention of her on any website thrown up by the search engine beyond the fact of her being Hatshepsut's mother. So I switched it off again, and texted Dan goodnight. The message would be waiting when he touched down at Gatwick. Then, feeling an odd little sense of displacement, I closed my eyes and drifted off to sleep.

***

I woke next morning with my sense of myself, and my purpose in still being here, much restored. I'd even own up to a small frisson of excitement. We'd arranged for Adam to come and meet me at the hotel mid-morning. He arrived looking clean-cut and crisp in loose cotton shirt and trousers not yet wilted in the heat, and smelling citrus-fresh. My stomach gave a little lurch at the sight of him. I'd said goodbye to him at Karnak believing I may never see him again. But here we were, and all because I'd dared to take a risk and do something different. And I was about to take another one; placing my faith in the hope I wouldn't live to regret it. I felt a bit giddy for a moment.

We sat in the deep cushioned wicker chairs under huge canopy shades on the hotel terrace overlooking the Nile. He looked around, taking in the spectacular view of the river with the Theban hills off in the distance, the closely manicured lawns, swaying palm trees and general botanical vibe. 'Nice here, isn't it?'

'Fantastic actually. And wait 'til you see Ramses the camel plodding by. He usually comes this way round about now.'

He raised an enquiring eyebrow.

'They have this great little children's petting zoo here. Ramses is the star attraction. He goes walkabout with his keeper every day, offering rides to all the guests.'

'And naturally you succumbed?'

'Naturally.'

He chuckled then broke off as a waiter appeared. We gave our order for peppermint tea, then smiled at each other. We both knew we were making small talk, filling time until I told him the purpose of my impromptu call to him last night; and why I was still here in Egypt, rather than unpacking my suitcase back home in leafy Sevenoaks.

The waiter returned with our tea and poured it into delicate cups. Adam thanked him and watched him out of sight then swung his gaze back to meet mine, 'Come on then, out with it, Merry. The suspense is killing me! You were very mysterious on the phone. What's this all about?'

The moment had arrived. I took a deep breath and plunged in. 'I know this is going to sound madly cloak-and-dagger, but you have to agree to a pact if you want me to tell you.'

He tilted his head to one side and regarded me searchingly. 'I'm intrigued.'

'Yes, well, not nearly so intrigued as you might be in a minute. So the pact has to come first.'

'Ok, what's the pact?'

'You have to swear not to repeat what I'm about to tell you to another living soul.'

He grinned. 'So, the dead ones are alright?'

I frowned at him. 'Can you please make some attempt to take me seriously?'

'Sorry Merry.' He wiped the smile off his face, and looked at me with a disarmingly open expression. 'You have no idea how theatrical you sounded, but I didn't mean to poke fun at you. So, what is it I'm promising not to reveal to another living soul?'

'Well it's one specific living soul you need to promise not to tell.' I qualified, only slightly mollified. 'I need your cast iron guarantee you won't shop me to your police friend.'

He stared at me. I don't think he was expecting that. 'Ok, well unless you're about to confess to murdering your boyfriend and burying him under the swimming pool over there, I guess I can promise to keep my lip buttoned where Ahmed's concerned. But now you've got me even more intrigued. What's the big secret you don't want him knowing?'

I fiddled with the braiding on the seat cushion for a bit. 'Well, you see, the truth is, there's a bit more to my breaking of the Queen Ahmes picture frame than your friend Ahmed knows.' It really would be helpful if he were called Mohammed, I decided. Ahmed and Ahmes really didn't roll off the tongue comfortably in the same sentence.

His eyebrows inched upwards above his rather lovely blue eyes. 'Ok Merry, what have you done?'

To give him credit, he didn't give me the lecture Dan had treated me to when I owned up to the stolen scrap of paper. Listening to me, his eyes widened in disbelief; then he went very still and quiet.

'So, you could be in possession of something to shed new light on who knows what, or it could be nothing at all, just some meaningless scribble?'

'That's about the size of it.'

If it's possible for someone's eyes to change colour, his did, from a deep blue, to a rather intense violet. 'Bloody hell, Merry, you've just set my brain on fire!'

'Sorry.'

'Don't apologise. It's incredible. I mean, wow! A hidden message, possibly from Howard Carter himself; that's a find-and-a-half!'

'Well, as I said, I'm not 100% sure the handwriting's his. And I guess the hieroglyphics could have been drawn by anyone. Carter might just have added his scrawl at the top of the page. Although the ink's the same.'

'You're making my head swim!'

'Sorry,' I said again. 'I've had a few of days to get used to it.'

He shook his head as if clearing it of cobwebs. Adam has rather thick glossy dark hair. So this was quite appealing to watch. 'Can I see it? I don't read hieroglyphics, as I said. But there's a slim chance if they're inscriptions copied from somewhere, I might recognise them. Of course, it's possible I'll take one look and laugh you into the next century...'

'Thanks!'

'Well, you have to admit it's one of the possibilities. It could just be a doodle.'

I remembered Dan said similar.

'But the way you found it does, I have to say, lead me to hope for something more thrilling. I presume it's tucked up in that ginormous holdall of yours right this moment, is it?'

I nodded, and unzipped my bag. I didn't need to rummage. It was right there on top of the other miscellany of possessions I dragged around with me every day. But - contrary minx that I am - I made it appear I was rummaging, wanting to draw out the moment. It never hurt to build a little anticipation, I told myself. I withdrew it on a small flourish and handed it over.

Once it was in his tanned hands, I realised how ridiculous I was - eking every modicum of drama from a rather straightforward situation. I must be feeling a stronger need for significance than usual, redundant from my job, my boyfriend back home, curiously rudderless, despite all my brave rhetoric about rollercoasters. Sad and tragic individual I can be sometimes!

Adam studied the paper intently. He was utterly still, totally silent.

'Well?' All of a sudden it was me the suspense was killing.

His eyes didn't shift from the document in his hands. 'Well, as predicted I can't make head nor tail of the hieroglyphs. But, as far as my untrained eye can work out, I don't think they're copied from anywhere. Something about them seems a bit odd. Like they're just a random jumble of stuff.'

'Probably just a meaningless scribble after all?' My disappointment was disproportionate really. I'd convinced myself they were more.

He tilted his head to one side, still frowning at the inscriptions. 'I don't know I'd go so far as to say meaningless. They've been drawn with remarkable precision. And I'm inclined to agree with you, this line at the top looks like Howard Carter's handwriting. And the ink looks the same, so I'd hazard a guess they were inscribed at the same time as the text. It looks and feels old enough to date from Carter's time. All in all, I'd say we have a mystery - could be something, could be nothing.'

I stared at him in frustration. 'I'm sure the "could be nothing" scenario is the most likely. But I can't get away from how I found that scrap of paper. I don't believe it found its way between the folds of the Queen Ahmes' portrait by accident. It just seems to me it was hidden there, possibly by Carter himself; then secreted inside the frame. And I want to know why.'

'Ok, so if I join you in making that leap, then we abandon the "could be nothing" conclusion, in favour of, what, seeing it as some kind of puzzle to be solved?'

I nodded slowly. 'I kind of think that's how I've seen it from the start. Probably from the moment I discovered it.

Call it instinct, intuition, whatever, but there's some hook in that scrap of paper that has me baited. I just know it means something. It has to. And I intend to discover what. That's why I'm still here.'

He gazed out across the silent waters of the Nile, reflecting. '"Find my equal here",' he breathed softly. 'Well, I can see why you latched onto the 'equal' bit of the parallel line between Hatshepsut's temple and Karnak. And I'll tell you another interesting nugget of useless information that might just give you pause for thought...'

'What?'

'If you extend that axis out even further, the other side of Hatshepsut's temple this time, under the cliffs, you'll find yourself slap bang at the entrance to her tomb in the Valley of the Kings!'

'Run that by me again...?'

'The Valley of the Kings lies directly behind Hatshepsut's temple, on the other side of the bay of cliffs. Once she had herself pronounced Pharaoh, she fixed on the idea of a tomb in the Valley. Her father, Thutmosis I, was the first pharaoh buried there. The fascinating fact is this ... If her tomb had been dug along a straight axis, as historians believe was the original idea, her burial chamber would have lain directly beneath her temple at Deir el-Bahri, and on the same axis as the Temple of Amun at Karnak.'

'But it wasn't dug along a straight axis?'

'Sadly, no. It seems poor quality bedrock forced the workmen to follow a corkscrew-like course in a vain search for better stone. The burial chamber ended up deeper and to the southwest.'

I sipped my tea for a moment, and contemplated all this. 'So, what you're telling me is there's another "equal and opposite", running backwards from Hatshepsut's temple this time.'

'Exactly!'

'Can we go there? We drew a blank at Karnak, but maybe there's some inscriptions in the Valley to match the ones on the paper.'

'Impossible, I'm afraid. Hatshepsut's tomb is closed to the public. I'm not sure it's ever been open, not since Howard Carter cleared it in 1903.'

I caught my breath. 'Howard Carter again! He cleared Hatshepsut's tomb?'

'Yes, although by all accounts it was a terrible experience. Not only was it filled with rubble, but the ceiling in the burial chamber had collapsed. The air was so bad and it was so hot the workmen's candles melted. Just to make things even nastier, dried bat-poo from centuries of bat infestation created suffocating clouds wherever the men worked.'

'Sounds hideous,' I agreed. 'But nevertheless, it's a link, isn't it? Carter worked on copying Hatshepsut's temple in the late 1800s, then on clearing her tomb in the early 1900s. Did he find anything? Specifically, anything relating to Queen Ahmes?'

Adam slowly shook his head. 'I'll need to check to be sure. But from what I remember, Carter found two stone sarcophagi, one for Thutmosis I and one for Hatshepsut. But neither of the mummies was there, nor any treasure, just a few broken fragments of wood and pottery.'

My shoulders slumped; then I had another thought. 'What about the mummy of Queen Ahmes? Has that ever been found? Perhaps by her 'equal' Carter meant the real her, or at least her remains.'

Again, Adam paused then slowly shook his head. 'No, no mummy of Hatshepsut's mummy that I'm aware of.'

I let his execrable play on words pass. 'What about inscriptions?'

'I think there were a few stone tablets lying about with scenes from the Amduat carved on them. I can't imagine they're what we're looking for.'

It seemed hopeless. I was unwilling to let go of the linked tomb-and-temple angle, and Carter's association with both, but couldn't see any way out of the dead-end.

'I think the only thing we can do is find a way to translate these hieroglyphs,' he said.

I looked up as his words sank in. 'You said "we". Does that mean you're going to help me? Even though it means being an accessory after the fact, or whatever it's called, and keeping that little piece of stolen property you're holding so reverently a secret from your friend Ahmed?'

He gazed at me for a long time, and a slow smile tugged at the corners of his mouth. 'Well I know it's not the choice I should make as the fine upstanding citizen of the world I consider myself to be. But I'm sitting here with this scrap of paper knowing my whole future could turn on what it says. What's the expression...? "I feel like I'm diagonally parked in a parallel universe." That's it exactly, because I agree with you. I don't think this scrap of paper is nothing, either. If Howard Carter hid it in the picture frame, he did so for a reason. So, even though we might find ourselves up to our necks in trouble, and Ahmed may never forgive me if he ever finds out, there's no way I can hand this back to you, and not take the next steps towards deciphering it. I'd spend the rest of my life wondering about it, and probably never get a sound night's sleep again!'

'So you're not going to turn me in?' I pressed.

'No, Merry, I'm not.'

'Pact?' I asked.

'Pact!' he agreed.

'So, we have to find a way of cracking the hieroglyphics.'

'Yes, and I've just had a thought about that,' he mused. 'I think I know someone who might be able to help us.

Chapter 6

'My old university professor retired out here to Cairo a few years back,' Adam said. He took me under his wing a bit because of, well, because of what happened to make me leave university early.' He didn't volunteer any further insight into what this was, and sensing it wasn't something he liked talking about, I let it go. 'I've stayed in touch with him sporadically over the years. I'm sure I could look him up.'

It sounded a high-risk strategy to me. I'd had a hard enough time persuading myself to confide in Adam. Here we were contemplating taking someone else – another complete stranger from my point of view - into our confidence. I started to wonder if I'd taken leave of my senses. I had no trouble at all imagining what Dan would have to say on the subject. Although, to be fair to myself, it was difficult to see any other way of getting the hieroglyphics translated. 'And what would you tell him about how we came by the scrap of paper?' I asked doubtfully. 'Because I, for one, am not opting for the truth; that information is strictly classified. I have no desire to be arrested. I've taken the one-and-only risk I'm prepared to take by telling you. And, believe me, I debated long and hard about that.'

He looked at me and grinned, and I could tell he was starting to enjoy himself. 'We'll just have to get creative then, won't we?' The warm breeze blowing across the Nile ruffled his hair, and brought with it some tropical scent I couldn't identify. I could almost see his brain whirring. 'The problem is, without knowing what the hieroglyphics say, and without being able to admit to where you got them, we're taking a massive leap of faith showing them to anyone at all,' he said thoughtfully. 'But I don't see another way of decoding them – at least, not quickly. I think my old professor it probably our best bet.' He stared at me for a minute or two, and I could sense the doubts raging inside him too. The enjoyment of a few moments ago was giving way to a few misgivings of his own. 'But I'll be honest Merry, I'd like to retain his good opinion. If this ends up being a total wild goose chase, I don't want to think I've wasted his time. And I don't want him to think I'm the village idiot. You've trusted me with this, so I'll level with you. I've come to this whole Egyptology lark rather late in life after a false start. I'd like to be taken seriously. I want to feel I could make a career out of it somehow. I've spent too much of my life doing something I hate to chuck it all to the wind now. I don't have a degree in Egyptology, just a half-achieved attempt at one. So I have to tread with some caution. I want to build a reputation for myself as a credible student of Egyptology, not as a laughing stock.'

I could see his point of view. For me, there was nothing at stake. Well, nothing if you discounted the risk of being banged to rights for stepping onto the wrong side of the law. It was a bald fact I'd come by the scrap of paper not by fair means, but foul. I sipped my tea, seeing the dilemma spreading in all directions. 'There is another possible outcome,' I said slowly as I returned my cup to its saucer. 'Those hieroglyphics could contain something to make your reputation as a budding Egyptologist, not break it.'

'How do you figure that one out?'

'Well, just suppose the inscriptions - for all they seem to be a random jumble of stuff - turn out to be important. Maybe they shed new light on Howard Carter, and you could somehow add to his biographical record. Or maybe they say something about Tutankhamun, or Hatshepsut, or Queen Ahmes - something the rest of the world doesn't know yet. Surely there's an opportunity for you to make a name for yourself.'

I could see he desperately wanted to sign up to this line of thought. 'You're holding out the ultimate bait. But that leaves us with the unavoidable problem of the provenance of the scrap of paper. How the hell would we say we came into possession of it?'

I shrugged eloquently. 'I guess I'd have to fall on my sword and come clean. I've never had criminal tendencies up to this point in my life. Maybe I could say it was a mental breakdown.'

He grinned at me. 'You're incorrigible! And, you know what? I think we have to take the leap of faith and keep our fingers crossed. To talk ourselves out of it at the first hurdle seems a bit lily-livered!'

'So we get the hieroglyphics translated, no matter what; and get ready to deal with any consequences. Right?'

'Right,' he said emphatically, the dashing, adventurous side of him coming to the fore again. 'Which means I need to make a phone call to the professor, and we need to urgently come up with a plausible story to tell him.'

***

We booked two berths on the overnight sleeper train from Luxor to Cairo. Over our tray-dinner - surprisingly good actually - in the lounge car, we puzzled over what we were going to tell the professor.

'I just said I was coming to Cairo for a couple of days with a friend to re-visit some of the sites. It's been a long time since I've been to Cairo, so it's natural I should want to look him up. We've not been in close contact over the years, but we've always exchanged Christmas cards, and we met up for lunch once or twice in London a few years back, before he retired out here.'

'You didn't mention the hieroglyphics at all?'

'No, I thought I'd save that for when we actually see him.'

'So we need to agree our pitch, so to speak.'

We decided to stick as close to the truth as possible, without admitting my part in it. We struck on the idea of throwing Adam's chum Ahmed into the mix, working on the assumption it wouldn't hurt to namedrop a policeman to add an air of authority to our story. As W.S. Gilbert famously quoted in the Mikado, this was "merely corroborative detail, intended to give artistic verisimilitude to an otherwise bald and unconvincing narrative", but we felt it might help.

So the tissue of semi-fabrication we finally agreed upon was to say Ahmed, as a member of Luxor tourist police, happened to be on site at the Howard Carter museum in Luxor when a tourist accidentally broke one of the display pictures. Supervising the clearing up, Ahmed spotted the scrap of paper, which had drifted underneath one of the display cabinets. He'd slipped it in his pocket, needing first of all to take statements from the tourist, and from the house attendant about how the accident had happened. Basically, he'd forgotten it was there, rediscovering it later that evening when he stuck his hand in his pocket for some loose change during a game of dominoes with Adam. He actually had no idea whether the scrap of paper was relevant to the breakage, or might have fallen from one of the other displays. He'd shown it to Adam, who was intrigued by the hieroglyphics. So, this being Egypt, and law and order being a little on the loose side, he'd agreed to lend it to Adam for a couple of days, provided he returned it so it could be restored to its rightful place on display in Howard Carter's house. We decided it would do.

I enjoyed the train journey; for all that I spent a fair bit of it fast asleep in my tiny berth. The track skirted the Nile on its northwards journey, passing rural scenes of farmers finishing their day's work in the fields, returning home with their donkeys, or in some cases camels in tow. The sunset was truly spectacular, as Egyptian sunsets always seem to be, a blaze of orange, fading through purple and navy blue.

I phoned Dan to update him on progress, and let him know I was on my way to Cairo with Adam to hopefully get the hieroglyphics deciphered. He'd had a heavy-duty day back at work, catching up on the inevitable backlog after a couple of weeks away. The UK is three hours behind Egypt, and he was knocking himself up a stir-fry when I called, having just got in from work. He sounded distracted and a bit grumpy, so I kept it short and sweet, promised to call again tomorrow, and rang off.

I was woken early by the train attendant, and given my breakfast box. The shadowy stretches of pale desert rock beyond the track gave way to more agricultural land as we approached Cairo; green fields interspersed with mud brick huts surrounded by livestock. Soon I was watching the grimy suburbs blur past the train window, huge posterboards in Arabic script, neon Coca Cola signs flashing from the tops of high-rise apartment buildings, and flyovers crammed with traffic snaking through the metropolis. Then, before I knew it, we were pulling in to Cairo station.

My lasting impression was of noise, flies, dust and heat. I guess a bit like busy stations anywhere in the world - although perhaps without the flies.

We'd had a bit of a debate about where to stay, but as it seemed we were both in the lucky position of having a modest cushion of money in the bank, we decided to live it up a little, and opted for the Mena House. We'd made our bookings before leaving Luxor, and Adam had invited the professor to meet him at the hotel for lunch. It was agreed I'd join them for coffee, to say hello and ask about the hieroglyphics, but let Adam do some proper catching up with his old mentor first.

The taxi from the station dropped us at the doors to the impressively grand foyer of this old colonial hotel. Reminiscent of an oriental palace, and in a truly unique location overlooking the pyramids, Mena House welcomed us to a sumptuous world of bygone opulence, complete with Arab mashrabia windows, brass embossed doors, blue tiles and mosaics of coloured marbles and mother-of-pearl. Originally a Khedive hunting lodge, it was re-styled into a lavish hotel, opening in 1886. The rich and famous have been staying there ever since.

I hadn't expected our rooms to be ready, considering our morning arrival; but we were immediately shown to them, each lavish in its dècor and with a jaw-dropping view across to the pyramids.

With a couple of hours to spare before the professor was due to meet Adam for lunch, we gave in to the irresistible allure of these last of the great wonders of the ancient world, and strolled the short distance up the road from the hotel to the Giza plateau.

The touts and hawkers started making a beeline for us when we were no more than a few paces outside the hotel gates. This time, it wasn't so much curios they were selling - although we did get the inevitable miniature pyramids waved in our faces - it was more horse or camel rides around the plateau. These poor creatures, ridiculously decked out in pom-poms and tassels, stood forlornly under some rigged up and ripped sheeting, unequal to the task of shielding them from the blazing sun.

I was starting to baton down the hatches into my normal non-responsive guise, head-down, eyes on the floor - really not the best pose for appreciating the massive mountains of stone rising from the desert sands. But Adam was having none of it. He stopped dead in his tracks, held up one hand in an unmistakeable "stop" sign. He barked out a few presumably well-chosen words of Arabic, in a tone of such command it nearly had me jumping to attention. Breathless with admiration, I spun to face him. 'I thought you said learning Arabic was an uphill struggle. That was awesome!'

'Yes, well, the first thing I got Ahmed to teach me was how to give these pesky so-and-so's their marching orders. I don't blame them really; they're just trying to make a living. But I don't always condone the way they do it, constantly shoving and pushing, and never taking no for an answer.' He glanced about him as we stepped into the shadow of the Great Pyramid, looming above us silent and rather forbidding in its immensity. 'And I don't condone the mess they let build up around the place either.'

I could see what he meant. Piles of refuse, water and soft drink bottles, crisp packets, horse and camel dung, and probably other unmentionables drifted against any obstacle preventing it blowing out across the desert. Even so, these modern distractions and detritus couldn't detract from the awesome spectacle of the pyramids. I suspect there are no more famous sites in Egypt, or for that matter anywhere in the world. They are, without question, the icon most associated with the land of the pharaohs. Since their logic-defying construction, they've embodied antiquity, mystery and speculation.

'The best view is from beyond the sphinx, looking back at the pyramids,' Adam said, so we wandered in that direction.

The hawkers must have some tom-tom system for passing on messages among themselves, because we weren't bothered again for the whole time we were there. There were a couple of tourist coaches there, and we passed a harassed-looking tour guide leading his group towards the entrance to the Great Pyramid. But generally, like the rest of the tourist sites, it was relatively quiet.

The sprawling metropolis of modern Cairo, noisy, smelly and dusty, and with its inevitable MacDonald's and Kentucky Fried Chicken outlets, spills literally to the foot of the pyramid plateau. If you stand with your back to the sphinx, the pall of pollution hanging over the city and, closer up, the brash neon signs of the tourist bazaars and souvenir shops hit you full in the face. But turn away from these modern eyesores and it seems the whole of history rises before you.

The sphinx seems to protect the huge mountains of stone rising on the desert plateau behind him. I've always thought there's something particularly unnerving about the sphinx - impassively watching civilisations rise and fall, perhaps secure in the knowledge he'll outlast them all.

Like the Hypostyle Hall at Karnak, it's impossible to do the pyramids justice with a camera. Adam and I larked about for a while taking touristy photographs, then glanced at our watches and decided it was time to head back to Mena House.

We both headed back to our rooms to clean and brush-up. But while I stayed luxuriating in the bath, Adam headed off for lunch with the professor. I'd agreed to meet them there a bit later. I ordered the most fantastic club sandwich I've ever tasted from room service, and sat out on my balcony, staring across at the pyramids, thinking it was actually far easier to appreciate them from a slight distance.

I took my time strolling through the hotel to meet Adam and the professor, noticing all the exquisite antiques, handcrafted furniture, original works of art and magnificent antiques displayed throughout the public areas. I joined them in the Khan el Khalili restaurant, billed in the hotel guide as a cafe-of-the-world and, again, with the stunning backdrop of the omnipresent pyramids.

Adam and the professor both rose to meet me as a smiling waitress showed to their table. This was a nice throwback to old-fashioned manners. Perhaps being in such historic surroundings brought out the best in them. Adam performed the introductions, 'Merry, this is professor Edward Kincaid. Ted, this is Meredith Pink.'

We shook hands. 'Please call me Ted,' he said, at the precise same moment I said, 'Please call me Merry.'

Smiling all round, we subsided into our seats, and ordered coffee.

'So, how was your lunch?' I asked.

'Historic!' Ted proclaimed. 'Food, location, and view - and the company wasn't bad.'

We all laughed, and settled back in our chairs. Ted appeared to be in his mid-seventies, a trim, dapper gentleman with silver hair, light blue eyes - quite startling in his tanned face -impeccably tailored, sporting a gold sphinx-shaped tie pin.

'In honour of the occasion,' he said, when he caught me admiring it. 'It's not every day I'm invited to lunch in a landmark hotel by one of my favourite ex-students.'

'Makes up for the time you took me for afternoon tea at the Ritz.' Adam grinned at him. The warmth of a genuine bond between them was plain to see.

'Adam's been telling me you bumped into each other at the Luxor museum, and again at Hatshepsut's temple, and discovered you share a mutual love of ancient Egypt.'

'Yes, although I'm trailing well behind him in the knowledge stakes. I'm just an enthusiastic amateur. I'm sorry to say most of what I know has come from reading fiction set in ancient Egypt.'

'Don't apologise,' Ted laughed. 'Story-telling is an age-old method of acquainting people with history. While artistic license allows the imagination to run free, the basic historical facts have to be correct. I'll bet you've learnt a huge amount of academic material through the media of popular entertainment. So don't knock it.'

I could see why Adam liked him. A stuffy cliché-of-a-professor of academia he most certainly was not.

Adam must've spied his opening in this exchange, because he sat forward. 'I've been telling Ted about those hieroglyphics Ahmed found on the floor in Howard Carter's house,' he said, 'And how they got our imaginations going.'

'Ah, yes.' Ted joined in. 'I'm interested to see what I make of them.'

Adam withdrew a folded sheet of A4 from his jacket pocket and handed it across the table. We'd taken the precaution of photocopying the original, and covering up the intriguing scribbled "find my equal here". So all Ted was seeing was a photocopy of the hieroglyphics, without any context whatsoever, apart from the where they were found. No Queen Ahmes link, and no Howard Carter handwriting. We'd decided this was safest, since we had no idea what they hieroglyphics might reveal.

Ted stuck a narrow pair of gold-rimmed spectacles on the end of his nose and studied the sheet of paper. 'Exquisitely drawn, aren't they?' he commented. 'It's quite a skill. Modern artists make a fair living painting copies of the ancient reliefs and inscriptions onto papyrus to sell to the tourists.'

I could well believe it. Adam and I had both attempted to hand-copy the inscriptions with a remarkable lack of success. It certainly proved just how skilled an artist you had to be to render them with any semblance of accuracy. Our attempts were toe-curlingly crude.

Ted frowned over them for a long time. 'I have to say, at first glance, they don't seem to say anything coherent. Each column of glyphs seems to bear absolutely no relation to the one before or after it. So I don't think you've got a story or a description here. But I'll need to do a proper translation to be sure - I'm a bit rusty on the old philology.'

We must both have looked a bit crushed.

'Tell you what,' he said. 'Why don't I zip home and consult my reference books. I'll meet you back here for afternoon tea - any excuse to indulge in a slice of Mena House cake - and we'll see what I've come up with. How does that strike you?'

I'd say we were in no position to refuse.

'Well...?' Adam said after we'd waved Ted off in a taxi. Not with indecent haste, I should add. We did let the poor chap finish his coffee. 'We've got a couple of hours to kill. We can either laze round the pool, or try to put our time to more productive use. What do you fancy?'

The thought of lazing round the pool with Adam was a trifle unsettling. There were no temples, pyramids, tombs or sphinxes there to divert my attention from his blue eyes. 'Is there time to visit the museum?'

He shrugged. 'We'd be cutting it fine. Tahrir Square is in downtown Cairo. I'm not sure we'll make it there and back by cab with time left to see anything. The traffic in Cairo is notorious. I suppose that's what comes of having something like fifteen million people all crammed into the city. But we could get a taxi to the nearest metro stop, and take it from there. I'm game if you are.'

So we replaced the thought with the action, and soon found ourselves squashed into a packed metro train careening at top speed into central Cairo.

Dusty, decrepit and higgledy-piggledy, the Egyptian Museum of Antiquities is definitely not state of the art. To my way of thinking, it's a thousand times lovelier for not being so. Housed in a late Victorian mansion house, which, Tardis-like, seems to expand to impossibly enormous proportions once inside, it's wonderfully old-fashioned. Occasionally artefacts lack any description whatsoever, but most have a short, just-about-adequate explanation printed in faded typewriter ink on small, yellowed cards.

'You know, there are as many objects packed away in storerooms as on display in this place,' Adam said. 'Incredible huh?'

Considering the priceless and exquisite nature of the artefacts, the museum did seem sadly unequal to the task of doing them any sort of justice. Some of the statuary looked to me as if it had simply been dumped there, probably by some tired and sweaty archaeologist more than a hundred years ago; and there it remained to this day, jumbled alongside relatives cast in stone from Dynasties past, present and future.

'Needs to be dragged into the twenty-first century, doesn't it?' he went on. 'Apparently they're planning to open a brand spanking new museum near the pyramids at Giza in 2015. They'll move all the artefacts there and be able to put more on display.'

'Translating that into Egyptian time, I won't start holding my breath for the grand opening until at least 2020,' I murmured drily, and he chuckled.

He was right though. Overwhelmingly, the museum had the feeling of a storage warehouse, just one in which the contents were visible rather than enclosed in packaging. But, to me, this added to its charm.

I guess due to nervousness about the political situation around Tahrir Square in particular, there were no crowds. We had the place practically to ourselves. But with so little time before we had to get back to Mena House, we didn't linger on the ground floor to study the immense collection of papyrus, or the displays of coins from the ancient world. Instead we made a beeline upstairs for the big draw, Tutankhamun's treasure. In the scant forty-five minutes or so we had to spare, it was impossible to make a detailed study of each item, as we'd have liked. So we darted among ritual golden figures of the boy king, amulets and royal regalia, clothing and textiles, cosmetic jars, games and game boxes, musical instruments, writing materials, chariots and weaponry, beds and headrests, boxes and chests, chairs and thrones. It was mind-boggling.

Despite the richness of some previous finds; I'm not sure anything could have possibly prepared Howard Carter for the opulence and sheet quantity of the funerary objects buried with Tutankhamun; or for the gold. Just about everything in sight gleamed with it. And we hadn't even entered the treasury yet.

The really priceless objects are kept behind bars and dark curtains in a separate, closely supervised room. They include breath-taking pectorals inlaid with semi-precious stones, the exquisite golden shrine showing scenes of Tutankhamun hunting birds and fowling with his queen Ankhesenamun, a solid gold coffin and - of course - the world-famous mask.

Where we'd exclaimed often and excitedly to each other as we moved between display cabinets in the main hall, now, entering the dark treasury, we fell silent. Absolute silence really was the only thing equal to the spine-tingling sensation of coming face-to-face with eternity.

We both moved to stand in front of the golden mask, as if drawn by a magic spell. Superbly modelled, Tutankhamun's portrait mask must surely stand as a masterpiece without parallel. Beaten from pure solid gold, it shows the young king as Osiris, wearing the striped blue nemes headcloth, with a vulture and cobra rising from his brow, the latter poised to spit fire at Pharaoh's enemies.

We stood speechless and star-struck for a long time; then moved off to inspect the other fantastic objets d'art. It was only when we were back in the main display hall I felt I could breathe normally again.

'I don't know about you,' I said, feeling curiously tight-chested and light-headed, 'but I found that eerie. Almost as if he was watching our every move.'

'I know what you mean. The mask emanates a kind of knowing serenity, as if he possesses some timeless secret we'll never know.'

That was exactly it: Adam once again proving his uncanny ability to tune precisely into my wavelength and put my jumbled impressions into words. Dan would've snorted and accused me of being ridiculously fanciful. And suddenly I asked myself if it was really the done thing to be here enjoying another man's company quite so much, when my boyfriend was at home, doubtless stuck behind some dreary computer screen in Canary Wharf.

We arrived back at Mena House, and were shown to a table outside on the terrace barely five minutes before Ted joined us. The pyramids glowed a mellow gold in the late afternoon sunshine, the air still and warm, and smelling powerfully tropical. I identified why when I spotted the huge display of hothouse flowers on the occasional table in the corner.

We ordered tea and cake all round, nothing more substantial since Adam and I were booked into the restaurant for dinner later, and Ted claimed to be still full from lunch. We told him about our lightning visit to the museum while we waited for tea to arrive and be poured, then all leaned forward as if part of some dark conspiracy - as perhaps we were!

'Here you go.' He handed the A4 photocopy back to Adam, and I could see he'd annotated the blank bottom half of the page. 'I wonder if what you've got there are perhaps a bunch of inscriptions copied from items found in King Tut's tomb. Or perhaps from elsewhere in Carter's recording of the monuments. They seem a rather random assortment of phrases, not seeming to relate to each other, as I said earlier.'

Adam scanned the sheet, then read aloud for my benefit, 'One of two ladies rising. Most esteemed of him who made himself alone. Manifest lord, resurrected of Re. Horizon of Ra Horus who rejoices in it. Four colours of earth and water at home in two. Of the place of pillars through darkness and light.'

His gaze lifted from the sheet to meet mine, full of bewilderment. I knew just how he felt. Not one single word made any sense to me. Then he grinned and shrugged, and shoved the paper into his pocket as if it didn't much merit further discussion.

'Thanks Ted; I appreciate your afternoon's work on this. I hope it didn't give you too much of a headache.' I figured this meant he was making light of the hieroglyphs, downplaying any significance they might have.

'I enjoyed it actually. It's a while since my old brain has had proper exercise. I'm not sure the daily Sudoku puzzle really counts. Well, I suppose it means you can return the scrap of paper to your policeman friend to put back on display safe in the knowledge you haven't stumbled across anything significant.' With that pronouncement he smiled, took a sip of his tea, and turned the conversation to Hosni Mubarak's trial.

But that conclusion was the last one Adam and I were willing to accept. We spoke of literally nothing else over dinner that night at the Moghul Indian restaurant, one of Mena House's signature dining venues. It has a reputation for serving the finest Indian cuisine in Egypt, a culinary reminder of the hotel's membership of the prestigious, Indian-based Oberoi hotel chain.

I'm sorry to say my appreciation of the delectable and aromatic array of dishes placed in front of me throughout the evening was not what it should have been.

'All those random phrases just have to mean something,' Adam exclaimed. 'They must have something in common, some theme or link or image. But I'll be damned if I know what it is.'

'Maybe the clue is in the "find my equal here" bit. It suggests it's a place we're looking for.'

We'd both gone back to our respective rooms between afternoon tea and dinner and Googled every part of the translation Ted had produced. Nothing the miracle search engine returned seemed to shed any light on the dilemma.

Adam took a thoughtful sip of his wine. 'You know, if I had to have a stab at what those phrases are supposed to represent, I'd say they look like cryptic crossword clues.'

'What makes you think that?'

'Well, it was Ted's mention of Sudoku that put the thought in my head. Brain teasers, that sort of thing.'

I groaned. 'I've never been good at crossword puzzles, certainly not cryptic ones.'

'My Dad used to be good at them,' he said.

'Not anymore?'

'Well, I suppose it's possible they do crosswords in Heaven, or whatever version of the afterlife he's gone to, but I suspect it's unlikely.'

I could have happily crawled under the crisp white linen tablecloth onto the floor. 'Oh God, Adam, I'm sorry. I didn't know.'

'Of course you didn't. You're not clairvoyant. At least, not that I've noticed.' He gave me a very charming lop-sided

131

smile. 'Anyway, my Dad always said there were conventions to cryptic crossword clues.' He frowned, 'Let's see if I can remember...'

I watched him dredge through his memory, wondering a bit about all the parts of his life story not known to me. Weird really, to be sitting here so intimately, feeling such a natural affinity with someone I'd known barely a week and, in reality, knew barely at all. Yet here I was, sharing some of the most adventuresome moments of my life with him, riding night-trains and metros, visiting ancient sites and historic museums, meeting new people, staying in a world class hotel, and feeling completely at home all the while.

'... If memory serves, it's something like a precise definition, and some word play. And that's it. Simples!'

'But with one big difference,' I pointed out dampeningly. 'In a crossword puzzle you know how many letters you're searching for. We're stabbing in the dark, hoping they're riddles for us to solve which, perhaps collectively, might give us a location for whatever is supposed to be "equal" to Queen Ahmes. And that's always assuming it's Queen Ahmes whose equal we're looking for. We're working on the premise he chose her picture specifically, rather than hiding his message in any old picture frame.'

'If we give up on the idea the "my" in "find my equal here" refers to Queen Ahmes, we might as well pack up and go home. Surely it makes no sense otherwise. The only other person the "my" could relate to is Howard Carter himself, if it's his handwriting. But what in heaven's name should we be expected to make of that?'

I shrugged and pushed my food round my plate a bit.

'You know Merry, I can't help wondering if this is all some elaborate hoax. As if someone's having a great laugh at our expense.'

'If my boyfriend Dan could write hieroglyphics, I'd be well inclined to agree with you. It would be right up his street.'

Adam concentrated on his food for a while, as if by so carelessly dropping Dan into the conversation I'd created a small space between us that hadn't been there before. I wasn't sure whether to regret it or not.

'I have to say, it's not a bad idea,' he said after a while. 'Cryptic crossword puzzles with ancient Egyptian clues; I wonder if there's a market for it. Perhaps something to keep the Nile cruise passengers occupied while their riverboat steams between one historical site and the next. I guess it could add a little je-ne-sais-quoi to the holiday experience.'

'I wonder if we shouldn't concentrate on trying to solve the clues we've got, before we get carried away by the idea of writing new ones.'

'Agreed, o wise one; so where do we begin? If the Internet isn't able to throw out any suggestions, I'd say we're stalled in the starting blocks.'

'Howard Carter didn't have the Internet, so perhaps we should have a go at getting on without it?'

'Okey dokey, so fire a suggestion at me.'

I rooted around in my head and kept drawing blanks. To buy time for inspiration to strike I asked him to quote the first phrase - now remodelled as a clue - back at me.

'"One of two ladies rising".' He said. 'I suddenly feel as if we've strayed into a Bingo hall!'

I let my mind go into free-fall. An image sprang up before me and I narrowed my eyes to fix it. I realised it was Tutankhamun's golden funerary mask I was seeing in my mind's eye. Perhaps not surprising it should be the first image to pop into my head. I'd spent long enough gawping at it that afternoon. And it is, after all, pretty memorable. But something about it snagged on my consciousness, and wouldn't let go.

My vision cleared and I found myself staring into Adam's darkly lashed eyes.

'What are those two creatures called that rise up above the pharaoh's forehead when he wears the nemes head-dress? We saw them today on Tutankhamun's mask. You know, the snake and the bird of prey.'

He went very still. I'd noticed that about him. He had this way of seeming to do a living freeze-frame when a significant thought struck him. 'The uraeus,' he said slowly.

'The divine cobra of Lower Egypt and the vulture goddess of Upper Egypt.'

'Do they have names?'

'Wadjit, the cobra, and Nekhbet, the vulture,' he breathed.

'Do you know if they were ever referred to as The Two Ladies?'

'Bloody Hell, Merry; I think you might be onto something!' There was a pleasing note of enlightenment in the way he said this. Then a frown creased his brow. 'But neither one's a place. They're part of the royal regalia.'

I was in no mood to be put off. My dampening spirits of a few moments ago gave way to the implacable zeal I get when I absolutely know I'm right. 'Let's not worry too much about that now. Besides, you said one was Upper Egypt, the other Lower Egypt. We know it's only one of them we need - the clue says so. So that narrows the field a bit, to my way of looking at things.'

'My God, Merry, you're a genius!'

'And I'm not the budding Egyptologist around here,' I remarked benignly.

Chapter 7

An Internet search of Wadjit, the divine cobra of Lower Egypt and Nekhbet, the vulture goddess of Upper Egypt revealed they were indeed referred to as The Two Ladies. There was no way of knowing which was the right one in the context of Carter's conundrums. But this did nothing to dent the euphoria of having cracked the first clue.

We downed another bottle of wine between us in the bar after confirming this discovery, and tossed the other riddles back and forth between us.

'"Him who made himself alone",' Adam said. 'Does that have a ring of Moses about it to you? He went wandering off into the desert for forty years. I struggle to think of a better way of making yourself alone.'

I shrugged, 'Ok, so who or what was his "most esteemed"?'

'Well, his God, I suppose; the God of the Hebrews. What did they call him? Yahweh, wasn't it?'

'Yes, that rings a bell. So, was Yahweh ever known as "most esteemed"?'

We'd brought Adam's iPad along to the bar with us. We entered a search on "Yahweh" + "most esteemed", but it didn't offer up anything that seemed helpful.

'Ok, let's add it to the maybe pile,' I suggested. 'What about "Manifest lord, resurrected of Re"? The only person I can think of who was resurrected was Jesus. But somehow I don't suppose He's who we're looking for.'

Adam's eyes gleamed. 'I read this crazy book once claiming Tutankhamun was actually Jesus. It put forward other great 18th Dynasty pharaohs as Solomon and David. You know, the Bible never actually names the pharaohs who feature so prominently in the Old Testament. To this day, scholars argue about who the pharaoh of the exodus might have been. Most seem to settle on Ramses II, but there are other contenders.'

'They probably settle on Ramses II because they've read the Christian Jacq novels,' I muttered. 'But I read an equally compelling case for Horemheb in a novel recently - killing the first born sons of the Hebrew because he believed Ankhesenamun, Tutankhamun's widow, might be hiding among them with an heir to the throne.'

Adam shook his head at me. 'You and your fictional history!'

'Your professor said not to knock it,' I reminded him. 'Ok, so let's run the scenario the "manifest lord, resurrected of Re" is actually Jesus masquerading as Tutankhamun. Does that help us at all?'

Adam pulled up the Internet and searched on Tutankhamun. He had another of those still, freeze-frame moments; then whacked the base of his palm against his forehead. 'My God, I'm a dimwit! And I call myself a would-be Egyptologist. All I'm good for is getting on the first flight home!'

'What? What have you found?' Electricity was zinging through my bloodstream.

'Listen to this. Here are Tutankhamun's throne names. My God, I've known these all along! Any of them sound familiar? "Strong bull, fitting of created forms", that's his Horus name. "Great of the palace of Amun, lord of all", that's his - get this - "two ladies" name! "The one who brings together the cosmic order", that's his Golden Falcon name. "Lordly manifestation of Re", that's his Prenomen - Nebkheperure.' Adam paused, looking at me meaningfully. 'Then Tutankhamun - his Nomen, which is "Living image of Amun".'

'Ok, I understand that on their accession to the throne each Egyptian king adopted a sequence of five formal names, the combination unique to each ruler. Nebkheperure seems to be the significant one here. But how do you account for the "resurrected" bit?'

'Well, if Howard Carter didn't resurrect him from the dead, what did he do? Tut went from minor and largely unheard of pharaoh, to one of the most famous names the world's ever known. I call that a resurrection, by anyone's standards!'

'Ok, so we think the solution to clue number three is Tutankhamun himself?'

'I'd put money on it!'

It was clear his certainty was equal to mine over the two ladies. 'But he's not a place either,' I challenged.

'No, but he was buried in Thebes,' Adam pointed out. 'That's Upper Egypt.'

'Yes, but I'd always understood he ruled most of his reign from Memphis,' I argued. 'That's Lower Egypt.' I've always thought it a bit counter intuitive for Cairo to be in Lower Egypt, when you look at it on a map. But it's to do with the direction the Nile flows in, from its source in Ethiopia downwards to the Mediterranean.

He glared at me, but had to concede. So, we were one apiece. But perhaps still no further forward in fixing a location.

'Next?' I asked. 'Something about the horizon?'

'"Horizon of Ra Horus who rejoices in it",' he quoted.

'Well the only "horizon" I know of in ancient Egypt, is Akhenaten's new city. If I remember rightly, he called it Akhet-Aten, meaning "Horizon of the Sun." Akhenaten's pretty much universally believed to be Tutankhamun's father now, isn't he? So we've made a link between Tutankhamun and the Two Ladies, through his uraeus crown and throne names. Doesn't it equally make sense to make the link to the city where he was born? You know, I'm starting to think your professor might be right. I wonder if Tut's tomb is the common thread.'

'Isn't that a bit obvious?' Adam challenged. 'I mean, it's the thing Carter's most known for. But I can't see a way of linking Queen Ahmes, Hatshepsut's mother with it.'

'Unless Queen Ahmes is a red herring.'

'Don't let's go there again. We surely need to have a couple of core beliefs to hang onto.'

'Ok, and so far they're Queen Ahmes and Howard Carter. But it seems to me Tutankhamun has to feature in there somewhere.'

'So let's Google Akhet-Aten, and see what we come up with.' He fitted the action to the words and clicked in and out of various websites without any apparent success.

'Nope. It seems the most likely solution, but it's not readily turning up anything I can latch onto.'

'Right, so let's move on. "Four colours of earth and water at home in two." What on earth is that supposed to mean?'

Adam seemed to drift off for a moment, as if he was with me physically, but somewhere I couldn't reach him mentally. 'Well, the pharaohs always described themselves as Lords of the Two Lands, meaning Upper and Lower Egypt. Those are the themes that seem to keep recurring in all of this.'

I caught his drift. 'Ok, that might explain the two, upper and lower, but what about the four, earth and water?'

'Well, I guess we have the Nile - that must be the water, surely.'

I could feel excitement zipping along my veins again. 'Doesn't the Nile have two sources? The White Nile and the Blue Nile?'

He looked at me with discovery in his expression. 'How do you know this stuff?'

'I watched a documentary with Joanna Lumley. She started out in Cairo, then tracked the Nile all the way to it's source, where she set some little carved souvenir boat free.'

'You've struck a chord again,' he said. 'So if the waters are the white and blue sources of the Nile. The earth must be the red and black lands of Egypt. Egypt was known as "Kemet", which means "black land", referring to the fertile black soils of the Nile flood plains. Distinct from "Deshret" or "red land", meaning the desert.'

'So "four colours of the earth and water at home in two", are the white and blue Nile, the red and black land, and the two lands of Upper and Lower Egypt?'

'Seems logical.'

'So, the solution is where they're all at home? So, surely that must be "Egypt"?'

'That's my reading of it,' he agreed.

'You know what? I think we're getting good at this cryptic puzzle solving lark!' I said with satisfaction, sitting back and nursing my wine glass.

141

'Let's take stock,' Adam suggested. 'So we have Wadjit and Nekhbet, of Upper and Lower Egypt. We have Tutankhamun, of Upper and Lower Egypt, and we have the Nile running through Upper and Lower Egypt. So we seem to be concluding so far that Queen Ahmes' equal is somewhere in Egypt. Does that make you feel we're any further forward? Because I, for one, am still totally flummoxed!'

'Don't be so defeatist! Let's have another go at the last clue; "Of the place of pillars through darkness and light". The only place of pillars I'm familiar with is the Hypostyle Hall at Karnak.'

'Which is dedicated to the cult of Amun-Ra,' Adam supplied, back in a mood to be helpful.

'So, what do we know about Amun-Ra? Does he have much to do with darkness and light?"

'Well he was massive in Thebes, coming to real prominence in the 18th Dynasty - so there's our link to Tutankhamun's time. Remember, Hatshepsut claimed divine birth from him. The Amun part of his name represented essential and hidden. Could you stretch that as far as light and darkness, do you think?'

I shrugged. 'What about the Ra part?'

'I think it's about creative power, the power of the sun. Amun-Ra was worshipped as one of the great creator gods; rising to such prominence other gods were seen to be manifestations of him. Part of that power came from being self created himself.'

'Run that past me again.'

'He was self-created. Without a mother or father.'

I sipped my wine and let the thought settle before I said it out loud. 'So you could say he made himself alone?'

Adam stared at me with a look of awe on his face. '"Most esteemed of him who made himself alone". Which becomes "most esteemed of Amun-Ra".'

'Any guesses?'

'You mentioned the Hypostyle Hall earlier. Karnak was known to the ancient Egyptians as Ipet-Sout, meaning Most Esteemed of Places.'

We stared at each other, letting it sink in.

'So nothing to do with Moses or Yahweh at all.'

'It never felt right,' Adam admitted. 'Whereas this does.'

'Which means in trying to solve the last riddle, we think we've actually cracked the first? The solution is either Karnak, or Ipet-Sout. That seems to narrow our location for Queen Ahmes' equal to Upper Egypt, doesn't it?'

'Which would mean the one of the two ladies we're looking for is Nekhbet, the vulture goddess.'

'Ok, so let's come back to the place of pillars and the darkness and light. If Karnak is the solution to the first clue, it seems unlikely to be what we're looking for here.'

'"Of" the place of pillars,' Adam mused aloud. 'Maybe it's the opposite of the first clue. That was a place, and we got to it through the god. Now maybe it's the god we're looking for - he who is "of" the place of pillars.'

'But you said it was stretching it to associate Amun-Ra with darkness and light.'

Adam's eyes sparked as a new idea hit him. 'In the first clue we concentrated on the Amun part of his name. But Ra, or Re, as he was sometimes known, was the ancient Egyptian sun god. And, guess what? He was thought to travel on two solar boats called the Mandjet, or morning boat, for his journey through the sky by day; and the Mesektet, or evening boat, for his journey through the underworld, by night.'

'There's our darkness and light.' I said triumphantly. 'Night and day.'

Adam was tapping on the iPad again. 'Thought so!' He looked up at me excitedly. 'The chief cult centre of Ra was Heliopolis, known as Iunu to the ancient Egyptians, which translates as "Place of Pillars"!'

'So, not Karnak at all. But, hang on a minute; ancient Heliopolis was around here somewhere, near Cairo, wasn't it? That's Lower Egypt, and everything else seems to be pointing to Upper.'

'But the answer to the last riddle has to be Ra. It fits perfectly. And there's still a link to Tutankhamun through his nomen "lordly manifestation of Re".'

I could feel the wine starting to go to my head. 'So, we've cracked all but one of the coded messages. Just one more to go, and we're both pretty sure the answer is Akhet-Aten, the sun-city of the heretic pharaoh Akhenaten.'

'Known nowadays as Amarna,' Adam put in. 'But we've Googled Akhet-Aten, and Akhenaten and Amarna, and nothing's coming up with Ra Horus in it. You know, I'm not sure I've even heard of Ra Horus. When I Google Ra Horus all I get is a load of guff about the eye of Horus, and the eye of Ra.'

'Here, pass the computer to me.' I reached across for it, and he handed it over.

I typed, "Ra Horus rejoicing in the horizon" into the search bar. Suddenly up popped the page of a book, an out-of-print handbook of Egyptian gods. I spent a couple of minutes scrolling up and down. Then I looked up at Adam, who seemed transfixed by something at the bottom of his wineglass.

'Listen,' I said. 'Ra Horus of the Horizon transliterates into Ra Herakhty. Have you heard of him?'

Adam looked up, and the gleam was back in his eyes, looking very dark blue in the dimly lit bar. 'Ra Herakhty is the ancient form of the Heliopolitan sun god. We've met him as Ra.'

'Well, it says here, when Akhenaten originally established the cartouches of the Aten - his new sun god - he defined Aten as Ra Horus, ruler of the horizon, rejoicing in the horizon in his name of "Ra, the father, who has returned as Aten".'

'Crikey Merry, how did you get to all that with a few swipes on the trackpad? I spent hours before dinner Googling everything I could think of.'

I smiled smugly. 'It's just a question of knowing what to put in the search engine. You can't have been specific enough.'

He scowled at me, but it was an affectionate scowl. 'So we must be talking about Akhenaten's new city. "Akhet-Aten" literally translates as Horizon of the Aten.'

'Would Howard Carter have known the Ra Horus stuff?'

He thought about it a moment, swirling the last of his wine round in his glass. 'In 1892, when he was only about eighteen, Carter worked for one season under the tutelage of the great Flinders Petrie at Tell el-Amarna. It seems pretty likely he'd have come across original cartouches on the boundary stelae. So, yes, I guess so.'

'So we were right all along in leaping to the conclusion the answer must be Akhet-Aten or Amarna, or, what did you just call it?'

'Tell el Amarna. I think that's what it was called in Howard Carter's day. More recently they think the "Tell" bit is inaccurate as nowhere do the ancient remains constitute a mound of eroded architecture that would warrant the description of a "tell", which is Arabic for "hill".'

I smiled in triumph, not really listening to this explanation. 'Well we've worked our way backwards and forwards through the riddle, and the answer's the same. So we must've cracked it!'

'But Amarna is mid-way between Luxor and Cairo, pretty much on the borders of Upper and Lower Egypt. So how does that help us with the location of Queen Ahmes' equal?'

'You know, I think all the Upper and Lower Egypt stuff is a red herring. I agree there has to be a link between these clues, something that ties them all together, but I don't think that's it. So let's have one last review of where we've got to, then I'm off to bed. My eyelashes are starting to feel like they've got lead weights attached to them.' It was true; I was suddenly overwhelmingly tired. Glancing at my watch, it wasn't hard to see why. It was nearly one o'clock in the morning, and I'd drunk pretty much a whole bottle of wine, counting the one we'd shared over dinner, and the one we'd almost finished between us now. I glanced round the bar. There was only one other couple over in the corner and, in truth they looked like they were nodding off too. The barman was too polite to give any indication we were outstaying our welcome. He was behind the bar polishing glasses with a clean white cloth.

Adam drained his glass and sat back. 'Ok, we have Nekhbet the vulture goddess; although maybe we should add back Wadjit the divine cobra if the Upper and Lower bits are really irrelevant. We have Karnak, known to the ancients as Ipet-Sout. We have Tutankhamun, under his prenomen of Nebkheperure. We have Akhet-Aten, known nowadays as Amarna. We have Egypt itself - which seems a bit vast as a concept in all this. And finally we have Ra, the original sun-god.'

I shook my head. None of it was landing anywhere helpful within my consciousness. 'Let's sleep on it,' I suggested. 'Maybe one of us will have a blinding flash of inspiration in the middle of the night.'

As it was, I slept like the dead, and woke with a stonking headache. I rolled over and groaned, and then remembered Dan. I'd promised to call, or at least text, every day - and I had patently forgotten to do both yesterday, caught up in all the excitement of decoding the clues. I groaned a bit more, and reached for my mobile sitting accusingly unused on the bedside table. Given the time difference, I might just catch him before he left for the office. I was in luck, he answered on the fourth ring.

'Hi sweetie. Sorry I didn't call yesterday. I...'

He cut me off abruptly. 'Meredith, your voice sounds the way it always does when you've had too much to drink the night before. Do you have a hangover by any chance?'

'A small one,' I admitted meekly.

So adept am I at reading Dan's expressions, he doesn't even have to be standing in front of me. His scowl made its presence felt wirelessly and across continents without me needing to see it at all. 'I know you're at the age where maturity should be a given. But in your case it seems to have given you the slip. Do I have to remind you again that you're sitting slap bang in the middle of a political trouble spot - especially there in Cairo. It wasn't so bad when you were down in Luxor. And now you don't seem to have the sense to stay sober. My God, Pinkie, are you asking for trouble?'

'I didn't phone for a lecture,' I said snappishly.

'No, yesterday you didn't phone at all,' he reminded me. He loves it when he has the upper hand, and can be all pompous and moralistic. 'Just do me a favour, will you, and stay away from Tahrir Square?'

I decided now was not the time to tell him about my trip to the Egyptian Museum. 'I'm not here for much longer. We're booked on the overnight train back to Luxor this evening.'

'Yes, well try not to get locked in any pyramids while you're there, and let me know when you're safely on board the train.'

And with that he rang off, saying he had an early meeting at work, and without even asking about the hieroglyphics. Piqued, I stomped across to the fridge in search of water.

***

'So, no blinding flash of light?' Adam asked later, as we clambered into the back of a taxi for our trip out to Saqqara.

We'd made a leisurely start to the day, both I daresay feeling the after-effects of the amount of wine we'd consumed the previous night. I'd ordered breakfast in my room, giving myself some time for my head to clear. He'd been out for a walk around the Mena House grounds, I guess for the same purpose.

I'd never visited the stepped pyramid at Saqqara, so was keen to see it before we headed back to Luxor. Adam willingly agreed to be my guide. So we were heading off into the desert, a few miles outside Cairo for our day's excursion.

'No blinding flash of light,' I confirmed regretfully.

Saqqara is a vast necropolis west of the ancient city of Memphis and known, rather unappealingly, as the City of the

Dead. It was used as a burial ground for something like 3000 years, from the Old Kingdom right up to Graeco-Roman times. It's famous as the site of the world's oldest stone structure, the stepped pyramid of Djoser, constructed by his visionary architect Imhotep. Dating back more than 4600 years, it was a prototype for the great pyramids of Giza, which came later.

I enjoyed the ride out from Cairo, through lush farmland and palm groves. There's an oasis-like feel to Saqqara, calm and tranquil after the chaos and smog of Cairo; and a beautiful view across the pyramid fields of desert rock, and back over the cultivated land.

The camel touts were less aggressive here, although the camels were plentiful, gaily bedecked in their pom-poms and tassels. Adam was spared the need to put his Arabic into use, the whole place having a more relaxed vibe altogether.

We spent a happy time exploring the sand-laden tombs and mastabas of the ancient burial ground. Some of the carving and artwork was exquisite and still brightly coloured, though dating from the earliest part of Dynastic Egypt. My favourite was a tomb with painted stars spanning the entire deep blue ceiling, and a row of carvings of royal cobras rearing up but looking surprisingly jolly.

'Howard Carter had a rather unhappy association with this place,' Adam commented, lowering his camera from the shot he'd taken of the stepped pyramid with a crotchety-looking camel sitting in ungainly pose in front of it.

'How so?'

'It became known at the Saqqara Affair, and it effectively ended his career with the Antiquities Service.'

'What happened?'

'Well, remember he'd had a rather meteoric rise until this point, appointed Chief Inspector for Upper Egypt in Luxor when he was only about twenty-five. In the autumn of 1904, when he was about thirty, he moved here to become Chief Inspector for Lower Egypt. I'm not sure why the decision was made to switch, but whatever the background, it all turned sour within a few weeks.'

I found a convenient stone jutting up out of the sand in the shade of an ancient ruined wall. Brushing the sand off it, I sat down and took a swig of water.

Adam leaned against the wall and continued his tale. 'The incident took place in early 1905. A group of young Frenchmen turned up here one afternoon. They'd been on a picnic, and drunk a lot of wine. They were rowdy and boisterous, and apparently rather offensive towards other visitors. They ended up in the Antiquities Service Rest House, still drinking and carousing and generally making a nuisance of themselves. Finally they decided they wanted to visit the monuments. The ticket inspector told them they needed tickets. This caused some fracas as some of them refused to pay. The upshot was, some bought tickets, some didn't, but they all went charging out to the Serapeum. The guide, or ghaffir as they were known then, at the entrance asked to see their tickets before admitting them. They refused and, still drunk and disorderly, rushed the door and forced it open, breaking one of the padlocks. Once inside, they complained about the dark and demanded candles. The guard said they didn't supply candles; and that seems to have been the tipping point. They started manhandling him, demanding their money back. The ghaffir called for help, and two of his colleagues came running. It seems the Frenchmen set about them too, knocking their tarboush from their head and trampling on them.

'They all charged back to the Rest House, where the Frenchmen barricaded the doors and set about the ticket inspector, attempting to get their money back by force. In the meantime, one of the ghaffirs ran off to find Howard Carter, who was showing round some upper-crust English visitors. Carter legged it back to the Rest House with the ghaffir, and forced his way inside. He demanded an explanation from one of the Frenchmen who spoke English. I think all he got was a mouthful of abuse. So he commanded them to leave. The Frenchmen made it clear they were going nowhere until they'd been given their money back. So Carter gave his ghaffirs orders to eject them. It seems the Arabs proceeded to set about them with sticks and stones - literally, sticks and stones - and an out-and-out fight broke out. Remember, the locals were thought of as natives, Bedouins. For them to attack European visitors was a scandal.

'The French party made an official complaint, and the whole affair was reported in the foreign language newspapers, sparking a bit of a diplomatic dust-up between the British and French authorities. There was an official enquiry and all sorts.

'Carter's bosses in the Antiquities Service asked him to express his regrets over the incident. But Carter obstinately refused to do so. As far as he was concerned, his actions were fully defensible and should be vindicated. I don't think he could see the subtlety in what he was being asked to do. He saw it as issuing a grovelling apology; whereas his superiors merely saw it as expression of regret, to smooth over troubled waters, a diplomatic gesture to allow the whole matter to be put to bed.

'Carter's stubborn intransigence came to the fore - he became well known for it later in life. He dug his heels in, despite direct appeals from Gaston Maspero, Director General of the Department of Antiquities, and resigned from the Antiquities Service; apparently to devote himself to painting.

'The next two years are always described by his biographers as his wilderness years. It wasn't until 1907

Maspero recommended him to the Earl of Carnarvon, who was seeking a concession to excavate in Egypt, and needed an archaeologist. And, as you know, they didn't get the concession to dig in the Valley of the Kings until 1914, when Theodore Davis gave it up.'

I'd continued to sip my water throughout this story. But something in the last part of Adam's narration made me pause with the water bottle poised halfway to my mouth.

'What is it?' he said. 'You look like you've thought of something.'

I looked up at him from my position perched on the jutting stone. 'What have you got whenever you've Googled Queen Ahmes over the last few days?'

He frowned at me, not following my switch in subject. 'Nothing, except a few words describing her as Hatshepsut's mother; usually it's just her picture comes up. That's what she seems to be famous for.'

'Exactly,' I said, as enlightenment surged through me. 'Her picture! Howard Carter painted her picture. Not once, but over and over again, to sell to tourists during his wilderness years. My God, it's been staring us in the face the whole time!'

'I'm not sure I'm following you.' Adam dropped down into a crouch so his eyes were level with mine, a sure indication I'd grabbed his interest.

'It said it right there on the legend under the picture I broke in Howard Carter's House. It said he originally painted scenes like the one of Queen Ahmes for the purpose of scientific recording; but later he produced pictures like it to sell to tourists. I even remember thinking I could see why it would be a popular souvenir - it's such a beautiful portrait with such lovely pastel colours. My God, I'm an idiot for not seeing it sooner!'

'You're saying "find my equal here" means we need to search for another portrait of Queen Ahmes - an exact replica of the one you smashed?'

'Yes! Absolutely that's what I'm saying! It's obvious, isn't it?'

'But Merry, there might be hundreds of them! How do we know where to start? There might be copies in private homes, or personal collections, and people's attics all over the world!'

'He's told us where to look. Somewhere in those hieroglyphic riddles is the location. We just haven't cracked the common link yet. Come on Adam,' I grabbed his hand as I jumped up from the stone. 'We have to take another look at those clues!'

Chapter 8

It wasn't until we were back on the train, rattling southwards towards Luxor, we really had time to turn our brains to the unriddling of the riddles. Our taxi-driver back from Saqqara was a chatterbox; wanting to tell us every thought he'd ever had on the subject of his country's revolution. We had the checking-out procedures at Mena House, effortless to be sure, but not conducive to puzzle solving. Then another taxi-ride to the station, this time with a Kamikaze driver who seemed to view the road as his own personal race-track, and all other road-users, whether in coaches, cars or buses, or atop donkey carts, camels or motorcycles, as skittles to be tossed aside by the rollerball that was himself behind the wheel of his taxi. It was frankly terrifying. I was concentrating so hard on clinging to the door-handle and staying alive, Carter's brainteasers never once entered my head.

But once safely on board the train, sitting in the lounge car with our tray dinners in front of us, and the Egyptian scenery zipping past the window, we could relax and re-focus.

I'd texted Dan, a short note to confirm my ability to visit the pyramids unscathed, un-trapped and unimpressed with him for suggesting otherwise. I made a short quip about the translated hieroglyphics being a puzzle within a puzzle - let him ask, I decided! And I pretty much left it at that.

'So, what links the cobra and vulture of the uraeus, Karnak, Tutankhamun, the City of the Sun, Egypt itself, and the god Ra?' Adam mused.

'Cobra or vulture,' I reminded him. 'We still don't know which it is.'

We were sticking to soft drinks tonight. Adam swirled his coke round in his glass.

'Granted,' he said. 'But, either way, I'm stumped.'

'Is there an image they all share? A common identifier of some sort?'

He racked his brains. 'Nothing springs to mind. I'd have thought the hieroglyphs would have given the game away on that one.'

'It's a place we're looking for,' I reflected aloud. 'Or perhaps a person, someone he knew he'd given a portrait of Queen Ahmes to. Of course, the most obvious person is Lord Carnarvon. We'll probably find the picture's on the wall at Highclere Castle.'

'Fat lot of good it will do us there!' Adam muttered. 'I can't quite see us bowling up to the current Earl and asking to see his painting of Queen Ahmes.'

'Ok, so let's hope it's not at Highclere.' I pushed my dinner tray away, and took out a notebook and pen from my canvas bag. 'You know, I wonder if it would help to write the crossword solutions down. So, let's take it one clue at a time. What did you say those uraeus creatures were called?'

'Nekhbet and Wadjit,' he said.

I wrote both names on a blank sheet, and added "vulture goddess" and "divine cobra" alongside, for luck. Underneath, I wrote "Karnak", then looked up at Adam. 'What was it you said the ancients called it?'

'Ipet-Sout', he supplied, and spelled it out for me so I could add it alongside.

Next I wrote "Tutankhamun".

'You should add his prenomen,' Adam advised. 'That's the part of his name the clue related to; Nebkheperure.'

So I faithfully scribed it onto the list alongside Tut's more common appendage. Underneath I wrote "Amarna" and "Akhet-Aten - City of the Sun". And, on the next line "Egypt." I looked up. 'What did the ancient Egyptians call Egypt?'

'Kemet,' he said.

I nodded and added it alongside; then, with a final flourish, I wrote "Ra" to the bottom of the list.

I held the sheet of paper away from me and stared at it, squinting slightly to narrow my gaze on the capital letters starting each word.

'What are you doing?'

I shrugged. 'I just can't help wondering if we're trying to be too clever, looking for a theme or a link. Maybe this jumble of apparently unrelated words are supposed to spell something.' I put the paper back down again and picked up the pen. He was watching me intently. 'So we've got N or W for the first letter, K or I for the second. So, ok, it would have to be I as that's a vowel. Starting from the beginning again, that's N or W, then I, then T or N, then A, then E or K, then R.' I wrote the letters out at the bottom of the page.

I could see he thought I was on to something. He turned the sheet of paper between us, so we could both read it at right angles.

I started writing out combinations of the letters on a separate sheet, pulled out of the notepad. N I T A E R. W I T A E R. N I N A K R. N I N A E R. W I N A K R. N I N A E R. W I N A E R.

Suddenly Adam's hand shot out and grabbed hold of the pen, and my hand with it. I jumped so violently it sent a black inked streak back up the page through all my careful notations. 'Bloody Hell, Merry, you've got it!' he yelled.

'What?' I yelped, my heart hammering in my chest, blood rushing in my ears, rather painfully aware of all the heads turned in our direction from other parts of the carriage.

'Sorry.' He let go of my hand, and grinned at me. But he was telegraphing excitement from every pore. 'It's not A for Amarna. It's T for Tell el-Amarna. Carter knew it as Tell el- Amarna.'

'So, if you replace the A with a T...'

'Exactly, in the last transcription you wrote, it becomes W I N T E R.' He wrote the words on the page with the pen he'd snatched from me as he said them aloud.

'But that makes no sense.' I spluttered. 'This is one of the hottest countries I know. I mean, I know they have winter here, and Carter used to do most of his work in the winter season, but I don't see...'

'Think Merry,' Adam laughed, holding up his hand to stem my meaningless gush of words. 'It's a place we're looking for. What place do you know, one that Carter knew well, with WINTER in the title?'

It hit me like an electric shock. 'The Winter Palace Hotel,' I breathed. 'Where Lord Carnarvon stayed whenever he visited Luxor, and certainly during the early days of King Tut's discovery; slap bang in the middle of Luxor.'

'Exactly! And what do you think are the odds of the hotel having artwork on display painted by one of the most famous Luxor residents of the day?'

'Pretty good, I should think. At least, pretty good back in the 1920's. I'm not so sure about now.'

'Well that, my lovely Merry, is what we have to set out to discover next; does the Winter Palace still have a copy of Carter's portrait of Queen Ahmes on the wall somewhere?'

* * *

In November 1922 Howard Carter stood on the staircase in the grand lobby of The Winter Palace hotel to announce the discovery of the tomb of King Tutankhamun to an astonished world. The hotel opened in 1886, a favoured winter retreat of European nobility and Oriental royalty. Lord Carnarvon first came for his health, advised to get away from the damp English winters after surviving a brush with death in a serious car accident. He soon considered it home away from home, staying for winter seasons onwards from 1907 when first granted his commission to excavate in Egypt. The Winter Palace combined the classical elegance of the nineteenth century with all the luxury anyone could possibly want when escaping the gloomy winters back home. To be honest, it still does.

Adam and I decided to combine our reconnaissance of the hotel's artwork with afternoon tea. We met at the foot of the curved marble staircase leading up from the Corniche to the hotel entrance. I was fresh from a lazy morning by the pool, Adam from a rather more focused few hours of Internet searching on Carter's artwork.

'There's nothing online to show if he ever gave paintings to the hotel. We'll just have to keep our fingers crossed they're not in some storage box gathering dust in the attics.'

'Or sold into some collection years ago,' I added, just to layer a bit more pessimism on top. 'We are talking eighty odd years between then and now. The hotel's probably changed hands loads of times, and done countless refurbishments.'

'What a cheerful pair we are!' Adam chided. But I think we were just steeling ourselves for inevitable disappointment. I mean, how likely was it really we could go bowling into this wonderful old grande dame of Victorian hostelry, spy Howard Carter's painting of Queen Ahmes hanging conveniently on the wall, and somehow persuade the management to let us take the back off it in search of more secret messages? Crazy to even imagine it! It was the thought I'd been batting away all day. Just because we'd come this far - figured out there must be twin of the portrait in Carter's house and figured out where it might be - didn't mean we hadn't hit the buffers now.

And even if - to stretch incredulity to its absolute limit - we were lucky enough to stumble across the twin painting; then what? Baksheesh might be a way of life in Egypt, but I have no doubt there are depths even the money-loving Egyptians won't plumb just to earn a few quid. So bribery and corruption were out of the question. This was, after all, a first class hotel run by an internationally reputed hotel

163

group. And having brought myself to the attention of the local police once already for smashing a framed portrait of Queen Ahmes, it seemed reckless and foolhardy in the extreme to contemplate a repeat performance.

Perhaps we'd just have to make them an offer for it. One they couldn't refuse. I wondered how much money Adam and I could raise between us. It wasn't how I'd planned on spending my redundancy money, but perhaps the ends justified the means. Then an image of Dan's apoplectic face popped into my head and I did a swift mental u-turn; perhaps not.

I gazed up at the impressive façade of the hotel as we climbed the staircase, shaking free of my ridiculous train of thought. Painted the colour of warm Sahara sand, it stretched away on both sides of the grand stairway, with deep terraces both sides. Palace is right; definitely not your normal hotel architecture.

Stepping from the blinding sunlight through the rotating door into the coolness inside was like entering a time warp. Where the Mena House in Cairo evoked a bygone age, this was like being transported to one. I had the impression I'd literally stepped back a century or so. The grandeur of the marble entrance hall was eye-popping, all glittering chandeliers, lofty ceilings, elaborate cornices, gilt furniture and with a sweeping staircase creating a gallery that seemed to frame it.

We'd dressed for the occasion, Adam in a stylish, cream silk-thread jacket over a light blue cotton shirt, open at the neck, and tucked into tailored trousers; me in a simple cotton shift dress in pale green, with a snazzy silk scarf tied with artful nonchalance at my throat. It took several attempts to achieve that artful nonchalance, I don't mind saying.

We were shown through to the Victorian Lounge for our afternoon tea. We'd worked on the principle it would be far easier to take our time scouting the other public rooms if we'd had the decency to partake of the hotel's hospitality first.

The Victorian Lounge opened off a huge corridor leading from the entrance hall. It was immense, opulently decorated and lavishly furnished. Painted a warm shade of ochre, elaborate gold drapes with acres of fringing hung from tall windows. We walked across a truly exquisite oriental rug the size of a bowling green to reach the arrangement of deep cushioned sofas and silken occasional chairs separated by a low antique side table, where we were invited to sit.

Afternoon tea was an indulgent affair served on delicate china plates and with genuine silverware, enhanced I'm sure by my certainty I'd turn to find Howard Carter pulling up a chair any minute.

'Carter used to come here with Lord Carnarvon regularly,' Adam said, picking up the thread of my unspoken thoughts in that uncanny way of his. 'I'll bet he knew every inch of this place like the back of his hand.'

'It doesn't look like it's changed much,' I said. 'If this stuff's not original they've done an amazing job of capturing the Edwardian style. I imagine he could walk in now and feel right at home.'

'You know, I don't doubt some of it is original. Perhaps not the sofas and stuff, but probably some of the more decorative furniture like the antique tables and chests, the Oriental lamps, and those huge urns over there.'

'So, you have hopes for the artwork?'

'Let's say I'm cautiously optimistic.'

A quick scan of the walls had already made it clear there was no Howard Carter artwork in here. After the last crumb of cake had been eaten and the last drop of tea drained, we wandered across to the other side of the wide corridor and entered the Royal Bar.

It was another hugely characterful and evocative room. Painted a deep red, and lined with dark mahogany bookshelves; its heavy, fringed drapes were rich gold and red this time, its parquet floor scattered with Oriental rugs, and its artwork a tasteful mix of birdlife and Bedouin desert scenes. There were no Howard Carter paintings anywhere in sight.

Further along the corridor, we took quick excursions into the famous 1886 à la carte restaurant and the only slightly less swanky Corniche restaurant opposite. Neither rewarded us with much in the way of artwork. Their ambiance relied instead on tall gilt mirrors, chandeliers, drapes and ornamental sconces holding decorative electric candles.

The corridor itself served as a mini Winter Palace museum. There were glass fronted wall niches containing paraphernalia from the hotel's early days: visitor books, glassware, photographs, uniform tarbouches and the like. And the walls were lined with black and white photographs showing the hotel in days gone by, looking remarkably unchanged by the passage of more than 120 years. Fascinating to study, but not what we'd come looking for.

Another huge corridor opened out on the other side of the entrance lobby, so we crossed the hall to see where it led. The answer was nowhere, although Adam said it was once a walkway through into the monstrosity that was the New Winter Palace hotel, a 1960's apology to architecture, since demolished. Guest rooms lined one wall. The other displayed a set of paintings. Seeing the frames from a distance hope surged; and was quickly dashed. The paintings were fabulous. But they weren't by Howard Carter. The artist was David Roberts and the frames contained vivid watercolour scenes of an Egypt people like me can only dream about. He travelled to Egypt in the 1830s, and captured scenes of the temples still in a state of ruin and filled with centuries of sand; long before modern archaeology really gained a foothold and the huge restoration project began. I was entranced by the sheer romanticism of the lithographs, with their sensitive rendering of the monuments, and even more so the be-robed and be-turbaned natives, not a single one of whom appeared to be there with any intention to hassle.

We strolled rather despondently back to the grand lobby. Adam did a quick scan of the reception desk, and seeing the receptionist deep in conversation with a couple of guests, grabbed my hand and pulled me up the stairway. It was an elaborate affair, sweeping from one wall round in front of the enormous windows, then curving back on itself up the opposite wall to reach the first floor landing.

'We might as well see as much of the place as we possibly can,' he argued. 'They can hardly turf us out just for walking along the public corridors.'

'They might think we're casing the joint,' I murmured.

He grinned, 'Isn't that exactly what we are doing? Come on, don't let your spirit of adventure abandon you now!'

We toured the long corridors on this floor and the one above. Doors led off on both sides to guest rooms which differed in scale and grandeur from classic rooms through to enormous and sumptuous suites, stayed in by royalty and other notables down the years.

'Look, this one is King Farouk's suite,' Adam pointed to the plaque on the wall alongside the door. 'I'll bet it costs a bob or two to stay there for the night!'

While artwork featured on most of the walls, none of it was the Queen Ahmes portrait. Most of the guest-room doors were firmly closed. The couple that weren't had cleaning carts parked outside them, and sounds of industry coming from inside. We managed to peep through the cracks of semi-open doorways, but only succeeded in getting an impression of more luxury, certainly no glimpses of the sought-after painting. Feeling dispirited but perhaps vaguely resigned to this as the inevitable outcome of our jaunt, we made our way back downstairs.

'Now what?' I asked.

'We might as well take a stroll round the gardens while we're here. I hear they're spectacular.'

Another heavy rotating door took us out onto a back terrace. The heat was like smacking face-first into a wall.

'Shade please, and fast,' I said. So we hurried down the curved steps leading down into the hotel grounds. Although, to be fair, gardens, as Adam described them, was far more accurate. Planted with exotic and unusual trees and shrubs, and forking left and right with walkways from an ornamental pond resplendent with lilies, it was a beautiful green oasis in the noisy dust-pot that was Luxor.

As we walked through the gardens in the dappled shade of tall, stately palms Adam said, 'Well, short of asking for a guided tour of all the guest rooms, I'd say we've hit a brick wall.'

'You know, I wonder if we're making this unnecessarily hard for ourselves. Couldn't we just find the hotel manager and ask him?'

'Trust a woman to take all the fun out of it,' he said darkly, but with a glint of humour in his blue eyes. 'I was getting on famously back there pretending to be MI5 on a secret mission!'

I grinned at him, 'Sorry to be a spoilsport, but I have to point out we're not getting on at all, let alone famously.'

'And here was me thinking we were friends!' He slapped his hand against his heart as if I'd shot him there.

I laughed and swiped playfully at his upper arm, 'Idiot! I just can't see how else we're going to find out if the painting's here.'

'And do you have a convincing tale to tell by way of persuading him to open the hotel's archives to us?'

'No, I admit I hadn't thought that far.' I racked my brains a bit and hit on an idea. 'Couldn't we say we're students of Egyptology, studying Howard Carter for our thesis. After all that's not so far from the truth for you, allowing for a break of twenty years or so.'

'Thanks for reminding me.'

170

'You're welcome.' But I didn't let the banter side track me. 'Maybe we could say we'd learned Carter once gave a picture of Queen Ahmes to the hotel. We might as well be specific about the painting we're interested in. We could pretend our particular field of research is tracking down the pictures he painted and sold during his wilderness years. That's not so far from the truth either.'

'Ok, and if by some miracle he swallows this bunch of baloney and takes us to wherever the painting is displayed or stored - always assuming he knows which one we're talking about - how are you going to convince him to let us un-frame it?'

We'd reached the hotel pool, at the far end of the gardens. A few people lazed about on sun-loungers, and there was a honeymoon-looking couple perched at the swim-up bar sipping cocktails. But otherwise it was pretty quiet. I sat down on one of the sun-beds under the shade of a vast awning, and kicked off my shoes. 'I was puzzling about that earlier,' I admitted. 'I suppose we could say we believe Carter made some annotation on the back of his paintings, and we want to take a photograph of it for our research? And we'll obviously pay for any re-framing necessary.'

Adam dropped down beside me. 'Ok, I like your thinking so far. But just suppose all this plays neatly to the admittedly inventive story you've concocted. What happens if we get the picture out of its frame and find a familiar-looking scrap of paper tucked inside? I don't for one second imagine the manager of this hotel is going to be so foolish as to leave us alone with the painting. How do you plan to spirit any message out from under his nose? Or have you been secretly practicing magic?'

I didn't have an answer. We sat in a rather depressing silence for a while, watching a small child splashing in the shallow part of the pool.

'We need to find a way of seeing inside the guest rooms,' Adam said. 'But without the company of a hotel porter.'

'What about Google Images? Or even TripAdvisor. Quite often people upload their holiday snaps of the places they're reviewing.'

I was rewarded for this suggestion with one of Adam's little freeze-frame moments. 'Merry, you're a wonder!'

'I try,' I said modestly.

We didn't have a laptop with us, but Adam had spotted a guest computer in the vast entrance hall, at the foot of the staircase. The heat didn't seem so oppressive as we made our way back across the gardens. I guess there's nothing quite like a renewed sense of purpose to distract attention from the temperature.

The computer was free; so we pulled up a couple of chairs, called up the Internet, and within moments were happily clicking through cyberspace.

We started with the hotel's own website. It seemed as good a place as any to expect high quality images of the guest rooms. In this assumption we weren't disappointed.

'Wow, the rooms are amazing,' I breathed as we flicked through images of classic, superior and luxury rooms, upgraded with a click of the mouse to vast prestige, opera and imperial suites. There wasn't much evidence of artwork on the walls at all in the lower category rooms. But once we started looking at the suites it was truly like looking at interiors fit for royalty. Picture the most sumptuous Oriental style soft furnishings your imagination can conjure up, then treble it. Add heavy drapes, brass four-poster beds, antiques-galore; oh, and views across to the Theban hills just as a little something extra. And artwork. Artwork everywhere.

I have to admit I'd almost stopped scanning each image for the Queen Ahmes painting, so caught up was I in the sheer decadent luxury of the interiors, each more lavish than the last. I tried to imagine the kind of lifestyle you had to have to spend your holidays in rooms like these. Not the lifestyle of a charity communications executive, that's for sure.

'There!' Adam's shout sent me out of my skin. 'Look! Reflected back in that mirror. There, you see?' And he stabbed his finger triumphantly at the screen.

It took me a moment to spot it. But he was right. The picture wasn't in full view in the shot, but was reflected back from an ornate gilt mirror above a mahogany ornamental desk. It wasn't even the whole picture, just half of it, and flipped backwards as a mirror-image. But it was unmistakeable.

'We've found her equal,' he breathed, the softness of his voice resonating with far more emotion than the shout of a few moments ago.

My own heart was hammering in my chest - a strange expression, that one; but it most definitely described the sensation. I looked at the typed notation under the image. 'Adam, that's the Imperial Suite. I think that's the one King Farouk stayed in. How the hell are we going to blag our way in there?'

He turned gleaming eyes on me. They'd changed colour again, I noticed. Back to the deep violet I'd first seen a few days ago when I told him about the hieroglyphics. It was quite hard not to get mesmerised by those eyes, especially when they were staring back at me with such passionate intensity. 'Why blag?' he asked. 'Why not book?'

'I beg your pardon?'

'Surely our money's as good as King Farouk's. If we want a chance to study that painting without some hotel flunky breathing down our necks, we need to be in that suite legitimately. And there's only one way I can think of to do that. We have to book.'

'But Adam, it's the most expensive room in the hotel!'

'So, some things in life are worth paying for. I'm game if you are.'

'Oh, what the hell! It's only money!' I flung caution to the winds, and decided I'd figure out what to tell Dan later. 'Let's do it!'

I wasn't expecting the kiss, quick though it was, just the briefest press of his lips against mine in the excitement of the moment. But I have to say it did my ego no harm whatsoever.

Chapter 9

We had to wait two nights for the suite to become free. Although, free it most certainly was not. We shelled out an eye-popping amount of money for our one-night booking, even after the massive discount Adam negotiated, these being hard times, and all that.

Adam talked me into agreeing to join him and Ahmed for the evening of the next day. He promised a game of dominoes I'd never forget. I figured if I was up to my neck in the consequences of pinching the scrap of paper from Howard Carter's house, then so was he. He'd certainly aided and abetted. So I decided to get over my reluctance to put myself in the way of the law, and to be sociable instead.

But that gave me the whole day free to go back to being a simple holidaymaker, with no hieroglyphics or clues to decipher and no paintings to hunt. I felt at a bit of a loose end, to be honest. So I called Dan.

'The Imperial Suite is vast,' I explained, after bringing him up to date. 'The Queen Ahmes picture looks like it's on the wall in the living room, so far as we can tell from the online photograph. If you log on to historic-hotels-then-and-now-dot-com you can see it for yourself. Anyway, the important thing is, there are two bedrooms, so that's ok.'

There was a short silence. 'You know, Pinkie, that thought wouldn't have entered my head if you hadn't put it there.' Dan's not the jealous type, as I may have pointed out before. But then, never having actually clapped eyes on Adam, he probably still pictured him as the archetypal boffin Egyptologist, covered in dust and cobwebs.

'Oh,' I said lamely. Actually I don't think it would enter Dan's head that another man might find me attractive. Which is not to say he doesn't. At least I don't think so. It's just ten years down track I daresay we're boringly sure of each other.

He sighed, 'I trust you, Pinkie. You know that. So reassurances on that score are unnecessary.' I ignored a tiny prickle of discomfort remembering the kiss. I decided it didn't count, since it was just an expression of euphoria, nothing more. 'What really worries me is that your determination to play detective is going to lead you into serious trouble. And I'm still not clear what exactly it is you hope to find.'

It was the one thought I'd not really confronted; one Adam and I seemed to keep shying away from, too. It was impossible to say. And I'm not sure hope really entered into it. The detecting, which seemed as reasonable a description for it as any, was not so much a quest for discovery, more about solving a puzzle that had presented itself. But I had to admit it must be leading somewhere. And Dan's certainty it was nowhere good was a bit of a downer.

After ringing off, I spent the day sun-lounging, swimming and generally lazing about. It felt a bit weird to be so inactive after the adrenaline rush of the trip to Cairo and the ultimate success of tea at The Winter Palace. I borrowed a very dog-eared copy of a Howard Carter biography from the Jolie Ville library and speed-read it to try to get more of a sense of the man.

A breeze blew up in the afternoon, a welcome respite from the suffocating heat. So I took advantage of the hotel felucca and joined a small party of other guests for a trip out on the Nile under the shade of its vast triangular sail. I let my mind drift, staring out over the water, across the strip of cultivated land along the riverbank, into the stretching desert and rock beyond.

I'd moved beyond assumption into certainty that Howard Carter was responsible for the hidden hieroglyphics. I'm not sure who he envisaged finding them, in what circumstances, or when. The simple fact being I was the one who had, presumably at least seventy years after he put them there.

I'd looked at pictures of him on Google Images. I know it was a more formal world back then, but his version of a smile was an infinitesimal lift of the corners of his mouth - by which I mean barely there at all - only evident in one or two photographs at most. Typically he looked severe, down at the mouth, a bit scary to be honest.

He seemed an intensely private person, hard to get to know - a man of few words, not one for expressing emotion, a master of understatement. His reputation was for taciturnity, stubbornness and obstinacy. That he was meticulous and a perfectionist were about the nicest things anyone ever said about him; both words with a definite sting in the tail, if you ask me. He doesn't seem to have had much need for close personal friendships, and never married.

I mulled on the hypothesis put forward by his biographer, that his defensiveness and abruptness stemmed from insecurity about his middle-class background and lack of formal education. He kept company with the aristocracy, but wasn't one of them. Yet, here was the man who made the greatest discovery of the twentieth century, perhaps the greatest archaeological discovery ever. But he received no public honours from the British government before or after his death, and was buried in an unremarkable grave in Putney Vale with few mourners.

A paradoxical chap, for sure. And now I found myself on the receiving end of a direct communication from him. I turned my mind back to Dan's question. What did I hope to find?

I tried to imagine Carter carefully penning the hieroglyphics, then sealing them up inside the picture frame. This was a procedure he undertook twice if, as seemed likely, he'd secreted something similar inside the twin picture he gave to The Winter Palace. Something on paper, in any event; hard to imagine much else being taped up inside a half-inch-thick glass frame.

Perhaps we'd find a hidden cache of love letters, revealing a more emotional side to Carter after all, I speculated. There was some suggestion of an attachment between him and Lady Evelyn Herbert, Carnarvon's daughter. Of course it would have been unheard of for an unqualified excavator of Carter's social class to pursue a romantic interest in an Earl's daughter. But the romantic in me was quite taken by the idea.

Adam said the hieroglyphics had the look of cryptic crossword clues. Actually, I was starting to wonder if it wasn't more like a treasure hunt. But that made no sense at all. Howard Carter famously and very publicly found the most fabulous treasure the world has ever known. From the moment of the tomb's discovery he lived his life under the spotlight of frenzied media attention. I doubted this was a search for buried treasure.

My thoughts were spinning in cartwheels taking me nowhere. So I gave up. There was no point imagining. Better wait to see what, if anything, Queen Ahmes' equal

180

had in store for us. So I turned my attention back to the breeze on my face, the flapping felucca sail above my head and the company of my fellow Jolie Ville guests.

***

I arrived a little late for my agreed rendezvous with Adam and Ahmed in downtown Luxor. My taxi got stuck behind a herd of shaggy brown-haired sheep being coaxed along the road by a herdsman clearly in no immediate need of his dinner. My first impression of the coffee shop where we'd arranged to meet was of dense tobacco smoke, stray cats roaming free, and the deafening chant of the Islamic muezzin blaring from the loudspeakers rigged up on the dainty minaret of the local mosque. I could see why Adam and Ahmed played dominoes. Talking was clearly out of the question. There was an overwhelming, and rather appetising aroma of cooked garlic drifting on the stifling night air. The busy street outside was lined with market stalls, piled high with sacks of spices and varieties of knobbly vegetables I couldn't identify. Even those I could looked exotic, and very fresh, no doubt pulled in from the fields on a donkey cart today and simply stacked up for sale. I could see why Adam chose this slice of life over mixing with the holidaymakers. The hotel seemed unbelievably sterile by comparison.

'Meredith! Over here!' Adam's yell reached me above the din. A moment later he appeared from the shadows under a broad canopy slung across the front of the coffee shop, weaving his way between closely grouped tables towards me. He grabbed my arm, dropped a casual kiss on my cheek, and drew me back with him through the throng. 'Great to see you; come and meet Ahmed.'

Ahmed rose to greet me as we approached the table. I'd been racking my brains trying to remember what he looked like. The minute I spotted him, I remembered. Dark brown eyes beneath rather heavy brows, snapping with interest as he looked at me; close cropped black hair, an engaging smile despite the rather serious need for some dental attention; but wearing a pale grey galabeya this evening, in preference to his police uniform. It rather robbed him of the authority he'd projected last time, and did little to disguise his protruding stomach.

'Meez Peenk,' he said politely, a definite twinkle in his eyes. 'We meeda agaaina. Bedda plaaca deeza tima, yes? And widouta beega mana een baada tempa!'

'Hello,' I said meekly. He was an officer of the law, after all. I hadn't understood a single word he said. It didn't bode well for a whole evening in his company.

'Cut it out!' Adam admonished, slapping him playfully in the upper arm, then turned to me. 'It's a sad fact he can't pronounce his t-h's for toffee, but other than that his English is a good as yours or mine. That's the voice he uses with the tourists. He bizarrely imagines it brings barriers down, or raises them, I can never remember which.'

Ahmed let out a bark of laughter and thrust out his hand to be shaken. 'Meez Pink, glad to meetd you. Ahmed Abd el Rassul atd your service.' It remained heavily accented, to be sure, although plainly discernible this time. But that wasn't what made me do a double take. I stared into his face suspiciously,

'Why is your name so familiar?' I demanded. This probably wasn't the politest thing I could have said on first acquaintance, especially when I had to shout it over the muezzin, but the certainty I knew his name was overwhelming.

This time it was Adam who laughed. 'She's outed you in one, buddy. Better own up!'

'You know a bitd aboutd our Egyptian history, Meez Pink?'

'Please, call me Merry, and yes, a little.'

'Pah! False modesty. She can tell you all the pharaohs of the 18th and early 19th Dynasty, in chronological order to boot.' Adam turned his smile on me. 'But I think the historical period Ahmed's referring to needs you to jump forward by a millennia or three, Merry. Nineteenth century to be precise.'

Ahmed gave a small bow, 'I have de honour to say my family helped de great Gaston Maspero witd his running of the Egyptian Antiquities Service.'

'What he's trying to tell you,' Adam grinned, 'is he's descended from the most notorious family of tomb robbers Egypt's ever known. He's your walking definition of the clichéd poacher turned gamekeeper.'

I think I gawped inelegantly at him. But it was definitely falling into place. Something about a mummy cache, if memory served. I'm sure it was included in the Amelia Peabody stories.

Ahmed grinned, 'Let's have someding to drink. Den I'll tell you de whole story,'

I glanced at the table to see what they'd been drinking before I arrived. 'Does it have to be coffee, or is beer acceptable?' I'd found the local Stella particularly good.

'Ahmed doesn't drink, good Muslim that he is. But I'll join you in a beer.' Adam disappeared inside for a moment, returning with two bottles, glasses and a promise Ahmed's coffee was on its way.

Ahmed pulled up a water pipe, using Adam's brief absence to fill the top with tobacco. He puffed contentedly a couple of times, and the water bubbled noisily in the upper glass cylinder. That's how I realised the muezzin had stopped. He settled back to tell his story, so I poured my beer and got ready to listen.

'In de late 1860's my several times great grandfadder, Mr Ahmed Abd el-Russel, was looking after his goats in de cliffs behind Deir el-Bahri. One of de goats strayed away from de herd; so my several times great grandfadder wentd to search for it. He heard de sound of bleating butd could see no goat. Following de sound, he found de goat fallen down a big hole in de cliffs. He cursed de goat, and scrambled down de hole to rescue it. He found himself and de goat in a cramped corridor, filled witd strange dark shapes. Dat's when he discovered he was inside a tomb shaftd.

'He lit a candle, and saw de shapes were made from dusty wooden coffins. Dey stretched as far as he could see, heaped on top of one anodder. My several times great grandfadder could see signs of royalty on de coffin lids, and lots of jars and shabtis from royal burials. He cursed no more, but prayed to Allah. Dis was a lucky goat.'

He broke off as his coffee arrived, and stirred several spoons of sugar into it. That accounted for the teeth, I concluded. Adam was watching him affectionately, taking occasional swigs of beer. I could tell this was a story he'd heard before, probably re-embellished each time.

'My family from long ago made a good living from de tomb shaft for many years. Dey sold bits and pieces of de artefacts found witd de mummies onto de antiquities marketd in Luxor. But after so long deir luck ran out. Important people started to ask questions aboutd where come from dese amazing objects. Not from any excavations dat were known about.

'Mr Gaston Maspero, head of de Antiquities Service, heard about dese treasures, and sent some people to investigate. But dey found notding. So Mr Gaston Maspero sentd in a spy. Dis man came to see my long ago family at deir home in Gurna pretending to be an antiquities dealer. My several times great grandfadder, Mr Ahmed, trusted him and showed him a new artifact from de tomb shaft. De spy immediately send a cable to Mr Gaston Maspero.

'Mr Ahmed Abd el-Russel was arrested witd his brodders Mohammed and Hussein. But dey refused to confess, and de local people spoke out to say dey were good men. Mohammed and Hussein were let go. But my several times great grandfadder was held longer. Still, he refused to confess. Eventually dey let him go. Den de brodders started to quarrel. Mr Ahmed wanted money to pay him for his time in prison.

'Mohammed, de oldest brodder, was not happy, so he became an informer, hoping to getd a reward. He showed de colleagues of Mr Gaston Maspero de location of de tomb shaftd. When dey entered dey could not believe deir eyes. Dere all wrapped up, were some of de greatest pharaohs of de New Kingdom. De priests had moved dem dere in ancient times when law and order broke down. Dere were more dan fifty mummies in total. Imagine dat! Dey included Ramses II, as well as some of de Thutmosis kings.

'Here is de funny part. My many times backwards uncle Mohammed Abd el-Russel went to work for de Antiquities Service as a foreman. Funny eh? In de early 1890s he led an inspector to yet anodder site in Deir el Bahri. Der dey found nearly 160 mummies who were once high priests from Karnak. De inspector was suspicious about Mohammed. He was sure Mohammed knew about dis cache for a long time. So he was fired from de Antiquities Service.

'Dis story has been handed down in my family from fadder to son ever since.'

I found myself a little spellbound, sitting so close to someone descended from a genuine slice of Egyptian history. 'It's a great story Ahmed. And not just for your ancestors' part in rediscovering the mummies for the world. The bit I find staggering is the priests moving them all there in the first place. And so many of them! And wasn't a similar cache of royal mummies found elsewhere?'

'Yes, the tomb of Amenhotep II in the Western Valley,' Adam nodded. 'There's still some confusion over both caches about exactly who everyone is. There's some suggestion the wrong labels got affixed to some of them. Which seems a bit unfortunate, considering how important the pharaohs name was to achieving the afterlife. But I'm sure the priests meant well.'

I sat back and sipped my beer. 'Do you think there are more hidden caches to be found?'

Ahmed stroked his chin, then took another pull on his water pipe, 'It is probably so. De cliffs are like a honeycomb of holes. We need anodder lucky goat to show us where to go!'

I laughed. 'Perhaps. Is it possible to walk on the cliffs behind Deir el-Bahri? I'd love to see Hatshepsut's temple from above, and see for myself whether it really does square up with the Valley of the Kings behind it.'

'Oh yes, it's possible. De cliffs are like a spiders web of criss-cross patdways and trails. De village workmen from Deir el Medina used to walk over de cliffs to work carving de tombs. I used to play dere as a boy wid my brodders. I tell you what. Why don't I take you and Adam dere one day soon. In-shallah, yes? God-willing? You can bring your camera and see de sights from an angle lots of visitors don't see.'

'That'd be great, Ahmed; thanks, I'd love that. It's amazing the stories this land has to tell.'

'And you have a story of your own to take home witd you,' Ahmed grinned. 'Your capture and release by Mr Howard Carter.'

What a strange way to put it, I thought, as the dominoes came out and conversation moved on to more prosaic things, like re-teaching me the rules.

***

'He's a good laugh,' I agreed when Adam and I met at the foot of the marble steps leading up to The Winter Palace lobby the following evening. 'And he has a knack for story-telling.'

'He doesn't often get the opportunity. Not many people know enough about nineteenth century Egyptology to leap on him the way you did. You'll be his friend for life now.'

'He has my taste in fiction to thank,' I reminded him. 'It was a great evening. I enjoyed it.'

We looked up at the grand hotel façade, lit golden and glowing by ball-shaped lamps in the fading light of sunset. 'Ready to do this?' he asked me.

Nervous excitement buzzed in the pit of my stomach. It had been buzzing there, on and off, all day. I couldn't quite believe we were doing this. We both carried small overnight bags; mine bought locally for our excursion to Cairo. For the second time within a week, we were checking in to one of the grandest old Victorian hotels in the world. But this time it was with illicit intent. 'Ready.'

The suite was stupendous. There really was no other word for it. I followed the porter who showed us around, trying to keep my mouth from hanging open. The décor throughout was in that dull shade of gold that's almost grey and manages to be at once classy, tasteful and very very opulent. It was all richly embossed wallpaper, silken Oriental carpets, heavy fringed drapes, quilted satin bedcovers, and deep cushioned sofas and chairs. It somehow pulled off a mixture of Edwardian stately home finery and Arabian Nights glamour. Enormous solid silver candlesticks decorated the mantelpiece, Oriental lamp-stands sat on antique side tables, and a display of fine porcelain plates graced the bureau top. The artwork was an eclectic mix of Arabian and Egyptian themed scenes; and there, above the dainty mahogany writing desk in the living room, was the painting of Queen Ahmes.

Adam tipped the porter, and we were alone with her. We both stared at her, then at each other.

'I don't know about you,' I said at last. 'But I'm having one of those weird out-of-body experiences. Like I'm standing on the outside looking in on all this. I keep thinking if I pinch myself I'll wake up and find I've dreamt the whole thing. It's surreal.'

He nodded slowly, and that curvy smile I was coming to know so well tugged at his mouth. 'Surreal, yes; but, hey, it's a blast too, isn't it?' He encompassed the room in an expansive sweep of his arm. 'I mean, this is incredible, don't you think?'

'It's certainly not what I'm used to. Although I'm sure I could become accustomed to it if I tried really hard. And it's all thanks to the twin of Queen Ahmes over there, for finally giving up the secret she's been keeping for the best part of a century.'

We both stared back at the picture and moved across the room to study it more closely. There she was, in pastel-shaded profile, in her beautiful feathered headdress, with the vulture Nekhbet rising on her brow, and Howard Carter's signature squiggled underneath her. 'Do you think this Queen Ahmes has a secret she's willing to share with us too?' I murmured.

He leaned forward to minutely inspect the painting. 'I wish I had x-ray vision. Then maybe I could tell without having to dismantle her. It seems a bit of an imposition if, as we hope, she's been safely tucked up inside that frame since Howard Carter put her there.' He straightened back and gave me one of those long looks of his. 'You know what? If there's nothing inside, I think I might just have to drink myself into oblivion tonight. I'm not sure I can handle that much disappointment. Especially after the last two days of anticipation.'

I could more than empathise. 'So, how do we go about this? I mean, do you think she might be alarmed?'

'I don't think she's alarmed, but it looks to me like she's definitely screwed to the wall. Just as well I brought a screwdriver set with me.'

'You didn't!'

'Of course I did! How else did you imagine I was going to get her off the wall?'

I realised I hadn't actually thought that far. The logistics of this whole affair were not something I'd cared, or maybe dared, to plan. The original Queen Ahmes conveniently fell off the wall at my feet, and saved me the bother. So I hadn't mentally transported myself into this moment to work through the finer details. Luckily, it seemed Adam had.

He unzipped his bag. 'I have screwdrivers, a utility knife, masking tape; all the usual picture framing paraphernalia. We need to put her back as we found her, as close as possible, so I figured this would all come in handy.' Then he swung a teasing glance back at me. 'Unless you were planning on another 'accidental breakage' - a staged one this time?'

I took a swipe at him, and he ducked, laughing. 'Your mate Ahmed's a great bloke. But I have absolutely no intention of inviting him here to join us tonight; or the hotel manager, for that matter! I've already paid for one repair. And with the way my bank balance is being hammered at the moment, I don't think I can afford another.'

'Ok, so it's just you and me then, and my screwdriver kit; come on, give me a hand.'

'You know what? I'm going to lock the door first!'

I had my heart in my mouth throughout the whole operation. I held the bottom of the frame so it didn't slip while Adam gently eased the gilt screws from their holes. I'm not sure I'd have spotted them; they were so well hidden by the ornately moulded frame. I half expected klaxons to start wailing any moment, or for someone to come banging the door down having spied us on a covert CCTV camera.

A few breathless moments later, Queen Ahmes was off the wall, held, rather reverently, in Adam's tanned hands. 'So far so good,' he breathed, and I noticed the sheen of sweat on his top lip. I have to say it made me feel a whole lot better to know he was terrified too.

'Let's take her into one of the bedrooms,' I suggested. 'She's less likely to get damaged on the bed than out here.'

I held the door wide open, so he could carry her through without knocking her against anything. He placed her face down on the silken bedspread and stood back. 'The moment of truth,' he murmured. 'If someone catches us now, we're in the brown stuff up to our necks.'

I really didn't need the reminder. Dan's voice was ringing in my ears yelling I'd finally gone over to the dark side. 'Just get on with it,' I muttered, trying to quash the instinct to keep looking over my shoulder.

Adam tested the tape to see if he could tease it away from the frame without having to cut it, a bit like peeling back sellotape. But it was stuck fast. 'I'm going to have to use the knife.'

I watched tensely while he pushed up the little triangular blade on the utility knife and carefully inserted it into the tape, between the frame and the backing mount. Working slowly and gently, he pulled the blade along one length of the frame. It was a bit like watching a surgeon perform a precision operation with a scalpel.

The whole room radiated with the raw nervous energy we were emitting. 'You know, if there are more hieroglyphics in there,' I said, in a strange high voice that didn't sound like mine, 'we're going to need a damn good story to tell Ted. I don't think the guff we gave him before will wash a second time.'

Adam didn't respond. His concentration was absolute, trying to release the painting without damaging it. 'There! Done it.' He straightened up and we shared another long loaded look. 'No turning back now, Merry.'

'No,'

'Do you want to be the one to look? I mean; this whole shebang is yours really. I'm just the lucky one you invited along for the ride.'

I moved closer to the bed, took a deep, shaky breath, and gently started to prise the backing mount out from the frame, using my fingernails. It came out fairly easily. Then there was a thick piece of card. I eased that out too, and laid it on the bedspread with the mount. The moment of truth had arrived.

I lifted the artist's paper from the frame, immediately noting the folded edge across the top.

It was a heart-stopping moment. Adam's breath seemed to quicken alongside me. I'm not sure I was breathing at all. I opened out the fold. A slip of paper fluttered down onto the bed.

'Oh my God,' I breathed. Finding nothing would have been a killer, as Adam said. But seeing that little scrap of paper, I felt a moment of pure panic; almost terrified to pick it up and see what it might say this time.

Adam did it for me in the end. I'm not sure how long we both stood there gawping, shifting between myriad emotions as we realised we really were onto something. What I'd stumbled across by accident in Howard Carter's house was now a definite and deliberate quest to discover where it led. Adam handed me the scrap of paper.

I turned it over with nerveless fingers. It took a moment for me to make any sense at all of what I was seeing, and even then, it didn't make sense. 'It looks like a spider's web?' I held it out for Adam's inspection.

He frowned over it for a moment, turning the paper round to view it from different angles. 'I think it might be a kind of topographic map,' he said at last.

'How do you work that out? It just looks like a lot of wavy lines to me.'

'Yes, but that's basically what a contour, or topographic, map is. It shows the man-made and natural features on the ground, with the wavy lines representing the elevation.'

'The key word you've used in all that, probably the only one I understand, is the word "map". We've found a map. Is that what you're telling me?'

He looked up and met my gaze. Slowly he nodded. 'And I think I know what it's a map of.' The darkening of his irises from pure indigo to deep amethyst gave away his excitement.

'What?'

'Well, I'll qualify this by saying if I wasn't looking for it to mean something, I'd probably think it was a bit of scrap paper with scribble on it, and toss it away. But because I think it has to be significant, I'm looking at it through the lens of possibility. I think it's a segment of the Theban Hills; basically the cliffs behind Deir el-Bahri leading through to the Valley of the Kings. I think this high elevation point here could be El-Qurn, the pyramid-shaped mountain above the Valley. I think this box-like marking down here could be

Hatshepsut's temple. And these small squares possibly indicate the tombs in the Valley.'

I stared at him, unblinking. 'Your friend Ahmed described those cliffs as a spider's web. And that's exactly what that looks like to me.'

'So, the question we have to ask ourselves is, what is this map telling us?'

I squinted at it. 'I'm not sure it's telling me anything. I don't see a route plotted on it, or an arrow, or anything.'

He grinned at me, 'What are you hoping for? X marks the spot?'

'Well, for it to make any sense at all, surely it needs something like that. On the original Queen Ahmes puzzle we had the instruction "find my equal here". So basically we were told what to do. We haven't missed any directions on this one, have we?'

He turned the paper over and re-scanned the back; then the front again, then shook his head. 'Nothing.'

'But that's crazy. If that's a map, it's certainly not showing us where to go. We must be missing something.' Then a thought struck me. 'What about the actual painting; Queen Ahmes' equal?'

I'd set the painting carefully to one side when the scrap of paper fluttered out from between its folds. I picked it back up and studied it minutely. There was nothing in the painting to give any help with the map. So I turned it over. The tiny hieroglyphics in each of the four corners leapt out at me so sharply, I nearly dropped it. 'Adam! Look!'

He peered over my shoulder, close enough for me to get a subtle drift of his aftershave. 'Well Merry, you know I don't read hieroglyphs. But I'd say they're numbers. If I remember rightly, the Egyptians had a decimal system using seven different symbols. I can't tell you whether they're map references, but I'd hazard a pretty shrewd guess they're either that or something very like it. I think our friend Howard Carter might be pointing us in the direction of something buried in the hills above Deir el-Bahri.'

Weak-knee'd, I sank onto the side of the bed, looking up at him a bit dazedly. 'So, it doesn't look like we'll be needing a lucky goat after all.'

Chapter 10

The most pressing need was to return Queen Ahmes securely to her picture frame. Adam took photographs of the hieroglyphics on both his iPhone and his iPad. I did likewise on my camera, so there was no chance of us losing the images. We took the same precaution with the scrap of paper, although that was coming with us.

Adam took his time re-framing the painting, making sure it was a precision job. I daresay if someone took the picture off the wall, they'd spot the renewed taping. But hopefully that wouldn't happen any time soon. From the front, Queen Ahmes looked just the same. I helped him screw her back to the wall, and we stood back and looked at her for a moment.

'Well, she gave up her secret easily enough,' Adam commented.

'It's weird though. I keep thinking had this been the frame to get broken, rather than the one in Howard Carter's house, this scrap of paper would probably have been chucked away. It's just so random. Why would anyone link those hieroglyphic numbers to it if they weren't positively looking?'

He shrugged. 'Seems to me our friend Howard Carter was willing to leave quite a lot to chance. Maybe he didn't expect quite such a long passage of time between him planting the clues, and us finding them. I mean; it's pushing the envelope a bit for both pictures to still be in their original frames and locations more than seventy years after his death. Especially since his house was used as a storage unit for donkey's years before being converted into a museum. They've done a great job of rounding up some of his personal stuff to put back there.'

'And what were the chances of them being found in the right order? The one from his house first, then this one here at The Winter Palace? We seem to have been incredibly lucky.'

'It makes you wonder if there might be another picture somewhere, pointing to the one in his house, the way that one points here.'

'If that's so, whoever finds it will be sorely disappointed. We've stolen a march on them. Queen Ahmes has divulged her secrets to us.'

'Either way,' he said, 'it appears Carter was pretty unfazed about handing things over to the whims of fate. After all, you could have found those original hieroglyphics, and thought nothing of them. Same for anyone. Even if you'd handed them over to the authorities, instead of brazenly walking off with them, there's no guarantee they'd have put two-and-two together the way you did. So the trail would have gone cold before anyone realised it even was a trail. Instead of which, here we are potentially nearing the end of it.'

'Unless we work out where the contour map leads us, only to find another whole bunch of clues taking us off somewhere else.'

'That's a possibility, of course. But I just have this feeling we're getting hotter. I mean; planting riddles inside picture frames in houses and hotels is one thing. Doing it in the cracks and crevices of cliffs is a different matter entirely. No, I think we're going to find whatever it is Carter wants us to find.'

'Assuming it's still there.'

'Well that's the chance we're going to have to take. I reckon he wasn't too bothered one way or the other. The sense I get is he left his clues, so there was a chance of discovery for anyone who had the wit to realise it and solve them. If not, I get an impression of him shrugging his shoulders and thinking, "ah well".'

'You make it sound as if he was absolving himself of something. As if he knew he'd be dead by then, so it wouldn't matter to him whether it - whatever "it" turns out to be - was discovered or not. It's so mysterious.'

'I don't have any more insight into his motivation than you do. I guess we'll have to find whatever "it" is before we can properly start psycho-analysing him.'

Which brought us firmly back to the matter in hand. 'So how do you suggest we do that?'

He rubbed the base of his chin with the back of his fingers. 'Ted's our only hope of getting the hieroglyphics translated quickly.'

'Surely you don't mean another trip to Cairo?'

'No, we do have the wonders of modern technology at our fingertips, Merry. I suggest we email him the images and ask him to email us back. We just need to figure out why we're asking this time.'

We poured ourselves a drink from the mini bar and went out onto the huge canopied balcony. The night air was warm and still, but noisy. Cars, taxis and buses sped along the Corniche, honking their horns with wild abandon. Caleche drivers, grouped at the roadside, shouted persistent invitations at all passers-by to come for rides in their horse-drawn carriages. The muezzin further along the road was chanting out its tuneless doctrine. Despite the noise, the haunting beauty of the Egyptian night time cast its spell. The view of the Nile from their balcony was like some exotic travel poster. The lights of Luxor played on the vast river, casting golden hues of light on the stirring inky waters. This was Egypt: nowhere else like it in the world. Nowhere else I'd rather be.

I leaned back in one of the cushioned wicker armchairs, sipped my drink and stared up at the pinprick stars in the cavernous black sky. Part of me would have been happy to stay here all night, feeling the soft breeze on my face, and soaking up the mysticism of this strange land. But the pull of the hieroglyphics was stronger, and I turned my mind back to the problem of what to tell Ted. 'Could we say we returned the original slip of paper to Howard Carter's house with the translations he gave us. And they thought it was a fantastic addition to the display. I mean to have the hieroglyphs with their translation typed underneath. So, they asked us to do the same with another example, just to add a bit more interest to the display?'

He frowned a mock disapproving look at me, 'You're getting frighteningly good at this making-up-stories lark.'

'You mean lying,' I said flatly. 'I know, and it doesn't make me proud, I can assure you. Now I've met him, I can honestly say if there's anyone I'd be willing to take into our confidence, it's Ted. But it just feels too soon. I'm not ready to relinquish the reins. But we need his help, and I don't want to stray too far from the truth. That's about the most plausible excuse for bothering him I can come up with. And it preserves the link to Howard Carter, just in case we do stumble across something we have to hand over to the authorities and fess up about.'

'Ok, hand me the phone. I can't think of anything better, and I'm with you all the way on this.'

I passed him the mobile, and a moment later listened in on him putting our plan into action. 'Hi, Ted, it's Adam. Listen, I'm having dinner at The Winter Palace with Merry, and we have another favour to ask...'

A few minutes later we'd zapped the hieroglyphic images off to him via email, and he'd promised to ping back the translations before bedtime if possible.

'Well, that leaves us at a bit of a loose end,' Adam said, finishing his drink. 'How about dinner? Not just to make another little falsehood true, but because all this excitement is making me ravenously hungry!'

Adam donned a jacket and tie to comply with the dress code. Definitely a man with a great sense of how to wear clothes; he looked suave and rather dashing with his hair freshly combed and his shoes highly polished. I guess years in the upper echelons of the City-based banking sector did that for him.

I touched up my make-up, added a silk wrap to the dress I was already wearing, and exchanged my sandals for killer heels.

We made a rather sophisticated pair, I think, though I do say so myself. I was so used to Dan's rather shambolic dress sense and unruly hair, it made quite a pleasant change to feel I'd stepped - if only for one evening - into the head-turning category alongside my dinner companion.

We ate in the 1886 à la carte restaurant. Its décor was pure French colonial, lots of ornate cornicing, tall gilt mirrors, and decorative candle sconces. The tables were set with yards of stiff white linen cloths, heavy silver cutlery and fine crystal wine goblets. The mood was set off to perfection by the guitarist standing unobtrusively in the background, serenading us with a repertoire of classical favourites.

I don't think we dared talk about what the hieroglyphics might reveal. So over my grilled seafood medley, and Adam's apricot-stuffed chicken, we started to fill in some of the gaps about each other.

'You never married?' he asked me quietly.

'It never really felt necessary,' I admitted. 'I knew early on I didn't want children. My goal's always been to travel and see a bit of the world. Dan's a happy-go-lucky sort of chap. Our life together fell into a kind of steady rhythm. I think we've pretty much worked on the principle "if it ain't broke, don't fix it". Besides, I have this rather fabulous surname of "Pink". Why on earth would I give it up?'

He grinned at me. 'Well, you don't have to nowadays, of course. My wife didn't. She remained Tabitha Hayes all our married days. She said Tabitha Tennyson made her sound like something out of a Beatrix Potter story, complete with whiskers and long bushy tail.'

I laughed. 'Tabitha. That's not a name you hear every day.'

'No, I think her parents had a warped sense of humour. Her younger brother's called Tarquin. He's a jobbing actor, as I suppose you have to be with a name like that. Her older sister's called Eleanor. Not Ellie, or anything friendly-sounding like that. It's Eleanor, and she's just about as prim as you'd expect. Get this; she's a headmistress in an upper-crust boarding school. You don't really associate that with the twenty-first century, do you? So school-mistress by name, school mistress by nature.'

'I'm getting the impression you don't much like Eleanor.'

'Well, I don't have anything to do with her now, of course; nor any of them - for which I can't say I'm particularly sorry. Tabitha did me a favour on that score when she left. But I think Eleanor always thought Tabitha married me on the sympathy vote, and I somehow stood in the way of her making anything of herself.'

I decided to fish for the sympathy vote reference a bit later. 'Tabitha didn't go to work?'

'No. I met her at a banking shindig, champagne flowing, and all that nonsense. Those were the heady days before the crash. I guess she fancied herself as the stereotypical corporate wife, playing hostess at all my lavish dinner parties. I'm not sure she realised that sort of thing died out in the eighties. It would never have been my scene even if it hadn't. So she mostly spent her time playing badminton, helping out at the local stables and taking our dogs for long walks. We had a nice place in a leafy part of Berkshire, and we rubbed along together happily enough like that for a few years. But I think we both knew it couldn't last. I felt increasingly disillusioned and trapped. I used to come home and escape into my history books. I can't have been much fun. She started going out more, increasingly without me, and met someone else. To give her credit, she was remarkably candid about the whole thing. There was no big showdown, or anything like that. She just packed up her stuff and moved in with her new boyfriend, a wealthy wine merchant, as I understand it. She took the dogs with her. We sold the house, split the proceeds, and went our separate ways. I hot-footed it out here at the first opportunity.'

He made it sound dizzyingly straightforward, but I sensed shades of emotion in the bits he left unsaid. 'Are you divorced?'

He took a slow sip of wine. 'Just about, I think. The decree nisi came through a while back. I think the final bit is pretty much of a formality.'

'And you never went down the children route, either?'

He screwed his nose up and shook his head, quite a compelling combination to observe. 'I think you know when it's not right. The subject never really cropped up. And since my Mum and Dad aren't around anymore, there was never any parental pressure from my side to start a family. Tabitha's still young enough to go ahead if she wants to. I'm not sure it's for me.'

He'd mentioned his Dad was no longer alive when we were in Cairo and talking about cryptic crossword clues. I hadn't realised he'd lost both his parents. Some sixth sense told me this must be something to do with the sympathy vote, the reason he'd left university, and why Ted had taken him under his wing. But I wasn't sure how to ask about it. I wanted to appear gently interested, not intrusive, but I couldn't think of a way to strike the right balance. 'You've lost both your parents?' I queried softly, contenting myself with checking I hadn't misheard or misunderstood him.

He looked at me for a moment as if he wasn't quite sure how I'd made the switch from Tabitha to his parents; then sighed; apparently realising he'd invited it with such a casual, throwaway reference. 'Yeah, they died in a car crash just before my twenty-first birthday. But let's not dwell on it.' He smiled at me across the table. 'It was a long time ago. I've had plenty of time to come to terms with it.'

Which wasn't the same thing as getting over it, I thought, looking beyond the smile and his determination to shrug it off and appear upbeat, to the sadness in his eyes. I'd wanted to know, but now I wished I hadn't asked. Acting on instinct I reached across the table to lay my hand over his. His turned underneath it, so we sat for a while in silence, gently clasping hands.

'Is that why you gave up university?'

He didn't answer immediately. He toyed with the stem of his wineglass with the hand not holding mine. I sensed he was reliving painful memories. 'Yes, in a roundabout way,' he said at last. 'Everything went up in the air for a while. Once the dust settled it became clear things were a bit fraught financially. It pretty soon dawned on me that no parents and no money equalled no university for me. I bowed to the inevitable, and got myself a job.'

I had the impression there was more to the story than he was telling me. But I figured I'd pursued my curiosity about as far as was reasonable. I felt overwhelmingly sad for him. Whatever the ins and outs, he'd lost not only his parents, but also his chance to pursue Egyptology at a young enough age to really carve a niche for himself.

'I think I've spent the last few years dreaming about Egypt the way some people dream about winning the lottery,' he went on after a pause. 'Then two things happened, pretty much simultaneously, and gave me the out I think I was subconsciously wishing for. Tabitha left me, and the credit crunch hit, seemingly overnight. Those two events were the catalyst I needed. I decided I had enough of a buffer in the bank to see me through a couple of lean years. So I packed up my old life, literally as well as metaphorically, and here I am.'

'Here you are,' I concurred; and very happy about it I was too, I realised. It had started out as a sense of amazing good fortune, running into someone who could help me with the hieroglyphics. But now I realised there was more to it than that. But it was too soon to say what exactly. So I didn't pause to examine the happiness too closely, smiling at him instead. 'And, you know what? I'm a firm believer in the adage it's never too late. You'll finish your online studies, and the next thing we know, you'll be blazing a trail through the world of Egyptology, and being interviewed for the next Discovery Channel documentary.' I squeezed his hand, fiercely certain he could make up for lost time.

He grinned at me, and the atmosphere turned a shade lighter. 'You make it sound so easy. It's one of the things I love about you, you know, your unshakeable confidence. The truth of the matter is though, Merry, until you turned up I was starting to think I might be having a horrible mid-life crisis.'

'What on earth do you mean?' I asked, genuinely shocked.

'Well, it's one thing being out of the rat race. And I guess just about every man on the planet must dream about being Indiana Jones at some point in his life. But dreaming about chucking it all in to pursue some big Egyptological adventure is a bit different from waking up at the crack of dawn every morning to the chanting from the muezzin, and wondering where the hell to start.'

I suddenly realised how alike we were, Adam and me. I could certainly empathise with his dream of escape from the daily treadmill. After all, the self-same sentiment prompted my spur-of-the-moment decision to take voluntary redundancy without a fall back plan. It seemed neither of us was content anymore to just go through life joining the dots to make a predetermined pattern. Egypt was the irresistible lure we both followed, exerting the magnetic pull of magic and mystery. It made me wonder if perhaps I was having a mid-life crisis too. Because I wasn't any clearer about where to go with my future from here than he was. But I knew for sure I wouldn't trade being where I was right now, this very minute; not for anything.

'You've been like a much-needed shot of adrenaline, Merry. I can't begin to tell you what these last few days with you have meant to me. For the first time in ages, I've woken up every morning with a clear sense of purpose, and a thrill of excitement about what the day might have in store for me. It's unpredictable, a little bit crazy even, but it's wonderful, too. Quite frankly, I'm having the time of my life.'

And, in those few sentences, he echoed my own feelings so exactly I might as well have been the one saying them. It was starting to dawn on me that getting locked up in

Howard Carter's house might just turn out to be the very best thing ever to happen to me. And, if I was reading Adam right, I was starting to suspect it might just turn out to be the very best thing ever to happen to him, too. A frisson of pleasure snaked up my spine. Catching it, I jolted-to into the rather belated realisation I was sitting here holding hands with a man who wasn't my boyfriend, looking dreamily into his eyes and drifting towards dangerously personal territory.

I withdrew my hand rather abruptly, and rushed into speech. 'Howard Carter had no idea what a favour he was doing us when he taped up those scraps of paper inside the picture frames, did he? We both arrived in Egypt longing for some excitement - however subconsciously - and he obliged us in a way we couldn't possibly have imagined.'

Adam sipped his wine, a subtle acknowledgement of my withdrawal. But he seemed less inclined than me to retreat to neutral territory. 'Didn't your boyfriend balk a bit at leaving you here?'

'That depends on your definition of "a bit".' I said, pulling my eyes away from his searching gaze. 'He did a bit of huffing and puffing. But I was pretty single minded about it. I don't think I left him much choice in the end.'

Adam's face was scrupulously devoid of expression. Even so, he managed to convey the strongest possible impression that in Dan's shoes he'd have reacted rather differently. I didn't so much read a criticism of Dan in this, as complete incomprehension of his blindness to what he was missing out on flying home; and I don't think it was just the hieroglyphics. Whatever; his lack of comment was eloquent and had the curious effect of making me feel as if the air conditioning had been suddenly switched off.

At some point during our conversation the waiter had unobtrusively removed our plates. I wasn't quite sure by what slight of hand he'd managed this without me noticing. Now he returned to offer us dessert or coffee. We opted for coffee, and the inevitable return to the subject of the hieroglyphics.

'You know what?' Adam looked across the table at me, and his smile was the soft, intimate caress I was getting to know, despite my earlier pullback. 'No matter where these hieroglyphics lead us; whether it's to a discovery to rock the world,' – he accompanied this with a theatrical gesture that made me smile; he was self-deprecating again - 'or to a total dead end; I'm wondering if we shouldn't combine forces, you and me. You're the one with the writing skills, the confidence, and the imagination. I'm the one with a knowledge of Egypt based on a bit more than fiction.' A huge grin lit his face at my mock-outraged expression. 'So, perhaps we should team up, Merry. What do you say? We could write novels together, or devise treasure hunts for the tourists, or write guide books to all the famous sites setting out the personality profiles of all the major players of ancient Egypt; we could devise murder mystery games, or –'

My hand held up to his face in an unmistakeable stop sign forced him to, well, stop. But I was laughing, enjoying his boyish charm and enthusiasm. 'And you reckon I'm the one with the imagination?! Perhaps we should see about solving the mystery we already have before we start dreaming up new ones. Then maybe we can decide how we both return to gainful employment, and whether this dream of Egypt we both hold in our heads actually has the capacity to pay the bills.'

He raised his eyes to the ceiling. 'Not only does the lady have charm; she speaks sense.'

'Oh stop!' I laughed.

Adam glanced at this watch, and smiled at me, stepping back from the play-acting into his more normal self. 'It's pretty late. Gone eleven. Ted didn't specify his bedtime. Do you think he's had time to work his magic?'

'There's only one way to find out.'

We gulped our coffee, Adam signed the bill, and we practically sprinted back upstairs to our suite. But none of this renewed anticipation could completely quell the knowledge we'd moved closer emotionally. I wasn't sure how I felt about this. Neither was I ready to confront the uncomfortable question of how Dan might feel about it. So, deciding if I ignored it, it might go away, I allowed the more pressing matter of Ted's hoped-for response to consume my attention.

Chapter 11

Back in the impossibly luxurious surroundings of our – sorry, King Farouk's – suite, it was immediately apparent there was an email waiting for us when Adam powered up his iPad. Seconds later, we were both peering at the screen.

"Make of these what you will." Ted had written. "To me they seem as random as the last lot you gave me. I hope the tourists enjoy them."

'Well, they're definitely numbers,' I remarked. 'But I can see what Ted means about random. They certainly don't look like map references, do they? There are no little degree signs for a start, although I don't suppose there's a hieroglyphic equivalent for them, to be fair. And no helpful compass points either.'

'No,' Adam frowned. 'They're just numbers.' He read them aloud, as if it might help us make some sense of them. '1,881. 1,458. 1,916. And 1,323.'

'Let's try writing them out in words again,' I suggested, hopefully. 'The letters spelt out the answer for us last time.'

'I'd be surprised if he used the same convention twice,' he murmured, 'but anything's worth a try.'

A frustrating half-hour later, we gave up. 'No, that's definitely a blind alley.'

We sat back on the deeply padded grey-gold sofa and stared blankly at the numbers. We'd tried everything we could think of. We'd written them out in ascending sequence, then descending sequence. Adam even converted them to corresponding letters of the alphabet to see if they were some kind of message in cypher. 'I don't know much about the enigma code,' he said glumly, 'except to say this isn't it.'

I nipped to the loo, opting out of the brain-ache for a moment in favour of marbled luxury, the softest Egyptian cotton towels imaginable, and, on my part, some rather star-struck wondering about the rich and famous who might have occupied the suite before Adam and me. Lord Carnarvon was a dead cert, which made me feel a bit goose-bumpy. And who knew how many other notable personages had preceded us. An awed feeling of unreality swept over me, and I knew Adam was right: I was having the time of my life.

It was as I returned to the sitting room, looking at the numbers upside down and from a distance, I was suddenly hit by the uniformity of them. 'Hang on, hang on!' I yelled. 'I think I've got it! They're not numbers. They're dates! Or years, anyway.'

'What?' Adam looked up at me as if I'd just landed from Mars.

'Take away the commas,' I commanded. 'What are you left with? 1916. 1458. 1323. And 1881.'

That characteristic stillness settled over Adam again. 'Ok, 1881 and 1916 I can run with,' he said slowly, thinking it through out loud. 'They were during Howard Carter's lifetime, although the first was ten years before he came to Egypt. But how do you account for the other ones. He was no historian of medieval history, so far as I'm aware.'

'You must be feeling tired,' I declared rather rudely, my elation permitting me the smugness. 'What about if you add a "BCE" after them?'

I pause here a moment to say I grew up understanding the term "BC" to mean "before Christ". But I understand it has been recently updated and reinterpreted to BCE to mean "before common – or Christian – era".

His eyes narrowed. '1458 BCE.' He gazed up at me, the radiance of a breakthrough shining through the confusion of a moment ago. 'That was about the time Hatshepsut died and Thutmosis III came to the throne.'

'And 1323 BCE?' I demanded excitedly.

'Bloody Hell, Merry; that's generally accepted as the year of Tutankhamun's death! I think you might have cracked it for us once again.'

'Not for the first time we were trying to be too clever,' I demurred. 'I'm getting the impression he was a pretty straightforward chap, our Howard Carter. Not one given to the highly convoluted mental gymnastics we've been torturing ourselves with.'

'So,' Adam said slowly, as I plopped back down on the impossibly deeply cushioned sofa alongside him. 'If we're trying to equate the dates with map references, we could deduce 1323 being Tutankhamun's tomb, KV62; and 1458 being Hatshepsut's tomb, KV20. If I'm right and those small boxes on the topographic map are tombs in the Valley of the Kings, then they're both on there.'

'Which means,' – I deduced cleverly - 'we just have to figure out what's significant about the years 1881 and 1916 in terms of locations within the range of that map.'

Adam stared off into space for a long moment. 'You know, I think Ahmed might unknowingly have pointed us in the right direction on that score. I'm pretty sure 1881 was the year the elder Abd el-Russel brother split on the others and coughed the location of the mummy cache to Gaston Maspero.'

A swift bit of Internet searching confirmed this, and added a few golden nuggets to our mine of information. The tomb shaft was known as DB320, due to its proximity to Hatshepsut's mortuary temple Deir el-Bahri. More latterly, it was renamed TT320, simply standing for Theban Tomb. Wonderful Wikipedia went one further, giving us precise co-ordinates 25° 44' 12.48" N, 32° 36' 18.13" E. Sadly living up to the female stereotype I'm not one for map reading; so these were a load of gobbledygook to me. But Adam seemed pretty au fait with the format, if his slow nods were anything to judge by.

Another speedy bit of zipping around Wikipedia confirmed the co-ordinates of Tutankhamun's and Hatshepsut's tombs, KV62 and KV20. So, with the wonders of modern technology at our fingertips, as Adam pointed out earlier, we had three of our map references in moments.

I was distracted for a while, wondering how an earlier discoverer of the riddles might have fared coming across Carter's conundrums in, say, the 1950s or 60s, before the great internet revolution. There was no doubt technology had helped me and Adam no end; and that was allowing for Adam's already encyclopaedic knowledge of ancient Egypt, and Howard Carter in particular.

'Merry, come back.' He nudged me with his elbow. 'Don't go drifting off into dreamland just yet. We're not done.'

'I'm not sleepy,' I reassured him. Although, glancing at my watch I realised I should be. It was well past the witching hour and creeping towards the wee small ones. 'So, what do you get if you Google Howard Carter and 1916?'

A little bit of scrolling later, we found ourselves reading about Hatshepsut's cliff-cut tomb.

'This is the one she had carved for herself when she was still queen,' Adam said on a note of discovery. 'She abandoned it in favour of KV20 in the Valley of the Kings after declaring herself Pharaoh.'

The location was given as Wadi-Sikkat Taka ez-Zeida, approximately one mile west of Deir el-Bahri. 'That's got to be approaching the Valley of the Queens,' Adam announced, consulting an internal map of the landscape. 'Fitting enough, I suppose.'

The website said the tomb was discovered by Howard Carter in 1916, when he was alerted tomb robbers had stumbled across a previously unknown tomb.

'It's all coming back to me now,' Adam said softly. 'I'd put money on it those tomb robbers were the next generation of Ahmed's erstwhile ancestors the Abd el-Russels. Carter caught them in the act, you know. He went to investigate with some of his workmen in the dead of night, lit only by moonlight. When they reached the site of the tomb, they found a rope dangling down the cliff-side, and could actually hear the tomb robbers at work.'

'How on earth did they manage to find their way in there?' I asked incredulously. I was looking at a drawing showing the location of the tomb, carved into a crevice about 42 metres down the sheer cliff face.

'I know, it defies belief, doesn't it? Even more so perhaps that the ancient tomb-builders conceived of constructing Hatshepsut's tomb there in the first place.'

'So, what did Carter do?'

Adam grinned at me, given an opportunity to lecture on his favourite subject. 'His first action was to sever the tomb robbers rope, cutting off their escape route. I'll bet that spooked them. Imagine being entombed, literally, half way down a sheer cliff face, with no rope! Here, look. There's a couple of paragraphs in Carter's own words.'

We put our heads close together to skim-read the small section of text in tandem.

"Making secure a good stout rope of my own, I lowered myself down the cliff. Shinning down a rope at midnight, into a nestful of industrious tomb-robbers, is a pastime which at least does not lack excitement. There were eight at work, and when I reached the bottom there was an awkward moment or two. I gave them the alternative of clearing out by means of my rope, or else of staying where they were without a rope at all, and eventually they saw reason and departed. The rest of the night I spent on the spot, and, as soon as it was light enough, climbed down into the tomb again to make a thorough examination. The tomb was discovered full of rubbish .... this rubbish having poured into it in torrents from the mountain above. When I wrested it from the plundering Arabs I found that they had burrowed into like rabbits, as far as the sepulchral hall ..... I found that they had crept down a crack extending half way down the cleft, and there from a small ledge in the rock they had lowered themselves by rope to the then hidden entrance of the tomb at the bottom of the cleft: a dangerous performance, but one which I myself had to imitate, though with better tackle ...... For anyone who suffers from vertigo it certainly was not pleasant, and though I soon overcame the sensation of the ascent I was obliged always to descend in a net".

Adam grinned delightedly at me again. 'He certainly wasn't overly risk-averse, was he, our Mr Carter? I reckon it takes a brave man to lower himself on a rope into a pit of eight tomb robbers.'

'Perhaps there was a more gentlemanlike code of conduct in those days,' I mused, 'even for tomb robbers. So, can we get a map reference?'

A pretty thorough search of Wikipedia and Google turned up nothing.

'This one's a bit obscure, it seems,' Adam concluded. 'But I'll bet there's someone of our acquaintance who'll know where to find it. In reality if not in cyberspace.'

'Ahmed.'

'Yes, and he promised us a walk in the Theban Hills, didn't he?'

'He did.'

Adam nodded, satisfied. 'So, we'll have to work out this last map reference for ourselves.'

'And then what?'

'Then, lovely Merry, by my reckoning we have to draw diagonal lines between the four sets of co-ordinates. The very fact Carter drew them in the four corners of the reverse side of the painting suggests to me he wants us to intersect them.'

'So, we really are looking for X marks the spot.'

His eyes gleamed violet. 'So it would seem.'

There didn't seem much else to say. A drowsy companionship settled over us. We both stared into space contemplating everything we'd discovered so far and where it might lead us next. It felt perfectly natural for his arm to slip round my shoulders, and for my head to tilt sideways to rest against his chest. The thought of turning in for the night skittered against my consciousness and drifted away again. Dan said he trusted me. But the sad truth of the matter was I could no longer be sure I trusted myself.

Adam, too, seemed perfectly content to let sleep steal over us where we sat, comfortably curled against each other on the deeply cushioned sofa. I sensed an unspoken closeness we were both unwilling to confront, almost as if fearful it might slip away; or perhaps nudge closer. Letting it drift, just below the surface, sensed but unacknowledged, seemed the safest bet.

I woke with daylight streaming through the shutters, to find my head pillowed against Adam's chest, his arm still holding me close.

He must've felt me shift against him, and he tilted his head to smile at me. He'd been awake before me, I realised. 'Good morning sleepy head, he said softly.

It was a rather lovely start to a new day. I smiled back; then gently pulled out of his arms, getting things back on a more familiar footing I didn't find quite so unsettling.

As I'd told Dan, there were two bedrooms in our suite at The Winter Palace. We hadn't used either of them. Yet I think there was a silent acknowledgement in that shared smile that we'd somehow spent the night together.

Innocently, I assured myself.

Chapter 12

Ahmed was only too delighted to play guide for our walk across the Theban hills. We met him in the afternoon, after he clocked off from his early shift. Adam and I fell back into our easy camaraderie as we refocused on our quest and left last night's intimacy behind us. Really all we'd done was fall asleep on a hotel sofa, nothing more. It seemed foolish to read more into it than that. Ahmed fussed over us for a few moments.

'Adam and Mereditd, you have water? You have hats? You have sunscreen? De sun here is fierce. You will burn easily.'

We reassured him on all points. 'Please, call me Merry,' I entreated, not for the first time. I didn't think Mereditd was something I could easily resign myself to. There's a formality to the Arabic language, I gather, which makes it difficult for them to comprehend abbreviations or nicknames.

Ahmed was robed in a white cotton galabeya, with a turban; also white cotton, wound round his head. It made his face look a bit like a walnut, very brown, with creased skin, hardened from years in this climate that sucked the moisture out of every pore. Adam was in his favoured outfit of chinos and a loose brushed cotton shirt, white again. He sported an Indiana Jones style hat, which made him look raffish and adventurous. I was similarly attired in cotton trousers and a flowing cotton shirt, with my broad-brimmed straw hat issuing a challenge to the sun to cast its rays on my face if it dared.

We met in the Deir el-Bahri parking lot. The trinket sellers started to approach, took one look at Ahmed, and hastily retreated in search of alternative victims. There were definite advantages to having friends in high places, I decided; well, in the tourist police, anyway.

'We are ready to go, yes?' Ahmed cast a look at our footwear. Adam was in scuffed walking boots, clearly a feature of his wardrobe for at least twenty years. I'd opted for trainers. Ahmed, I saw, was in open-toed sandals. Ah well, he'd grown up here. And I'd noticed the locals seemed to have feet of leather, watching one of them shimmying barefoot up a palm tree at the Jolie Ville to hack off bunches of dates.

A path ascended the slope north of Hatshepsut's temple, and this was where Ahmed led us now. It wasn't particularly steep, but covered in a thin layer of loose shale and shingle blown from the surrounding hillside, so we had to watch our step.

Half way up I stopped to admire the view, and take photographs. The temple was on our left, nestled in the curve of the cliffs like an oyster in its shell.

Ahmed grinned toothily at me. 'Dis temple, it is beautdiful, yes?'

'Stunning,' I agreed. 'Particularly from this angle, where you can see the terraces side-on.'

'From de top of de hill, de view is even more beautdiful,' he assured me. 'Come, I show you.'

We continued up the path. Adam pointed to the caves and excavated holes we passed, some gated, some gaping open. 'These are 11th Dynasty, if I remember rightly. So they were here when Hatshepsut was.'

The pathway curved as we reached the top. Following it, we found ourselves standing on the cliff-top directly above Deir el-Bahri. I gulped at the sight. Way below us, down the sheer cliff-face the lower terraces of Hatshepsut's temple jutted out from the rock. I could see little knots of tourists scurrying around like small insects. The view was spectacular. The whole of the West Bank was laid out like a carpet at our feet. We could see a patchwork of memorial temples in the valley below us, with the Nile snaking through the landscape beyond them, and the city of Luxor in the haze beyond.

Adam came to stand behind me and pointed across my shoulder, so we could pick out the landmarks together. 'There, on the left, that's the Seti I temple. A bit further along to the right, the bigger one there, see it? That's the Ramesseum. Keep scanning right, that's the excavation around the old palace of Amenhotep III, where the Colossi of Memnon still stand. And right over there to the right,' he turned me slightly, 'is the Medinet Habu, temple of Ramses III.'

'On a clear day, you can see far far across de Nile to de Red Sea hills on de horizon.' Ahmed added. I scanned the green fields and brown villages bathed in strong golden light and thought it one of the most breath-taking landscapes I'd ever seen.

Ahmed led us a short distance southwards, with the Nile valley on our left, the Theban hills stretching away as far as the eye could see on our right, an expanse of buff coloured rock deeply creased with bronze shadow. 'We are circling de eastern side of de Valley of de Kings,' he said. 'A bid furtder along, you will see.'

The terrain was rocky and barren. The path meandered across the high, shale covered cliffs, bleached by the sun to a dull gold, without so much as a blade of grass to relieve the glare. The sun hammered from the densely blue sky above us, sucking all the moisture from the air. It was an arid, dusty, inhospitable furnace of a place, but curiously awe-inspiring. After a few more paces we reached a fork in the path and turned westwards, further into the hillside. The ground was littered with stones, fragments of what looked like pottery, and something else I didn't expect to see. I scooped one up, the size of my fist. 'This looks like a shell,' I exclaimed.

I handed it to Adam, who studied it intently for a moment. 'I'd say this is a fossilised clamshell,' he remarked. 'It's probably been here for something like thirty million years, a reminder of a time when this whole area lay beneath the sea.'

'That seems impossible to imagine. Just like the stories about flash floods in the Valley of the Kings burying some of the tombs under layers of silt. Wasn't that what was supposed to have happened to Tutankhamun?'

'Oh yes,' Ahmed nodded. 'Sometimes torrential rain and sudden floods. What is your English expression? When itd rains itd pours?'

Adam smiled and nodded. 'Flood water still poses a very serious threat to the tombs in the Valley,' he said. 'There are all sorts of projects underway to construct flood barriers to protect the area. Ahmed's right. Sometimes here you can get several inches of rain dropped in a matter of minutes. The ground's so dry it can't absorb the water, so it washes in torrents down the hillsides into the ravines. And, of course, one of the handiest ravines of all is the Valley of the Kings.'

'De flood water is frightening,' Ahmed agreed. 'It poses much risk to de low-lying tombs. Id washes into dem, bringing tons of sand and stdone and rubble and debris wid

230

it. And it leaves a deep layer of siltd and sludge behind it.'

'Scary yes,' I agreed. 'But surely a useful natural feature to take advantage of if you want to build a tomb to lay hidden and undisturbed for all eternity. Especially if you're clever enough to make the tomb water-tight, as Tutankhamun's seems to have been.'

Adam nodded, 'They believe some of the tombs were cut directly into the upper cracks and crevices in the cliffs, rather than into the Valley floor, because they were underneath ancient dried up waterfalls. The idea was these were a drainage channel for flood water, so would quickly become hidden behind huge deposits of rock and other debris.'

My imagination started firing like a rocket launcher. 'It really makes you wonder what else might still be buried down there, doesn't it?'

'I'll bet there's tombs still undiscovered in the Valley,' Adam agreed. 'Howard Carter had to clear away the surface detritus of thousands of years, and get right down to the bedrock to find Tutankhamun. In a valley as big as this one, clearing away millennia's worth of silt and flood deposits is an almost impossible task.'

As he spoke, Ahmed led us around a slight curve in the rocky path and there, below us, spread out like a giant oak leaf was the Valley of the Kings. Natural veins in the rock branched out from a central stem, with the Valley slopes rising sharply all around.

We were standing on the hilltop at the southern end. In the blinding sunlight it resembled nothing so much as a science-fiction moonscape; a white shale ravine pockmarked with the pits and squared-off brick entrances to the tombs.

I giggled, 'You almost expect one of the Clangers or the Soup Dragon to make an appearance, don't you?'

Ahmed looked at me blankly, but Adam smiled one of his mock disapprovals. 'Where's your sense of reverence? You're looking at the most ancient graveyard in the world. Try to show a suitable level of decorum.'

I knew he was teasing, so got busy with my camera again. 'This is amazing Ahmed. I'll bet there aren't too many tourists who get to see it from up here. I feel very privileged.'

We took a quick rest break to gulp down some water. The heat was like a fourth member of our little party; silent, for sure, but dogging every step. Not for the first time, I found myself wondering how on earth the necropolis workers coped toiling in the broiling heat and blinding light, chipping away at the cliffs until they could reach the dimness of their rock-cut sepulchres. An appealing fact I remember being told on my first visit to Egypt, was the ancient Egyptians pencilled heavy black kohl around their eyes to reduce the glare from the sun; the ancient version of sunglasses. But I have no idea how they managed the temperature. Even underground in the tombs I knew the heat didn't let up. I remember my surprise on that first trip, descending into a tomb for the first time, expecting the damp coolness of a medieval dungeon, to find instead a stifling, and suffocating dryness, even hotter than outside.

Ahmed gestured us onwards again. 'Dis is de soutdernmost pointd of de Valley,' he informed us a few moments later. 'We are above de tomb of Thudmosis III. See dis here? Dis is de remains of a stone hutd. De necropolis guards in de ancient times watched over de Valley from dis spot.'

The small pile of rocks was indeed hut-shaped. I tried to imagine what it might be like to stand here through the long, silent night, with the whole solar system spanning the arc of the heavens above, and the dead kings of five hundred years buried below. A ghost-ridden, spine-tingling, terrifying sort of place, I should think. No wonder the ancient Egyptians believed in the afterlife so ardently. Hard to imagine too many other places on earth where the whole universe appeared quite so close, eternity something you could reach out and touch.

'Which way do you wish tdo go now?' Ahmed asked. 'If we continue along dis patdway to de west and de nortd from here, we will be on de lower slope of de mountain called "de horn".

'That's Arabic for El-Qurn,' Adam put in. 'It's the pyramid shaped rock that looms over the Valley, although it's shape's not so clear from here.'

I nodded. 'I've always wondered whether the New Kingdom pharaohs selected the Valley as their burial ground because of this natural feature, harking back to the Old Kingdom pyramids of Giza and Memphis.'

'I shouldn't be at all surprised.'

'Dere are still some small stone shrines dere,' Ahmed said, 'where de ancient workmen from Deir el Medina placed small statdues and stelae to worship de mountain goddess. Dis patd will take you around de edge of de Valley past anodder guard hutd. Finally we will reach de Valley floor near de tomb of Ramses II.'

'And if we go the other way? Back the way we came?'

'Den we fork off towards de soutd, and follow de patdway towards Deir el Medina and de Valley of de Queens. I can show you where de mummy cache was discovered by my long ago ancestors.'

'Sounds good to me,' I concurred, wondering how we could lead the conversation round to asking about the cliff-cut tomb of Hatshepsut.

'Do you know where Hatshepsut's cliff tomb is?' Adam came right out with it.

Ahmed's eyes gleamed. 'Of course,' he said proudly. 'Itd was found by my family nearly one hundred years ago.'

234

'Told you so,' Adam grinned at me. 'He's descended from a family of mountain wolves and jackals.'

'Dey handed itd over to Mr Howard Carder demselves,' Ahmed defended hotly, his black eyes snapping.

'Yes, well that's not the story I heard,' Adam said mildly. 'But I'm willing to go along with your version for the sake of friendship.'

'Dis way,' Ahmed pointed, mollified, and started leading us back along the path.

He was right when he'd described the network of pathways as a spider's web. From our high vantage point we could see them criss-crossing the slopes and gullies, as no doubt they'd done for millennia.

'We're literally walking in the footsteps of the ancients,' Adam said quietly, picking up on my thoughts in that uncanny way of his. 'These are the same footpaths taken by ancient craftsmen on their way to work in the tombs, by priests who came to make offerings, and by the guards on their tours of inspection of the temples and tombs.'

And by Howard Carter, I thought, when he was working out a secret location for whatever it was his clues were leading us towards.

Ahmed paused again as we came over the brow of the slope and the Nile valley hove into view again. 'Dis is de remains of a small village built for de workmen digging and decorading de tombs in de Valley of de Kings. Somedimes dey chose to stday for de night here, insdead of walk all de way back to Deir el Medina.'

I gazed around at the stone remains of their encampment, really little more than a few low intersecting walls and some rubble. The ground around what remained of these huts was strewn with scraps of ancient pottery, and what looked like stone tools, reminding me of the stone-age flints in display in museums at home. They brought it to life, somehow, and I could picture those long ago craftsmen, story telling around a campfire, weary from a hard day's labour in the sepulchres they were creating below.

The path continued southward, downhill towards Deir el Medina. We hadn't gone too far along it, when Ahmed suddenly branched off along a barely discernible side track. 'Dis is de way to de mummy cache. Follow me pleaze.'

I don't really know what I expected, hearing Ahmed describe it the other night as a tomb shaft. But I'm not sure it was the gaping hole in the rock, jagged edged and rock strewn that he showed us. It looked as if someone had exploded it out of the hillside with a stick of dynamite. I couldn't see how a goat could possibly survive a tumble into that yawning stone pit.

'My God, they don't believe much in health and safety round here, do they?'

'The shaft's about thirteen metres deep,' said Adam, who'd been studying it on the Internet this morning. 'It opens out into a series of corridors and chambers underneath where we're standing.'

'And they found more than fifty mummies re-buried in there? Some of the most famous pharaohs of ancient Egypt?'

'Yup, a lot of the A-listers.'

I stared into the gaping chasm. My mind struggled to grapple with the knowledge of how the ancient priests rescued the mummies from the routine plunder going on in the Valley as law and order broke down. They must have had this catacomb cut out, then dragged the mummies up to this barren, inhospitable place, presumably on some kind of make-shift sledges, and lowered them reverently into this treacherous shaft.

Adam stepped forward to peer over the edge. 'You know, Gaston Maspero's sidekick, a chap called Èmile Brugsch, cleared out the cache of all fifty-odd mummies within 48 hours of being shown it by Ahmed's erstwhile relative Mohammed Abd el-Russel in 1881. They rigged up some kind of ladder and pulley system down the chimney here. Nowadays the same exercise would probably take months. It's reckoned he caused incalculable damage in his unseemly haste.'

Ahmed's dark eyes flashed, 'Dat man, he did not trustd my many times removed uncle nod to cheatd him and keep robbing from de tomb under his nose!'

I took a few photographs; then Ahmed led us onwards again, along another barely visible track branching off at right-angles. We trudged further this time, accompanied every step of the way by the pounding heat. We were a long way from the beaten track now, the cracks and crevices in the rock baked dry and filled with desert sand blown in from the Sahara. Suddenly fearful of snakes and scorpions, I trod carefully, watching every step; supremely grateful I was wearing trainers, not envying Ahmed his open-toed sandals one jot.

Because I was watching my feet rather than where we were going, I ran headlong into Ahmed's back when he stopped abruptly.

'Dere. You see dere?' He waved away my apology and pointed up at the cliff face. I realised we'd entered a narrow valley, this time viewing the hills around us from below. 'You see dat crack in de rock?'

There was indeed a long vertical fissure in the tawny-brown cliff-face where he was pointing, a few hundred metres away. 'Dat is where my last century relatives discovered de original tomb of de queen-pharaoh Hatshepsut.'

'Did they find anything inside?' I asked. Last night I'd been so caught up in reading Howard Carter's story of how he'd caught them in the act, I hadn't read on to see if they'd actually found anything of value.

'Only a massive sarcophagus made of quartzite,' Adam supplied. 'Inscribed for Hatshepsut as queen.'

I stared bug-eyed at the crevice. I knew the tomb channelled horizontally backwards from its entrance halfway down the cliff-side. But, even so. Getting up and down that sheer cliff on the end of a rope was one thing. Manoeuvring an enormous flippin' great quartzite sarcophagus inside was altogether another. It was beyond my imagination to conjure it up.

'Although it's always possible of course the relatives of our friend here had already made off with anything worth stealing.' Adam added.

Ahmed beamed at him, as if this possibility was something to be truly proud of.

'The tomb was undecorated, and never used for a burial. So the chances are there wasn't much to take.' While he said this, he was digging about in his pocket. He drew out a compass and after a bit of searching, brushed the sand off a relatively flat-surfaced rock and set it down.

I know one fact, and one fact only about a compass. This being it has some kind of magnetised pointer showing the direction of true north, and from which you can presumably plot other bearings.

Luckily Adam's knowledge was more comprehensive. He turned it this way and that a few times, and jotted some notes onto a tiny pad, then straightened and nodded at me.

'I think that will give us enough to be able to plot it fairly accurately on a map.'

Ahmed watched these shenanigans without comment. He knew Adam was an aspiring Egyptologist. So I guess if he thought anything at all while he stood puffing contentedly on his roll-up cigarette, it was to assume we were simply carrying out part of Adam's researches.

'You are ready to go back now, yes?'

We nodded, swigged some water, and started to retrace our steps. The heat kept us company all the way, although the sun was starting its slow descent across the Theban hills, burnishing them with the lustre of old gold. I was glad to reach the main footpath, assuring myself, perhaps misguidedly, we were less likely to step on an unwary snake here.

'You wantd to finish your walk back at Deir el-Bahri, or in de Valley of de Kings?' Ahmed asked, as we passed the scattered remains of the little workers encampment.

'The Valley,' I decided, without consulting Adam. 'Then I'll feel we've done the whole trek.'

Adam nodded, quite happy to go along with my decision.

The path descended quite steeply for the last 100 metres or so. Adam took my hand to steady me as we slip-slided our way down to the Valley floor. We emerged beside KV17, the closed-to-the-public tomb of Seti I.

The Valley was deserted, it being late in the afternoon by now, just past closing time to visitors. Sunset was starting to redden the sky above us, sending crimson streaks across the heavens. The sinking sun cast long pools of shadow across the Valley.

'I arrange one lastd special treatd for you, yes?' Ahmed said, eyes gleaming in the golden light. 'You would like to visitd a tomb justd de two of you?'

Adam and I looked excitedly at each other. 'That would be great Ahmed. Are you sure it's ok though? You won't get into trouble?'

Ahmed grinned, showing off his rather disconcerting lack of dentistry. 'You give me a liddle baksheesh, and I go and fix id for you. Which tomb do you wantd to see?'

'Tutankhamun,' I breathed. I'd been inside before, of course, and considered it decidedly underwhelming compared to the others. But that was before my association with Howard Carter.

Adam handed him some notes and Ahmed scooted off to organise this little piece of skulduggery. Adam and I gazed at each other. 'Well, that was a productive afternoon's exercise,' Adam concluded. 'Even if I do feel like a wrung out dish-cloth.'

'Me too,' I sympathised. 'Unlike your friend Ahmed; he's like a mountain goat, for all his bulk.'

'Yes, well he's been scrambling all over these hills since he was a nipper. And he's not likely to feel the heat the way we do. It's what he's used to.'

'So you reckon Howard Carter's whatever-it-is, is up there in the hills somewhere?'

His eyes scanned the bleached cliffs rising around us from the creeping shadow of the valley floor. 'I've been trying to mentally draw lines between the four landmarks Carter gave us while we've been walking. I can't be sure until I plot them on that contour map, but I reckon if you connect Tut's tomb with Hatshepsut's cliff-cut tomb; and KV20, her tomb here, with the mummy cache, there's a cross-over somewhere off behind that guard post we stopped to look at. The one with the great view down here to the Valley.'

I digested this in silence. It was impossible to imagine, if he was right, what we might find up there. Or quite how we might find it.

Ahmed returned gleefully brandishing a key. 'You mustd notd be too long,' he cautioned. 'Butd you can have de tomb to justd de two of you alone. I will waitd here for you.'

He unlocked the metal gate with a rather theatrical flourish. So, somewhat unexpectedly, we found ourselves descending the almost mythical sixteen stone steps. They're cut steeply into the Valley floor, leading to the tomb entrance along a short corridor.

Tutankhamun's tomb, for all its fame and undoubted fortune, is totally unremarkable. It's small for a start. Just four small interconnecting rooms, only two of which are accessible to visitors, the antechamber and the annexe. And it's almost completely undecorated, except for the apparently hasty painting of the burial chamber. Otherwise, it's just stark white stone walls, with a stark white stone floor and ceiling. Unplastered, with chisel marks still plain to see showing how it was carved from the bedrock.

But it has one remarkable feature. And that is Tutankhamun himself. He's still there, enshrined in his golden outer-coffin, resting like a Russian doll inside his red quartzite sarcophagus in the burial chamber.

We stood at the little wooden gate, barring us access to the burial chamber, and the empty treasury leading off it. It was impossible not to succumb to a sense of awed wonder. I tried and failed to imagine what it must have been like for Howard Carter and Lord Carnarvon, stepping over the threshold of more than three thousand years; the collapse of time into just a single moment as the past collided with the present. How like intruders they must have felt, as if they were trespassing into an ancient room with life still clinging to it.

A few short days ago I was walking goggle-eyed around the Cairo museum, struggling to take in the sheer magnitude of treasure displayed there. Now here I was, inside the tomb where it was discovered, and I was struggling again. This time it was to comprehend just how the thousands of beautifully crafted objects I'd seen could have possibly been crammed into such a small space.

'How on earth did they fit it all in?' I gaped.

'It was piled higgledy-piggledy and every which-way,' Adam said, knowing immediately what I meant. 'Especially through there in the annexe, where furniture, jewellery, jars and baskets were heaped so haphazardly it looked like a hurricane had blown through.'

'You'd think they'd take a bit more care when burying their king.' I felt a little indignant on Tutankhamun's behalf.

He smiled at me. 'Well you, of all people, have read enough novels to know there's all manner of speculation about the suddenness of his death and hastiness of his burial.'

'True. But didn't Zahi Hawass prove pretty conclusively it was a combination of a deadly malaria and a broken leg, possibly caused by a fall from his chariot?'

'Yes, that's the latest thinking.' He grinned at me. 'Of course, it doesn't mean the chariot accident wasn't rigged.'

'Oh stop it! You're making fun of me! Still, it defies belief, doesn't it, that such a young king should have amassed such an incredible collection of grave goods to bring into his tomb with him?'

'Yes, perhaps,' he conceded. 'The sheer quantity of objects stuffed in here certainly gave our friend Howard Carter a challenge. He said it was like playing a massive game of spillikins. It took him ten years to clear the tomb.'

'And that's allowing for the stuff that was presumably removed by the ancient grave robbers. Wasn't it supposed to have been broken into twice? I wonder how much booty they got away with.'

Adam shrugged. 'They reckon both robberies were fairly quickly discovered by the necropolis guards. So I guess some of whatever was stolen may have been put back. Carter found eight gold rings lying on the floor of the treasury, wrapped in a piece of cloth. He believed they were part of the robber's haul. He figured they tossed them back into the chamber when they knew they'd been caught red-handed.' Adam gazed into the burial chamber for a long moment. 'I certainly prefer the theory of ancient tomb robbers to the more recent claims that Carter and Carnarvon were the ones doing the thieving.'

I gaped at him. 'What are you talking about?'

He turned and leaned back against the wooden gate, folding his arms and crossing his legs at the ankle. 'Certain hack writers started speculating that Carter and Carnarvon discovered the tomb long before 1922 and were secretly plundering it. Finally, thinking they might get caught, they allegedly "staged" its supposed "discovery". Honestly! These people who see conspiracy theories round every corner drive me nuts!'

I felt my mouth drop open, and hastily snapped it shut again. 'How on earth were they supposed to get in?' I looked around at the small set of interconnecting rooms, and back towards the corridor and staircase we'd come through. 'Surely they don't think they burrowed through that entrance passageway?'

'No, it's even more fantastical than that. We're supposed to believe Carter was in league with your friends and mine the Abd el-Russel family. They're claimed to have either discovered or carved out a passageway leading from the tomb of Ramses VI, which overlays this one, as you know. Carter and the Abd el Russel are supposed to have broken through into this very room, the antechamber, and systematically set about emptying it of its contents. Not only that, we're supposed to swallow some garbage about them re-patching up the wall then making a mess to cover their tracks and make it look like the tomb was robbed in antiquity.'

'But that's crazy,' I said. 'We're already struggling to see how all those grave goods were crammed in here. If Carter and Carnarvon were plundering it for years, it must have been absolutely rammed to the gunnels. There's simply not enough space.'

Adam looked around him, 'We're supposed to believe there are more rooms opening off these ones. Apparently this is just a small section of a much larger tomb.'

I stared about me, seeing the tomb in a whole new light. I rapped my knuckles against the wall next to me. It felt and sounded reassuringly solid. 'But those hack writers must have had something to base such wild fantasies on, surely? That's not the kind of rumour you start spreading without anything at all to back it up.'

'They base it on a ring given by Lord Carnarvon to a chap called Edward Harkness. He was Chairman of the Board of the Metropolitan Museum in New York. Apparently Carnarvon gave him the ring as a gift in 1921, a year before the tomb was discovered. The ring bore the cartouche of Tutankhamun, and was supposed to have been in circulation for some seven years by that stage. The conspiracy theorists claim it can only have come from the tomb.'

'But you don't believe them?'

'Absolutely not. What they conveniently forget is the discovery by Theodore Davis in 1907 of a small burial pit near the tomb of Seti I. You've seen for yourself how close it is to here. The pit contained a dozen or so large sealed storage jars. These held floral collars, embalming materials and linen containing text dating to the final years of the little-known pharaoh Tutankhamun. I think it's more likely the ring came from there, and Carnarvon bought it on the antiquities market. Remember, Carter and Carnarvon weren't randomly digging in the Valley just to see what might turn up. They made a systematic search for Tutankhamun. Why? Because they believed the embalming cache found by Theodore Davis was a clue to the existence of the tomb. All I'll say on the matter is there's plenty of evidence for the ancient thefts in the way the entrance was re-sealed, and none at all to support these wild conspiracy theories.'

I felt a tiny sense of deflation, and brushed it away.

'You seem disappointed, Merry; why's that?'

I shrugged. 'Well, I was just wondering, if Howard Carter was systematically plundering the tomb for years before the official "discovery" whether those intriguing clues he's left us might be leading to a hidden stash.'

He gaped at me. 'You can't be serious!'

'I have no idea whether I'm serious or not. It just struck me as a possibility listening to you, that's all. And, you know, I'm not sure Howard Carter was always entirely on the straight and narrow. He's known to have dealt in antiquities, isn't he?'

Adam nodded. 'Yes, that's pretty well documented. He certainly acted for private collectors and a couple of the major museums.'

'And wasn't there some story about one of the artefacts from Tutankhamun's tomb turning up in a wine case in the tomb they used for preservation work? I read about it in the biography I was skimming the other day. Wasn't there a suggestion he might be intending to steal it?'

'Yes,' Adam admitted slowly. 'But he was fully exonerated. It happened when he famously downed tools after the authorities refused to let the wives of his fellow excavators visit the tomb. Events escalated out of all proportion, and Carter was temporarily sacked. While he was out of Egypt the Minister of Antiquities made an inspection and found an undocumented sculpture of Tutankhamun in a Fortnum and Mason's red wine crate. It raised a few questions for sure. But Carter's telegraphed response was immediate and emphatic. He said the sculpture was found in the debris blocking the passageway in a very fragile condition. He conserved it; then set it aside until it could be properly registered. His explanation was accepted without question and the matter dropped.'

'Well, I just think it's suggestive, that's all. I mean, it raises a bit of a question about his record keeping if not his honesty, doesn't it? And with that quantity of artefacts, you could hardly blame him and Carnarvon for filching one or two small items. Especially watching everything else they'd searched for years for being carted off to the Cairo museum.'

Adam was looking at me strangely. 'It is true,' he said finally, 'that when Carter died they found a few small objects from the tomb in his private collection of antiquities in his flat in London. But nothing of any great intrinsic value, except perhaps a small headrest that was a unique item. All those items were presented to King Farouk after the war, and are now in the Cairo museum.'

'See? It's got to make you wonder just a little, hasn't it?'

'But nothing from Tutankhamun's tomb turned up in Lord Carnarvon's private collection. You'd think he'd have had one or two illegal items if they were spiriting them away. Besides all you're suggesting is a few random items pocketed here and there during the clearance of the tomb, possibly after Carnarvon's death. It hardly points to wholesale plunder for years before a "staged" discovery.'

'You're probably right.' I admitted consolingly; then grinned broadly at him. 'But those clues are leading us somewhere. And it's starting to feel more and more like a treasure hunt. I mean, I ask you; X marks the spot! And if Carter was performing wholesale daylight robbery, he can hardly have flooded the items onto the open market before the tomb was discovered, can he? He must have stashed them somewhere. So, tell me. What can you usually expect to find at the end of a treasure hunt?'

Chapter 13

My euphoric mood evaporated rather quickly back in the real world outside the claustrophobic, eternity-laden atmosphere inside the tomb. I started to get decidedly cold feet. If there was any chance at all we were going to come across a hidden stash of treasure from Tutankhamun's tomb, then I didn't for a second doubt the avalanche of trouble we'd bring crashing down on top of us.

Adam went home for a shower; then came to meet me for dinner at The Jolie Ville. We sat at a corner table in the buffet restaurant, away from everyone else. It was modern, spacey and fairly brightly lit. I began to feel better. My imagination was probably just running away with me.

With the help of his compass, a walking map of the Theban hills, and the three sets of coordinates we already had, Adam set about plotting the reference points on Carter's topographic map. He calculated the fourth set of coordinates, Hatshepsut's cliff-cut tomb; absently forking salad into his mouth while he concentrated. He plotted it on the map; then looked up. 'Ready to draw some lines?'

It wasn't a perfect X. But there was a definite point where the two lines crossed over. If Adam was right and the more densely drawn wavy lines represented El-Qurn, the pyramid-shaped mountain overlooking the Valley, then it seemed our destination was just off to the east of it. He was probably right in his earlier deduction that it wasn't too far away from the guard post we'd looked at.

Now it was just a case of going there. It was the only way to find out if there was anything to be discovered. It was impossible not to start speculating again. Adam remained steadfast in his refusal to believe his hero Howard Carter capable of any serious wrongdoing. I wasn't so sure.

'There's one thing that's been bugging me,' I said, scratching my earlobe. 'Carter cabled Carnarvon saying he'd made a "wonderful discovery" of a "magnificent tomb". At that stage he'd found some stone steps leading down to a doorway with the necropolis seals stamped on it. Behind it was a corridor filled with rubble. So, I'll concede the possibility of a "wonderful discovery". I accept it looked promising. But how could he possibly have known it was a "magnificent tomb"? Doesn't it rather support the conspiracy theorists' view that he'd already been inside?'

Adam tilted his head to one side, looking thoughtful. 'Not necessarily. Before Tutankhamun, the most spectacular find in the Valley was the tomb of Yuya and Tjuya, the in-laws of Amenhotep III. Theodore Davis excavated it in 1905. The story was pretty similar to Tutankhamun. It had been robbed in antiquity, but was otherwise an intact tomb. The two mummies were preserved inside, along with some amazing artefacts, including lots of gold. I expect Carter knew the signs. He was an experienced archaeologist, approaching fifty years old. Looking at those necropolis seals, and with the experience of Yuya and Tjuya already chalked up, I see no reason why he shouldn't have concluded he'd found another magnificent tomb.'

It was hard to combat this logic. And, like Adam, I didn't want to sully Carter's reputation. But the very fact of our quest to solve the riddles he'd hidden pointed to some sort of secret. Something he'd needed to hide.

'Ok, but how do you account for the Tutankhamun artefacts in museums all over the world? The Egyptian authorities refused to divide the spoils with Carnarvon, and made it clear everything found inside the tomb had to remain here in Egypt.'

Adam stared at me. 'What artefacts?'

'I was reading about it online while you went home for your shower. As recently as 2010 some German Egyptologists were pointing accusatory fingers at Carter. They claimed he smuggled objects from the tomb out of the country, entering and disturbing the burial chamber without the presence of Egyptian officials. Apparently there's a funerary figure in the Louvre with Tutankhamun's name on it. And a museum in Kansas City, Missouri, has two golden falcon heads, which they think came from a collar around the mummy's neck. And that's not all. Have you heard of someone called Thomas Hoving?'

253

'Yes, he was the Director of the Metropolitan Museum in New York in the late sixties and early seventies.'

'Well, he wrote a book citing some dodgy dealings by Carter and Carnarvon.'

'I know. I've read it. He blew the whistle on their unauthorised dead-of-night visit to the burial chamber.'

'Yes, well, he also claimed some of the small-scale items in the Metropolitan collection may have come, illegally, from Tutankhamun's tomb. His allegation prompted a bit of an investigation. The upshot was a joint announcement made by the Met and the Egyptian authorities in November 2010 that nineteen objects would be returned to Egypt. Admittedly the objects were small-fry. Mostly study samples sent to the museum for analysis, by the sound of it. But nevertheless, it does suggest Carter might have indulged in a bit of contraband, doesn't it?'

'Ok, reluctant as I am to believe you, I can suspend disbelief far enough accept he was perhaps guilty of smuggling a few small items for himself and one or two Western museums. Small-fry, as you said yourself, and probably pocketed during the clearance. But it doesn't come anywhere close to convincing me we're going to find a hidden stash of tomb treasure up in the hills behind the Valley.'

'But he had the opportunity to spirit away a few more significant items before the clearance started. Like you said, that story about their nocturnal visit to the burial chamber is an accepted fact nowadays. Aren't they supposed to have knocked a hole in the wall to creep through, then covered it up with a load of reed baskets for the official opening?'

Adam nodded, looking decidedly unhappy about where my reasoning was leading us. It was the first time we'd not been in complete accord. I have to say it lent a certain je-ne-sais-quoi to the conversation that was quite refreshing. 'You can hardly blame them,' he said, with sympathy in his voice. 'They were only human after all. It was on the night after they first made the hole in the doorway, stuck a candle through and realised they'd discovered a tomb. It was the famous "wonderful things" moment, when Carter said he could see the glint of gold everywhere. They knew they weren't supposed to enter the tomb until the officials from the Antiquities Service arrived the following day. But they were desperate to know whether the pharaoh still lay buried there. Until they found him, they couldn't be sure they hadn't just discovered some kind of fabulous storeroom. There were signs on the ancient plasterwork to suggest thieves might have broken in during antiquity. So Carter, Carnarvon, Lady Evelyn Herbert, Carnarvon's daughter, and a chap called Pecky Callender, Carter's friend, sneaked back in the dead of night. I'd say it was wholly understandable - if not entirely honourable - they should want to take a peek.'

'Granted. But surely it was also a prime opportunity for a bit of hasty pilfering. I won't go so far as to call it theft. I mean they'd been searching for the tomb for years. If anyone had a right to lay claim to it, they did. And Carnarvon started out his excavations believing anything they found would be shared out, the way it used to be in Gaston Maspero's day. It wasn't his fault the Egyptians were getting all nationalistic and starting to resent the pillage of their antiquities by European and American dilettantes. Maybe they saw the opportunity to pocket a few of the choice objects and took it. Like you said, hard to blame them, they were only human. But perhaps having helped themselves to a few precious items there was no way of getting them out of Egypt. Especially with Carnarvon dying so quickly. We know Carter bitterly resented the spotlight he was forced to work under, with both the press and the Egyptian authorities dogging his every move. His bad temper is well documented. Perhaps some of the reason for it was his knowledge of being in possession of, let's say, misappropriated items, and not being able to offload them.'

Adam looked at me for a long moment, then shook his head and started to laugh. 'I know you love your fiction, Merry; the more far-fetched the better, by the sound of it. But I refuse to believe Howard Carter guilty of tomb robbery. He dedicated ten years of his life to clearing that tomb. Years more to writing it all up, and going on lecture tours of

America. I don't think he was a treasure hunter. I think he was an archaeologist.'

I felt a momentary stab of defiance that he could pooh pooh my brilliantly articulated hypothesis quite so offhandedly. But Adam's good humour was infectious. And he was probably right. Who was I to cast aspersions about the most famous excavator of all time, despite the persistent rumours of skulduggery I'd come across on the Internet? Howard Carter was dead and couldn't answer back. But it did leave the small matter of the puzzles he'd secreted inside a couple of picture frames.

'Ok, seriously then Adam. What are you expecting to find up there in the hills behind the Valley?'

He rested his chin in the palm of his hand. A rather dreamy expression settled over his handsome face. 'I don't know,' he admitted softly. 'I suppose I'm daring to hope for a tomb shaft, perhaps another mummy cache. Who knows, maybe even a tomb?'

And he'd accused me of indulging in far-fetched sensationalism! I gaped inelegantly at him. I know he yearned to be an Egyptologist but this was surely taking wishful thinking too far. I wasted no time saying so. 'As an archaeologist I hardly think those are discoveries Carter would have left behind without trumpeting to the world. What on earth makes you think otherwise?'

He shrugged. 'Maybe he didn't have it in him anymore. Perhaps he was tired, and wanted to go home. The good old days of Victorian and Edwardian archaeology were long gone. The Second World War was looming. Egypt was a place of nationalistic fervour. And Carter was ill. He left Egypt in 1932 and died of lymphoma in England in 1939. Perhaps if he stumbled across another discovery late on, he decided he simply didn't have the energy for it any more. But by leaving those clues behind, he could still lay claim to it.'

'Unless someone else stumbled across it in the meantime; we are talking more than seventy years ago.'

'Yes, well, that's true. And we may have to face up to the fact there's nothing there to discover. It may have been found, cleared and documented years ago, and not of enough intrinsic value to make it into the reference books.' He tilted his head, and smiled at me, 'But it's a nice dream though, isn't it?'

* * *

Adam left me after our buffet dinner with a quick hug and the tantalising prospect of tomorrow searching the Theban hills for whatever Carter had hidden there. I waved him off on his scooter into the darkness outside the hotel reception building, trying not to think about this time last night, when there'd been no need to say goodbye until tomorrow. I spent a restless night dreaming of buried treasure and pharaoh's curses, and woke at the crack of dawn, feeling ridiculously nervous and excited, and counting the minutes until I could meet Adam again for the next step on our search.

I decided it was time to bring Dan up to speed. I'd been putting off phoning him for reasons I chose not to examine too closely. I called him early, catching him before he left for work. I chatted away quite happily for a few minutes, making light of both Adam's speculations and my own, and basically describing it all as a great big adventure including today's plan for another scout around in the Theban hills behind the Valley of the Kings.

When I finished there was a deathly silence on the end of the phone. 'Meredith, you're not seriously telling me you're going to indulge in a spot of tomb robbing of your own, are you?'

That pulled me up a bit short to be honest. 'I have no intention whatsoever of robbing anything,' I told him primly.

'It's a bit late for claims like that,' he reminded me unkindly. 'You turned thief the moment you left Howard Carter's house with that scrap of paper in your pocket. Don't get all high and mighty now just because I carry that little insight to its logical conclusion.'

'There's a big difference between shoving a piece of paper into my pocket in the heat of the moment, and deliberately removing antiquities from a tomb, or a tomb shaft, or a cache, or a secret stash, or whatever the hell it turns out to be!'

'Are you sure about that? Because from everything you just said that sounds like exactly what you've been planning.'

'It does not!' I defended indignantly. 'We just want to see what's there. Everything I've told you is just our wild imaginings. If by some miraculous spin of the wheel we turn out to be right, then of course we'll go straight to the authorities.'

'You're stark raving mad! Meredith, why will you not see you're running headlong into a hornet's nest? I accept it started out as a bit of fun. But I'm not laughing now. Translating the hieroglyphics was one thing. I was willing to go along with that. But in the last couple of days you've wilfully tampered with hotel property, and now you're about to start lowering yourself into tomb shafts, or God knows what, in search of buried treasure. It seems to me there are only two possible outcomes. Either you'll fall and break your silly neck, or you'll get caught red-handed and spend the rest of your living days behind bars.'

'Thanks for the vote of confidence,' I muttered sarcastically.

'Meredith, see sense! It's time to call it a day. Stop pretending to be Lara Croft, or whatever other fantasy image of yourself it is you're acting out, and come home.'

I could feel my temper rising, and for once I made no attempt to check it. 'How dare you tell me what to do?' I snapped out angrily. 'Just because I've dared to break out of my hamster cage and live a little, all you can do is heap scorn on me! If it were down to you, I'd be back on the treadmill, with only your warped practical jokes to relieve the tedium. No' – when he tried to interrupt me – 'don't start telling me I've taken leave of my senses. You're starting to sound like a broken record on that score. And, yes, I am aware this is post-revolutionary Egypt. You've rammed that down my throat at every opportunity, too. Although what the hell difference you think it makes, I'm not sure! You were happy enough to leave me here! And thank God for it, because for once in my life I'm having a ball. So, no, I'm not coming home. No way!'

'What on earth's got into you, Pinkie?' He sounded shocked to the core. 'This isn't like you at all. You're usually so sunny and settled. But recently some demon seems to have got hold of you and–'

'I'm bored,' I found myself yelling, tears springing into my eyes. 'Crashingly, stiflingly bored!

'With me?'

'With everything!'

There was a short silence while we both absorbed what I'd just said. I swiped at the tears now spilling down my cheeks, but it didn't stop them silently falling. I'd shocked myself, to be honest; unsure where the sudden burst of emotion sprung from.

'Thanks a bunch,' he stormed, his anger rising to meet mine. 'Perhaps you need reminding, there was one reason, and one reason only, why I agreed to come home and leave you there. And that was because you basically ordered me to. No other outcome was acceptable to you. Remember?'

'So what are you, a man or a mouse?' I shouted. 'You could at least have put up a token fight. Instead, all I get from you is wisecracks about getting locked up in pyramids and pretending to be Lara bloody Croft!'

'So, what did you want instead? His voice was tight and uncharacteristically furious. 'Some grand gesture; that I couldn't go home because I couldn't live without you; even for a few days? Or to give it all up to join you on this crazy treasure hunt you've got yourself mixed up in?' While he fumed I found myself having to forcibly squash a mental image of Adam's scrupulously bland face asking if Dan minded going home without me. I had a sneaking suspicion a grand gesture might be precisely what I wanted. 'Meredith; get a grip! This is real life. Not some Lawrence of Arabia fantasy!'

'And there you go again with your smart Alec comments!' I blazed. 'You simply refuse to take me seriously. Well, I've got news for you! This is real life! I know, because I'm living it. You may be content with the daily grind of work, commuting and cooking, with just the occasional round of golf or pub quiz to liven things up; but I'm not. I want more.'

'So, you are determined to pursue this reckless quest through to the bitter end, regardless of the danger; and hang everything else.'

'I'm not giving up now,' I said mutinously, drying my eyes with the back of my wrist. 'Not until I know what's there. If you knew me at all, you wouldn't ask me to.'

'And where does that leave us?'

'I'm not sure,' I said; and hung up before I let the heat of the moment carry me somewhere I might not like. I'd think about that later.

I stared at my red-rimmed eyes in the bathroom mirror and tried to follow Dan's advice and get a grip. I don't know where the tears came from. And I'm not usually one to pick a fight. His browbeating obviously hit a raw nerve of one sort or another. Poor old Dan; it wasn't his fault. He made very few demands on life, and it rewarded him by never throwing him any curve balls. I wish I could be such an uncomplicated character. But I dare say I'd just thrown him a curve ball; and I didn't want to dwell on it, or ask myself how he was feeling.

* * *

By the time I met Adam later that morning, I was on more of an even keel. I put my falling out with Dan to the back of my mind. A disquieting little voice told me I might have been a little unfair. But something was holding me back from probing it too deeply. For now, I wanted to live in the moment, and leave other considerations to bide their time.

Adam and I decided to start our walk into the Theban hills from the Valley of the Kings, not Deir el-Bahri. It was the most direct route to the sentry post, from where we'd follow the compass to the point where X marked the spot.

We had a bit of kerfuffle at the entrance to the Valley. The gatekeeper demanded to see our tickets to the tombs. Adam explained in careful Arabic we were there to walk, not visit the tombs. The guard looked suspiciously at us, and called over a couple of his chums from the tourist police. I didn't much like the way they kept stroking their big black guns while they looked us over. But eventually it seemed we passed muster, and we were allowed to enter.

We found the footpath marker next to the tomb of Seti I, and started to climb. It was hard going for the first hundred or so metres, but then the path levelled off and we were back in reasonably familiar territory. We skirted the western and southern ends of the Valley, to the southernmost limit, and found the ancient remains of the small stone hut once used as a lookout point by the necropolis guards.

Sun-bleached and barren the landscape stretched away, dry, desolate and more than a little intimidating. Perhaps it was the thought of snakes and scorpions making me think so. Adam busied himself with the contour map and his compass. We left the path, and struck out across the desert rock. The Valley of the Kings vanished behind us, beyond a high rocky outcrop. We were alone in this silent furnace of a place. Well, I say alone. It was certainly just the two of us. But there was also the omnipresent sun. It made an uncomfortable threesome as it beat down mercilessly from above.

It was a treacherous landscape for hiking. The ground was uneven, strewn with stones and more of the fossilised shells we'd noticed yesterday. We were forced to climb a couple of steep inclines then clamber down the other side, using our hands to steady our descent. We'd been walking about ten minutes, picking our way among boulders, sand and shale, and in and out of cracks and rivulets in the rock, when Adam stopped. 'It's somewhere around here,' he announced.

We both scanned the small gully we found ourselves in. Rocky slopes rose gently on either side, leading to a sheer cliff face a few hundred metres away. I looked for a gaping hole in the ground, like the one we'd seen yesterday, which might betray the presence of another tomb shaft. If it was there, it wasn't giving itself away. 'I suggest we tread very carefully,' I said.

Adam studied the map, then the compass, then looked up and narrowed his gaze on the cliff-face. Water-worn for millions of years, and buffeted by the hot desert winds, it had eroded into an intricate pattern of crevices and deep vertical fissures.

'We can't possibly climb up that! Adam, this is madness. It's got to be almost a hundred metres high! Howard Carter might have been quite happy shimmying up and down sheer cliff-faces dangling on the end of a rope, but this is where I draw the line.'

He turned to smile at me. 'Just as well I didn't bring a rope along with me then, isn't it? No, don't worry; I don't think we have to climb it. Although it is a bit reminiscent of Hatshepsut's cliff-cut tomb, don't you think?'

'A bit too much so for my liking; so, do you think that's what it is? Another cliff-tomb?'

Adam squinted in the intense sunlight. 'I'm not sure. No, I don't think so. None of those vertical cracks looks wide enough to conceal an entrance. But look closely. See those deep crevices towards the bottom over there, underneath that slight overhang jutting out above them?'

I peered in the direction he was pointing, following the line of his outstretched arm, and nodded.

'Notice the way they overlap towards the bottom? Do they look like a cross to you?'

I swung an incredulous gaze on him. 'You mean X marks the spot?'

'Yeah, that's kind of what I'm thinking.'

I stared back at the cliff-face. 'If you're right, I'm starting to think our friend Howard Carter had something of the theatre about him.'

Adam smiled, 'Yes, he seems to have had a taste for the dramatic, doesn't he? Come on, shall we investigate?'

We picked our way across the pebble-strewn bedrock towards the base of the cliff. Nervous anticipation crackled through my bloodstream, and my skin prickled with a shivery itchiness that wasn't heat rash. I suddenly had the overwhelming feeling we were being watched. So much so, I swung round and scanned the hillside and ravine behind us.

'It's probably the Gods,' Adam grinned, noticing the movement. 'Or perhaps Howard Carter himself, taking a break from strumming his harp.'

I tried to shake the feeling off, but couldn't dislodge it. It felt like eyes were drilling woodpecker holes in my back.

But every time I glanced back over my shoulder there was no one there.

The crossover in the two long cracks in the rock was at about a man's head-height. It was protected from the baking sun, the burning wind, and the occasional torrential rains by a canopy of rock jutting out in a small ledge a couple of metres above it. Standing on tiptoe, Adam peered at the shadow of the overlap. 'There's definitely a hole,' he said excitedly, and reached out.

'Stop!' I yelled. 'Are you mad, or what? That's exactly the sort of spot I'd choose if I were a cobra intent on an undisturbed daytime nap. I'd check it out with something other than your hand if I were you.'

'Good point,' he acknowledged, and dropped a swift kiss on the end of my nose.

There was nothing so handy as a stick or a bit of driftwood lying about on the barren desert rock. Eventually he drank the last of his litre of water, and used the plastic bottle to tentatively prod at the hole. I could tell by his stance he was ready to spring back ten paces in one giant leap if anything reared up and spread its hood. There wasn't a snake, but a couple of tiny black scorpions scuttled out onto the rock-face.

'See?' I couldn't help crowing.

He conceded the point with a grimace, and dug about a bit more with the water bottle to ensure he'd emptied the hole of its occupants. Finally satisfied it was safe he reached up with his hand. 'I feel like I did when I unscrewed Queen Ahmes from the wall,' he admitted. 'If there's nothing here, I'm not sure I'll be able to bear the disappointment. You might have to send me for therapy.' And with that, he stuck his hand into the hole. What he drew out surprised us both. It was a small metal tobacco tin. We both stared at it. Considering the passage of time, it was in remarkably good condition: just a small line of rust along one join.

'Well, it's not nothing,' I said. 'It's definitely something. I think we can say for sure it was put there by human hand. And we can have a pretty safe bet about whose it was. Beyond that, all bets are off.'

'It doesn't look much like buried treasure, does it? Not unless it's something very small. I mean; it doesn't have to be big to be priceless. Just look at those pectorals we saw in the Cairo museum. Although, to be fair, some of them were pretty big.'

'Adam, you're babbling,' I said gently. 'Why don't we just open it?'

This little operation proved more difficult than it sounded. The lid was pretty much welded onto the tin. Eventually Adam used his belt buckle to prise it off. Inside was a closely folded sheet of paper.

'If this is more hieroglyphics, I'm going to scream,' I announced. 'I really don't think we can call on Ted's good nature a third time.'

But it wasn't hieroglyphics, although the writing was almost as indecipherable. Adam unfolded the paper to reveal a letter. It was written in Carter's own distinctive hand, the ink somewhat faded but legible.

'Oh my God,' Adam breathed. 'I never for a second imagined this.' And with that, he plopped down cross-legged on the sand-blown rock, as if his legs wouldn't hold him up a moment longer. 'A letter from Howard Carter to me.'

I sat down beside him. 'What do you mean, to you?'

'Look, it says "Dear Sir".' His sense of humour hadn't left him, I noted, despite the tense exhilaration of the moment.

'Yes, well that says much about Howard Carter's lack of emancipation, and little for your own judgement. If you think you're going to cut me out of this now, you've got another think coming!'

I was teasing him, but his arm came around my shoulder, and he pulled me snug against him. 'I wouldn't dream of it,' he murmured against my hair, dislodging my straw hat, which slid sideways off my head. I left it, much more intent on sharing the moment, and reading the letter. It took us a while; sometimes pausing for long moments to puzzle over a particular word but the gist of it was this.

Dear Sir,

I find myself impaled on the horns of a dilemma; whether to take this matter with me to the grave, or entrust it to you. Forgive me, sir, I don't know who you are, or the circumstances in which you come to be reading this. Few years may have passed, or many. My name is Howard Carter. I'll place my faith in your having heard of me, arrogant though it may sound.

Perhaps you are reading this now because you have indulged me in the folly of advancing years and followed the little trail I have left. Perhaps you have stumbled across my hidey-hole entirely by accident. I cannot say, but you will know.

By the time you acquaint yourself with the content of this missive it may be too late. My secret may be already revealed. You'll know if this is the case. The discovery of the item on which I am about to confide, bricked up in its wall, is unlikely to pass into the world without comment. There is, in truth, only one place on earth it can have come from. It's a place closely associated with my recent history. If you know of me at all, you'll know to what I refer. So, let me share my story.

It may be known by now that I, accompanied by my close associates, made illicit entry into the place to which I refer above. Just once. There were those who were suspicious at the time. These were my respected colleagues, good men, who toiled with me in impossible circumstances, and knew me well. I suspect knowing me well may place a heavy burden on a man. But I digress. These colleagues were kind enough never to enquire of me directly. But they knew the moment of discovery had just passed, and the officialdom of protocol was about to descend.

Like them, I'll implore you not to judge me too harshly for my aberration of integrity. The excitement that night was without equal. We knew we should not sleep. We knew all too soon the madness would be upon us. And so it proved. The intrusion was to become intolerable.

So, this was to be our one moment alone with the occupant, assuming you know to whom I refer. This, of course, was assuming from our point of view, he should be there. We had to know. And we wanted desperately to make our peace with him; to beg his forgiveness for our trespass, and perhaps introduce ourselves, in a manner of speaking; as indeed we did.

I'm ashamed to confess we removed something from his presence that night. This, sir, is the object to which I refer, the purpose of this communication.

My esteemed patron took this item back to our homeland. The intention was to study it, and bring it back. Our objective, of course, was to return it from whence it came. But fate has a way of charting its own course, does it not?

My esteemed patron returned here to Egypt without the object, believing there to be time aplenty to reintroduce it. Time, sadly, there was not. Not for him.

I was given the task of executor-of-sorts, for his collection soon needing to be sold. I undertook the negotiations on behalf of the widow, a lady I regret I am unable to speak of with affection. The particular item to which this letter refers, being unethically come by, was outside of these negotiations. But, I may assure you it set off negotiations in its own right. The lady refused to hand it over. She disdained to tell me why. She was no lover of my profession, that much I know. Perhaps she saw it as the cause of her widowhood. Or perhaps she felt I may misappropriate the item for some nefarious purpose of my own.

I waited in vain for her to change her mind, delaying the removal of certain items from the original location until the last possible moment. But now it is done, the location is cleared.

I cannot claim to understand the workings of a female mind. I am not acquainted with it. So I shall make no comment on this being the moment she has chosen to return the item to me. She has entreated me to swear an oath I will not reveal it to the world while she still lives. In all fairness, I believe she wants to protect the memory of her husband from any slur. None can support her in this intent more than me. Perhaps had she returned it earlier I could have reintroduced it without any hint of subterfuge. This is no longer possible.

The lady lives, and the location is cleared.

So, this is the conundrum with which I am faced. Do I present this item to an unsuspecting world? To do so is to break a faithfully sworn oath, and call into disrepute my own professional integrity and that of my highly regarded associates. Or do I leave it for later discovery?

I have made my choice. I am not a man to easily break a promise. So I am entrusting the item to you. But I need to know you are deserving of it. So, forgive me, I have one last undertaking for you.

I must entreat you to find my equal one more time. If you have followed my trail to arrive at this intersection, you will know to whom I refer. If you are an accidental recipient of this letter then, forgive me; you may never find yourself the custodian of the all-important item.

Here is my final offering:

"In a place of thwarted dreams, in line with the God, two spirits ascend to the imperishable stars."

I entrust this knowledge to you.

Howard Carter

Chapter 14

'He likes to play the man of mystery, doesn't he?' I remarked, sitting back from the circle of Adam's arm to reflect on everything we'd read. 'He's certainly not one for just coming out with it. It's all circles within circles, wheels within wheels.'

There was an air of barely suppressed elation about Adam. 'I'm not so sure. He's told us plain as day there's something from Tutankhamun's tomb bricked up in a wall somewhere. You've been right one two counts, Merry. First, we're on a treasure hunt. Second, it's for something they took from the tomb on the night they broke through into the burial chamber.'

'I was thinking about that. Isn't there some suggestion there should have been a statue inside the exquisite golden shrine they found? You know, the small one, with the beautiful engravings of Tutankhamun and his wife all over it. There's just a pair of tiny carved footprints inside, and no explanation of what happened to the statue. Carter was always silent on the matter, remarkably tight-lipped, in fact. I was reading about it when we were in the Cairo museum. He never pointed the finger at tomb robbers, but equally he could offer no explanation for the absence of a statue inside what was a bolted shrine. Adam, that statue would be solid gold, and small enough to slip in your pocket!'

'It's a possibility, for sure. But I've got another idea.' The aura of excitement around him was almost palpable. He seemed to be radiating raw energy.

'Don't keep me in suspense. What?'

He shook his head. 'No, I don't want to jinx us. And I might be wrong. But I think a couple of bits of this letter are quite suggestive. Forgive me Merry, if I keep it to myself for now? If we can crack this last riddle we'll know soon enough. I don't want to tempt fate.'

He looked so appealing, hair hotly plastered against his forehead, shirt damply sticking to his chest, clutching the letter in his lap as if it was some sort of talisman, and with such naked hope shining in his eyes, I didn't have the heart to coax him into telling me.

'So, we're looking for another portrait of Queen Ahmes,' I said instead. 'Somewhere on a brick wall, by the sound of it.'

Adam stood up and brushed sand and dust from his trousers. 'Come on; let's get away from this hot-hell-hole. We can try and work it out as we go.'

I snatched up my hat, and followed him. 'That widow-woman sounds like a bit of an old witch.'

'Almina Carnarvon,' Adam said. 'A very rich, rather frivolous socialite, by all accounts; she was the love-child of Alfred de Rothschild, an unmarried member of the fabulously wealthy American Rothschilds. She inherited his fortune when he died. Chances are it was her money Carnarvon used to fund his excavations here. Perhaps that accounts for her hostility towards Carter. Theirs was the typical Victorian society match: she was the American heiress, Carnarvon the English earl. He got her money. She got his title, and a place in the English aristocracy. But I'm not sure it was a love-match. Carnarvon was still warm in his grave when she went scooting off to South Africa to marry her lover. And she sold off Carnarvon's private collection of antiquities with unseemly haste. That's the negotiations Carter refers to in the letter. It was offered to the British Museum in the first instance, but with an impossibly tight deadline to raise the asking price. So it went to the Metropolitan Museum in New York instead.'

'All except one key item.'

'Which wasn't hers to sell. I wonder why she held onto it. And then extracted that promise from Carter. I can hardly see what skin it was off her nose. Maybe she just liked having a hold over him. Anyway, she died in her nineties in 1969, some thirty years after Carter, so he was right not to try to wait her out.'

We plodded on in sun-drenched silence for a while; although I'm sure our thoughts were similarly occupied. Finally, we stepped over the brow of a small incline and the Valley of the Kings hove back into view. A few more paces, and we were back on the cliff path close to the ancient sentry hut. We followed the footpath and skidded back down to the Valley floor, heading straight for the shade of the little rest station opposite Tutankhamun's tomb. Adam replenished our water from the small refreshments stall, and we started to feel human again.

'Read me that clue again, would you?' I asked.

He didn't need to read it. He'd memorised it. '"In a place of thwarted dreams, in line with the God, two spirits ascend to the imperishable stars."'

'You know, there's something awfully familiar about all of that,' I mused.

He turned gleaming eyes on me. 'That's what I've been thinking. So, go on, you first.'

'Well, we started this whole quest to solve Carter's riddles looking at the original Queen Ahmes carving on the wall in Deir el-Bahri. It did go through my mind to wonder whether Carter bricked his artefact up in the wall behind her. But I don't think that can be right. I know they say the best hiding place is in plain view, but with all the restoration work undertaken on Hatshepsut's temple for the last century, surely someone would have found it. And I'm not sure anyone could describe Hatshepsut's temple as a place of thwarted dreams. Quite the opposite, I should think. She must have viewed it as a dream come true. That said; Deir el-Bahri does line up with the God; that was our first line of enquiry, remember? When you said the Temple of Amun at Karnak was equal and opposite Hatshepsut's temple.'

'I remember,' he agreed, blue eyes glinting. 'Although I didn't know we were on a quest or pursuing a line of enquiry at that stage. I just thought you were a delightfully engaging kindred spirit, and I wanted an excuse to get to know you better.'

A warm, fuzzy feeling came over me, and threw me off track for a moment.

'Anyway, go on,' he prompted. 'I'm with you so far.'

I shook the fuzziness away, took a swig of water, and re-focused. 'You told me the Temple of Amun wasn't the only thing to line up with Hatshepsut's temple. You said here, in the Valley of the Kings, on the other side of the bay of cliffs, her tomb entrance was also carved out of the rock on the same axis as Karnak. You also told me the original plan was for the burial chamber to be carved on the same axis, so it would be sited directly under her temple. But the workmen hit a fault in the rock, and had to curve away. Eventually the burial chamber ended up some distance from the original axis.'

He was grinning at me. 'And your conclusion is?'

'My conclusion is that's a thwarted dream by anyone's standards.'

'And the "two spirits" ascending to the "imperishable stars".'

'Hatshepsut and her father Thutmosis I obviously. Didn't you say she arranged burial for them both in the same tomb?'

'I did.'

'And from my understanding of ancient Egyptian beliefs, it was the pharaohs whose spirits ascended into the heavens, to become one with the imperishable stars.'

'And so we're looking for Queen Ahmes equal, where?'

'Here in the Valley, in Hatshepsut's tomb: KV20.'

He let out a small whoop, causing a few tourists to turn curiously in our direction. 'My conclusion exactly! Tutankhamun may have been the one to make him famous, but I've always believed Hatshepsut was the love of Carter's life. He copy-painted every inch of her temple, and he excavated both her tombs. If there was anyone he was going to entrust his treasure to, it had to be her!'

I wasn't feeling quite so delirious. 'Didn't you say her tomb was bat infested, with foul air, and as hot as Hades? You said the workmen's candles melted.'

'Well yes, when Carter excavated it in 1903; I don't think that's the case now. But it's a perfect place to hide something; don't you think? Carter can't have known it back then, but no conservation work has been done on it since he stopped work there in 1904. He must have realised it was of no particular archaeological interest. The walls weren't of good enough quality for decoration because the rock was a soft shale, rather than strong limestone. The few texts he found there were on limestone blocks, which he removed. So it was the ideal place to brick something up and not expect it to be stumbled across by accident. But we do have one small problem.'

'What's that?'

'I read somewhere that the burial chamber was completely flooded, some time in the last twenty years. It's full of debris, and completely inaccessible. So, we'll have to hope and pray Carter bricked up his artefact in one of the corridors.'

I tilted my head to one side, 'You know, I think we have more of a problem than that. You said KV20 has never been open to the public. How on earth are we going to get in?'

It was clearly the first time this little obstacle had struck him. He jumped up and snatched my hand, tugging me after him. 'Let's go and take a look!'

KV20 lies high in the easternmost branch of the Valley, cut into the base of the cliff-face. Standing there, I knew if I could cut a tunnel straight through the rock, I'd emerge on one of the ramps of Hatshepsut's temple on the other side.

We stood and stared at the metal grille firmly welded in place across the entrance. It seemed hopeless.

Adam let out a little puff of breath. 'There is one person we know who might be able to get hold of a key.'

I stared at him in open-mouthed concern. 'We can't possibly ask Ahmed. He's a police officer. We'll lose him his job!'

'Oh, I don't know, I have a feeling he might be game; he's descended from a long line of professional tomb robbers, remember. I'll bet this sort of thing will be right up his street.'

'Are you suggesting we take him into our confidence?'

'I'm not quite sure what I'm suggesting yet. Only that he seems like our only chance of getting inside this tomb.'

* * *

An hour later we were sitting outside a coffee shop in Luxor, swatting flies away while we tucked into a rather delicious vegetable tagine, mopping up the juices with fresh bread baked in a clay oven by the roadside.

'Ahmed, we need your help with a spot of breaking and entering into a tomb,' Adam said baldly.

'So, you have decided to tell all to de lovely lady, yes?' Ahmed favoured me with a beaming mega-watt smile, marred only slightly by his unfortunate lack of a good dentist's attention.

If I hadn't looked away from this disconcerting spectacle to glance at Adam's face, where, admittedly, my gaze was coming to rest more and more these days, I might have missed the warning look he shot back across the table.

But I didn't miss it, and it made me replay what Ahmed had just said. 'What do you mean? Tell me what?'

A quizzical look passed across Ahmed's nut-brown face, and he frowned at Adam. 'You have notd told her?'

Adam wasn't just still; he was positively statue-like.

'Told me what?' I said again, conscious of a little hollow feeling opening up in my chest as my eyes narrowed on Adam's frozen countenance.

Adam sighed. 'I'm sorry to say I haven't been entirely honest with you, Merry.'

My gaze swung from Adam's face, to Ahmed's, and back again. They both looked incredibly uncomfortable. Ahmed was twitching. Adam was avoiding my eyes.

'I think you'd better start talking,' I said woodenly, 'And fast.'

Adam swallowed hard, and looked at me with a pained expression on his face. 'It started the night you broke the Queen Ahmes picture in Howard Carter's house. Ahmed thought you were acting suspiciously, as if you'd made a discovery of some sort. He said you had some kind of light in your eyes. You have to understand; he knows the signs. It's in his blood. He thought there was more to the accidental breakage than you were telling him. But your boyfriend was there. Ahmed described him as a big man in a bad temper.'

My gaze swung back to Ahmed. He was looking rather sheepish, but nodding his head. 'Yes, biga mana in bada tempa.' His accent obviously got thicker when he was feeling guilty.

'Ahmed had no wish to cause a diplomatic incident by falsely accusing you of something and asking you to turn out your pockets. The tourist industry here is badly enough hit at the moment, without him adding to it. But he said you were very quiet and thoughtful on the ride back to your hotel. He told me the story, and asked me to keep an eye on you for a day or two.'

I have no idea what the expression on my face was like at this point, but it brought an apology rushing from his lips.

'I'm sorry, Merry; I know it must sound awful. But Ahmed's my friend, and he asked me a favour. I had no idea who you were. Ahmed's instincts are usually spot on, so I agreed to see if I could find out more. At that stage, I didn't know you were the girl I'd bumped into at the museum. Ahmed and I hung about in the lobby of your hotel until he spotted you and pointed you out. We saw you jump in one taxi, while your boyfriend got into another.' He smiled rather shamefacedly. 'I jumped on my scooter and followed you. I knew you looked familiar, and I racked my brains until I could place where I'd seen you before.'

'So you engineered that little meeting with me at Hatshepsut's temple.'

'Yes. And I'll be honest, Merry, I thought you were acting a bit strangely, too. You seemed to be on a mission of some sort. Especially when you started asking me if I could translate the hieroglyphics around the Queen Ahmes birthing scene. My curiosity was piqued, and I could see why Ahmed thought there was more to you than met the eye. And then you seemed to latch onto something I said about Karnak. I know now, it was the whole equal and opposite thing. But at the time I couldn't account for the way your ears seemed to prick up. The rest you know.'

So much for me being a kindred spirit he wanted to get to know better. 'Does Ahmed know about the scrap of paper?' I asked tightly.

Colour flamed in Adam's tanned face, but he levelled his gaze on mine. 'Yes. I'm sorry Merry, I told him –'

I didn't give him a chance to finish as anger surged through me. 'But we had a pact!' I bit the words out, feeling sick and dizzy, and with red dots dancing before my eyes. 'I made you promise not to tell anyone, specifically Ahmed! And you agreed! And now I find you've been playing me for a fool the whole time!' I jerked my chair back from the table, leaving my half-eaten tagine, and jack-knifed up from my seat. There was no clear thought in my head other than escape.

I heard Adam's shout behind me, and it just made me move faster. I barely felt my feet connecting with the dusty, cracked paving. My only focus was to put as much space between me and Adam and his duplicitous friend as possible. I needed to get away to somewhere I could get my brain functioning normally again. It felt like one moment I'd been standing on solid ground, only to find a pit shaft had suddenly opened up beneath me. Now I was tumbling headlong into a gaping chasm of nothingness, with nothing to hang onto, nothing to break my fall.

I pelted round the corner, ducked between two horses munching greenery in the shade while rigged up to their carriages. I leapt over a steaming pile of horse dung, and made a beeline for the first taxi to come hooting down the street. I threw myself into the back seat, gave the name of my hotel, and sat swamped in perspiration and shock, immune to the discomfort as we bounced over potholes, and the driver crunched up and down through the gears without once seeming to depress the clutch.

Back in the sanctuary of my hotel room, I flung myself facedown on the bed, and surrendered to the riotous turmoil raging through me. For the second time today hot tears slid down my clammy cheeks.

Adam had been taking me for a ride the whole time. My poor brain could scarcely register it; kept batting it away as if rejecting it would somehow stop it being true. The suddenness of the revelation took my breath away. It seemed impossible one minute I'd been excitedly contemplating how to break into a locked tomb, and the next here I was, alone in my hotel room, staring into a dark pit of disbelief. Adam had tricked me, betrayed me; lied to me. And I'd never once, not for a single moment, suspected.

Dan always said gullible was my middle name. He claims it's the reason I'm such an easy target for his practical jokes. I fall for them every time. And this just proved it. Only this wasn't a joke, it was wholesale deception.

And unbelievably Adam was the perpetrator.

I rolled onto my back and stared at the ceiling. I simply couldn't come to terms with it. Images kept flashing before my eyes; mental snapshots of Adam's face; the self-effacing charm he'd first greeted me with; his boyish excitement as we decoded the clues; his wistfulness about his past and hopefulness about his future; his claim that life burst into Technicolor when he met me. A few more tears squeezed under my lashes and trickled into my hair. I couldn't square that whole beaten-up-but-trying-not-to-let-it-show aura, and the flashes of a Boy's Own spirit of adventure of the Adam I thought I knew, with a man who'd deliberately set out to dupe me.

It just went to show what a naïve dolt I was; all bright-eyed and bushy-tailed, and desperate for a storybook adventure of my own. I'd presented myself like a lamb to the slaughter - stupid little innocent. I'd all but come gift-wrapped. And Adam looked into my dazzled, trusting eyes, and swore the silly, Enid Blyton pact I demanded; all the while knowing he'd been set up to trail me by the very police officer I was desperate to avoid.

Dan was right to say gullible. Actually, I was beyond gullible. I was positively suicidal ... which, I guess, was what Dan had been trying to point out all along in his rather oafish manner.

At the thought of Dan, I reached for the telephone. Dan might be rather more prone to hectoring than I'd ideally like, but I knew where I was with Dan. His uncomplicated, between the lines outlook was suddenly just what I needed. Dan represented solid ground. All at once it was an attractive alternative to the shifting sands I found myself on. He'd lecture me on my gullibility, tell me he'd told me so, and ask if I would please now have sense enough to come home. Then I remembered I'd fallen out with him. My hand connected with the receiver, but didn't lift it from its cradle.

I wasn't having a good day. Somehow I'd managed to fall out with Dan and now with Adam too. Everything was unravelling. I dragged myself off the bed, stumbled through to the bathroom, and splashed cold water on my face.

For the second time in a few hours, I stared at my red-eyed reflection. This time, it was with a stinging pain between my ribs, as if I'd been poleaxed. I asked my mirror image where this whole debacle left us.

Adam had Howard Carter's letter. Adam also had his dodgy friend Ahmed on his side; who could somehow square his tomb robbing ancestry with his police officer's badge; and would no doubt help Adam gain access to Hatshepsut's tomb. It hit me square between my bleary, bloodshot eyes: they had no further need of me. I was surplus to requirements - redundant once more; only this time not voluntarily.

My forlorn thoughts were harshly interrupted at this point. The pounding on my hotel room door sounded loud and violent enough to lift the paint off the walls.

My first instinct was to jump into bed, pull the covers over my head and ignore it. I stood undecided for a few moments. But the relentless pounding kept up its assault on the furnishings as well as my eardrums.

'Merry? I know you're in there! We've got to talk. You've got to let me explain.'

Hard to describe how I felt hearing Adam's voice; the little traitorous leap in the vicinity of my chest.

I dried my face with a soft towel, and walked on curiously jerky legs towards the door. All the rooms at this end of the Jolie Ville complex are in ground-floor bungalows. I opened the door to blinding sunshine shielding the beautiful gardens, and the three men standing silhouetted on the doorstep.

Adam had been hammering so hard on the door he nearly fell through it and into me as it suddenly swung back in front of him. He righted himself, and stood staring at me, no doubt taking in the swollen eyes and damp hair. 'Merry.'

It was all he said; just my name. But the depth of meaning and emotion he invested in it nearly had me bursting into tears again.

Behind him, Ahmed loomed like a large, rather rotund bodyguard. But it was the third man who stepped forward. I recognised him as one of the reception staff.

'These men refuse to leave before they see you,' he said, in faulting English, but with a better grip of the accent than Ahmed had achieved. 'I try to call your room extension. But dead tone.' I glanced at the bedside cabinet and realised I'd knocked the receiver off the hook; it must have been when I was dithering about calling Dan. 'I accompany them here to see if you want receive them; yes or no.' He looked at me enquiringly, and I realised this was a question. I wondered if I refused, just how he'd manage to frog-march them away from my door. From the intense way Adam was staring it me, feet firmly planted on the doorstep, it was obvious he wasn't going anywhere. And Ahmed's bulk looked as immoveable as one of the granite Pharaonic statues I admired so much.

'I'll see them.' I muttered. 'But not in here.' The thought of Adam and Ahmed in my hotel room was too unnerving for words. 'I'll come out.' I scooped up my room key, and looked pointedly at their feet to get them to stand back so I could step out of the room. 'Thank you,' I said politely. I smiled at the receptionist. 'I'll see them over there.' I pointed across the manicured lawns towards the Pergola set at the edge of the gardens overlooking the dark waters of the Nile. It was furnished with deep-cushioned wicker sofas, and shaded from the sun by its ornate, bougainvillea-strewn, roof and the canopy of majestic palms swaying gently above it in the imperceptible breeze.

'You want that I send refreshments?' the receptionist asked.

I looked at the sheen of perspiration on Adam and Ahmed's faces. 'No, thank you.' I said firmly. I wasn't hosting a tea party, for goodness' sake!

The receptionist acknowledged my decision, cast a faintly condescending look at Adam and Ahmed and took his leave. He was no doubt heartily relieved to be rid of them, and spared the need to find a handyman to repair the hinges on the hotel room door; much more of that hammering, and they'd have been in serious jeopardy.

With such ridiculous thoughts to occupy me, I managed to lead the way across the gardens to the pergola, where I sat rather thankfully in the deepest part of the shade, choosing a wicker armchair over the deeply padded sofas. My legs still felt vaguely numb, and somehow detached from the rest of me. I stared out across the silent waters of the Nile towards the distant Theban hills beyond the narrow strip of cultivation on the far bank. The cliffs glowed bronze in the early afternoon sunshine; the self-same cliffs where Howard Carter hid his mysterious letter; and stashed whatever it was he found in Tutankhamun's tomb but was unable to put back there. The scene exerted an almost magnetic pull on my gaze; and just as well, because I was determinedly avoiding eye contact with my erstwhile companions. But even so I could feel Adam and Ahmed's stiff rigidity in the same tangible way I could feel the heat. They were both sitting bolt upright alongside each other on the sofa, like two naughty schoolboys expecting the cane.

Adam sighed, and leaned forward, resting his elbows on his knees, hands clasped together. 'Merry, I'm going to ask you to hear me out before you hammer the final nails in the coffin of your judgement on me. I can see how much I've upset you, and I'm truly sorry I let it come to this.'

The appeal in his voice pulled my eyes from the distant cliffs to his face. But I didn't quite trust myself to speak. It was enough. He had my attention.

He looked square into my eyes. 'The first thing I should say is I haven't betrayed our pact; well, not to my way of looking at it, anyhow. I should, of course, have come clean with you from the start, and the need for a pact would have been totally unnecessary. But at that stage I still couldn't be sure you were for real. Once you told me about the scrap of paper and showed me the hieroglyphics I knew we'd been wrong about you. You have to understand; our first thought was you'd taken something from Howard Carter's house on purpose. Perhaps even arranged to be locked up in there deliberately, just making it look like an accident. If there was any chance you were some kind of international thief, a professional con artist, we had to tread carefully. Your knowledge of ancient Egypt seemed too good to be coincidental, and we worked up a theory you were searching for something specific.'

I narrowed my eyes on his face as a sudden thought struck me. I managed to voice it without my voice cracking or faltering. 'Are you a police officer too?'

'Me? Good God no. I'm exactly what I appear to be. A fortyish failed Egyptologist, sitting in the last chance saloon and hoping for a lucky break. It didn't take me long to realise you're exactly what you appear to be too. A lovely tourist unwittingly caught up in the adventure of a lifetime. Even before you showed me the hieroglyphics I already doubted our original supposition. And when you handed them over to me so candidly, I suddenly realised if you'd gone to Howard Carter's house intent on making off with something he'd secreted inside a picture frame, you'd hardly need a buffoon like me to help you decipher them. And I'd attached myself to you, not the other way around. Your reasons for not wanting to come clean about the scrap of paper to Ahmed were perfectly understandable. So I made the pact with you. Later that same night I told Ahmed we were barking up the wrong tree. I told him you'd found a scrap of paper – but not that it was inside the picture frame you smashed. I said there seemed to be a mystery attached to it, and I was going to try to help you solve it. But I'd promised you not to tell him about the hieroglyphics, and I didn't. I've kept that part of the pact until now.'

I looked back at Ahmed. 'Are you going to arrest me?'

He'd been following Adam's confession intently, a deep frown creasing his face. But now he surprised me completely by letting out a shout of laughter. 'Arrestd you? Why would I do dat? You have been giving me de adventure of a lifetime, trying to work outd what is dis mystery Adam refuses to tell to me! You are my friend, no? I do notd arrestd dose who are my friends!'

My gaze swung back to Adam. 'So he doesn't know everything?'

'No Merry. And what you need to know is he's been badgering me all week to come clean with you, especially after he met you the other night. He thought you deserved to be told the truth. That's why, when I brazenly asked him to help us get inside the tomb, he thought I must have confessed. He's figured out we've been following a trail, and for the last few days he's been content to let us get on with it. He knows I'm in too deep to back out now. If he's going to arrest you, he has to arrest me too.'

We sat in uncomfortable silence for a long moment while I digested all of this. I watched a heron stalk along the stone embankment leading to the Nile. Fishermen were out in a small skiff on the river. One of them slapped the surface with a long pole; drawing up the fish from the depths for the other man to catch in the net he swung wide over the dark water. It was a scene as timeless as the Nile itself. 'So, why didn't you come clean with me?'

Adam reached out and lifted my hand into his. I let it rest there, unresponsive and limp. He looked at me for a long time; then sighed. 'I'm not sure really; bad judgement, I guess, and supreme selfishness. And perhaps something about the way you've been looking at me with an expression a bit like hero-worship in your eyes. It's not an experience I've had before. I told you my boyhood fantasy of being Indiana Jones. You've made me feel as if I was living it. It's been addictive, intoxicating, exhilarating; I didn't want it to stop. I'm sorry, Merry; the truth is, it was all about me. Somehow you reached inside me and found the twenty-year-old kid still full of dreams and hopes and plans. I lost him once, and I didn't want to let him go again. I thought if I told you the truth, that I'd started out trailing you on behalf of my police buddy, you'd stop looking at me as if I was your soul mate, and start seeing me as some kind of psycho stalker, who'd just latched onto you as a way of fulfilling his sad boyhood daydreams. I didn't want to take the risk. But if it's a choice between giving up my Indiana Jones fantasy or losing you...' He stalled, and I watched his Adam's apple bounce in his throat at a couple of times. But I still didn't quite trust myself to speak, although whether it was now from the sick sense of betrayal, or something else, I wasn't quite sure. Adam's blue eyes were brimming with an emotion he hadn't quite admitted, and my insides felt a bit like some unseen hand was feeding them through a juicer. Ahmed was watching us, sitting stock still; with his lips pressed together, and a deep frown on his walnut face.

The sprinklers came on in the lawns behind the pergola. The suddenness of them springing to life made me jump, and my hand jerked in Adam's. He gave me a small, sad smile as I withdrew it. 'I've ruined everything, haven't I?' But he didn't give me a chance to reply, and went on, 'I don't blame you. I know how I'd feel if I thought someone wasn't playing off a straight bat. It's the one thing I despise most in others. I can't stand any sort of fraud or treachery. So I can understand you running away. It's what's making it hardest to come clean to you now; knowing I've been guilty of exactly the kind of duplicity I loathe in others.'

There was a deep bitterness in his voice. It gave me the clue he had more to say, so I stayed quiet, waiting for him to go on. He stared out across the Nile for a few moments, his gaze drawn by the same view of the mighty river, the strip of dusty green cultivation on the far bank, then the desert and tawny rock stretching beyond it. It seemed to give him strength. When his eyes came back to meet mine they were lit with a new purpose.

'Merry, I think I need to tell you a bit more about my past. I think it might help you understand my cowardice and bad judgement. I told you my parents died in a car crash, but I didn't tell you the circumstances; or why it cast such a shadow over my and my brother's early twenties.'

'What happened?' I asked, part of me suddenly wishing I hadn't withdrawn my hand from his just now. There'd been something reassuring about the way he'd been holding it. And the deep, instinctive part of me felt he might feel better for it right now, too.

He drew in a deep, measured breath, and I guessed this was something he didn't like talking about; something he kept deeply submerged inside him. 'I don't know for sure,' he said at length. 'That's the worst part about it. Toby – my brother - and me never got to the bottom of it. My suspicion is they were victims of a cunningly contrived fraud. But if so we've never been able to get a handle on it. Any tracks were too well covered. So whether they were on the receiving end of some gross deception, or whether they went in with their eyes wide open, the upshot's the same. They liquefied all their assets, including the house and all their savings, and invested in some South African mining company. They must've believed it was a guaranteed get-rich-quick scheme. It was either a scam or a disastrous error of judgement. Either way, the mining company went bust, taking all my parents' worldly goods with it.'

'Adam, that's terrible!' The words were out of my mouth before I'd even registered them. Ahmed sat forward on the sofa alongside Adam; but my attention was fixed on Adam's face. Adam's eyes never left mine, but I could see he was re-living the memories.

'Yeah, but that's not the worst bit. My Dad couldn't live with it. Whether his own foolishness or the knowledge he'd been duped, we'll never know. He drove his car off a cliff with both him and my Mum inside. They didn't leave a note. So we have no way of knowing whether they made a joint pact to end it all, or whether he just lost the plot in a moment of madness and took her over the edge with him.'

I didn't know what to say. At a total loss for words, I gave in to the instinct urging me to offer him some comfort and reached out for his hand. His fingers closed over mine, but I'm not sure he was consciously aware of it. He seemed caught in the sadness of his loss.

'It was all a bit of a circus for a while,' he went on. 'The press got hold of it, of course. And the police had to do their bit, understandably. Toby and I lived one day to the next in a kind of shellshock. As I told you before, it pretty soon dawned on me that no parents and no money equalled no university for me. Toby was already out in the big wide world, making a name for himself in computing. So I decided to follow suit and sign up for a career with the biggest pay packet on offer. I think I had some reckless notion of getting back everything my parents lost. Of course, it slowly dawned on me it wouldn't bring them back. That's when I started to see I'd sold myself down the river. I spent all my time dreaming about getting back to the one thing I still loved - Egypt. The rest you know. I wouldn't tell you all this; except I hope it helps explain why I feel so bad. I got myself into a crazy situation where I hadn't told you the truth from the start. And then I just kept putting off telling you because I didn't want the Indiana Jones fantasy to end. And now I feel like the worst sort of lowlife imaginable because I realise I'm no better than those pond scum my parents put their trust in. I never set out to deceive you, Merry, please believe me. Knowing you as I do now, you're the last person in the world I'd betray.'

Looking into his deep blue eyes, I believed him. Both his hands clasped mine, and I knew every word was heartfelt and true. 'I'm really sorry about what happened to your parents,' I said quietly.

He squeezed my hand. But he didn't say anything more, and I knew he was waiting for me to digest it all and decide how I felt.

'So, what happens now?' I asked. It was perhaps a dumb question to ask after the emotional intensity of his confession and the way he'd laid himself open to me. But I needed to know for sure before I could completely cast off the doubts, and submit to the spiralling relief and happiness his words were unravelling inside me. I knew I hadn't misjudged him completely. He was still the same mix of Boy's Own adventure and knocked-about-a-bit vulnerability I found so attractive. Perhaps more so, now I'd seen he had king-size feet of clay. I think he was right about the hero worship. And, let's face it; it's never a great idea to put a man up on a pedestal.

'Now I beg your forgiveness,' he said sincerely, 'and appeal to your better nature to let us carry on where we left off. We've come so far along this trail together. Please can we just forget about the despicable circumstances of our meeting? Speaking for myself, it may not have been an accident, but I'm still counting my lucky stars it happened. And that's not because I love the thrill of this treasure hunt we've been on, although that would be true. It's because I'm, well I lo...' He broke off suddenly, and glanced quickly at Ahmed, as if shocked to see him sitting there rapt and statue-like alongside him. I had the feeling he'd forgotten all about the cosy little threesome we made with Ahmed staying so uncharacteristically silent. Whatever he'd been about to say, he modified in favour of his next words. 'All I'll say is this. I wouldn't have missed a moment of it for the world, or for all the treasure in Tutankhamun's tomb.'

There's no doubt about it; I was feeling a whole lot better.

'We're in this together, you and me, Merry; all the way. At least, we are if you'll let me see it through with you. Please?'

I looked into his darkly lashed eyes and the last of my misgivings melted away. 'Oh, alright then,' I said grudgingly. 'But only if you promise to quote ancient texts to relieve the boredom in our prison cell.'

His smile of relief was heartfelt and genuine. He reached forward and pulled me into an awkward sort of hug. 'I promise,' he whispered against my hair; and I had a feeling if it wasn't for Ahmed shifting uncomfortably on the sofa alongside him not knowing quite where to look, the hug might have developed into something else altogether. I was crushed up against his rather damp shirt, breathing in the fresh, slightly citrus scent of his aftershave, aware of very little but a spreading sense of peace.

Ahmed coughed and leaned forward. 'So, everytding it is ok now, yes?'

Adam and I pulled back to grin a bit goofily at each other; and I knew that, yes, everything was ok again. I could surrender myself to the simple joy of getting back on track with how to break into a locked tomb.

'So, you wantd my help to enter dis tomb?' Ahmed leaned forward to peer eagerly into my face, his black eyes snapping with excitement.

While my rampant gullibility was fully expelled where Adam was concerned, I had to admit a few latent qualms lingered about his friend. I looked at his beaming face a bit suspiciously, and decided to sound him out a bit. 'Why would you do that Ahmed? You're risking your job and your livelihood.'

His face cracked into another exuberant grin and he puffed out his chest. 'Once a tomb robber, always a tomb robber, no?'

Despite the gleeful way he delivered this pronouncement, almost as if it was a badge of honour, I remained more than a bit nervous. It was hardly the reassurance I'd been looking for. For a start, I had no intention whatsoever of robbing a tomb. For both Dan, on the 'phone this morning, and now Ahmed to have suggested otherwise was a bit troubling.

'I want to make one thing crystal clear,' I said firmly. 'Adam and I don't know exactly what it is we might find in that tomb, but we're not robbing it. We're just discovering it, ok? And once we know for sure what it is, we can decide the best thing to do with it, and how to extricate ourselves from the whole affair.'

I don't suppose Ahmed knew the word extricate, but it was clear he understood. 'I do notd rob,' he said proudly. 'I am a touristd police. I justd help you wid de discovery, yes?'

He seemed blissfully unaware this was a direct contradiction of what he'd just said. Perhaps he'd meant he had the instincts of a tomb robber, without actually being one.

'Yes, well if you can find a way to make that happen without us all getting into shedloads of trouble, that would be great.'

'Yes, yes, don'td worry. I fix itd for you. I fix itd for tonightd, yes?'

'Will you be able to stand guard for us while we go inside?' Adam asked.

Ahmed wrinkled his face. 'Dat may be more hard. Tonightd I am on dutdy in Luxor at de police stdation. Butd I find a way to open de tomb for you, and maybe I try to meetd you dere later. We can be like de tdree muskatdeers, yes?"

Chapter 15

Booking into King Farouk's suite at the Winter Palace had been surreal. But staking out a spot in the hills above the Valley of the Kings at sunset and waiting for the last tourists to leave and darkness to fall took it to a whole new level.

Adam and I sat in the shade of a rocky outcrop, hidden from the footpath by an overhang in the rock, sipping our water, and letting the nervous tension build.

'You know, if we're caught, we're in deep shit,' I said. 'Are you still sure you want to see this thing through?'

'I've never been more certain of anything in my life.' And he reached for my hand. 'I meant what I said, Merry. I wouldn't have missed a moment. Put the whole you-and-me thing to one side. I told you, Howard Carter has always been a hero of mine. And here I am living a bit of his life. Well that's kind of how it feels anyway. I'm touching things he touched, following a trail he laid, even receiving letters from him. To anyone else it might sound bonkers, but to me it feels like the adventure of a lifetime.'

I was quite happy to go along with his suggestion to put the-whole-you-and-me-thing to one side. It was hovering there, shyly in the background, as if reluctant to intrude and demand attention. We could both feel it. But for now it seemed best to let it bide its' time; waiting patiently to be acknowledged and explored. We had a tomb to examine. And I had one or two other matters to consider. So I let my hand rest warmly in his and concentrated on the other part of what he'd said. 'I feel a bit sorry for Carter,' I mused. 'I can't help thinking that one act of sneaking into the tomb unofficially, and taking whatever it is they took, blighted his whole experience. Perhaps if Carnarvon had brought it back, and they'd been able to return it to the tomb without anyone knowing, he might have been free to enjoy himself. But it seems he lived out the whole thing under a bit of a shadow.'

Adam nodded slowly. 'I think the tragedy was Carnarvon dying when he did. It was barely four months after the tomb opening. He was only fifty-six. Perhaps if he'd stuck around a bit longer the whole story would have ended differently. But then we wouldn't be sitting here today. And, speaking for myself, I'm rather glad we are. I'm hot, and dusty, and uncomfortable, and a little bit petrified of what we're about to do. But there's nowhere on earth I'd rather be.'

I squeezed his hand. 'Carter and Carnarvon are supposed to have quarrelled, aren't they? I wonder if it was because Carnarvon left the item behind in England, rather than bringing it back to Egypt with him.'

'It certainly makes you wonder. Apparently Carter turfed the earl out of his house, so it must have been about something pretty serious; neither one of them ever admitted what. And no wonder, if it was about an item they misappropriated from the tomb. Carnarvon was the one to write the pretty letter of apology. It suggests he was in the wrong. So, yes, their quarrel could well have been about whatever-it-was they took.'

'And to only get it back after he'd finished the tomb clearance, ten whole years later,' I said, feeling Carter's helpless capitulation to a set of circumstances beyond his control. 'That Almina sounds to me like she had a bit of a spiteful streak.'

'Yes, or else she had some other reason for hanging onto it.'

'Such as?'

He shrugged and shook his head. 'I honestly don't know. Maybe once we know what it is we'll find out.'

'Do you still think you have an inkling?'

He smiled and shrugged again. 'Let's say I'm daring to hope.'

'You're turning into as much of a man of mystery as Carter was.'

'Sorry.'

'Yes, well, as you said earlier, hopefully we'll know soon enough. Poor old Carter: getting whatever-it-was back only to have to hide it away again. I think that's why I feel sorry for him. I have this picture of him carefully framing those coded messages in the Queen Ahmes pictures, and writing that letter. It all seems horribly sad, somehow. Despite the drama and mystery of the hieroglyphics and the trail of clues he laid. It's still part of his life's work, handed over to complete strangers, at some uncertain point in the future, with absolutely no certainty of how they'd treat it. I'm not sure he deserved that.'

'So the responsibility falls to us to do right by him,' Adam said vehemently.

And, looking at his impassioned face, I suddenly stopped feeling sorry for Howard Carter. There was no one better on earth he could have entrusted his secrets to than Adam Tennyson. And I hoped that I, Meredith Pink, might in some small way measure up too.

Darkness fell with the swiftness typical to Egypt. There really is no twilight to speak of. Just blazing sunset, and sweeping night-time. The sun took some of its heat with it as it disappeared behind the western Valley, but a balmy warmth remained, soaked up by the rock during the day.

Stars spangled the heavens above us, and I remembered thinking how spooky it must have been for the necropolis guards, keeping watch through the long, ancient nights. I was right. The Valley was an eerie, silent, immortal sort of place in the darkness. Eternity hung heavy in the still night air. The imperishable stars kept watch; just as they'd done for countless millennia. I shivered, and moved closer to Adam's reassuring presence.

He put his arm round my shoulders and I tucked myself in against him.

'Does your boyfriend Dan know what you're up to tonight?' he asked softly.

I couldn't see his face, but I sensed it was a question he felt more comfortable asking in the shadowed, starlit darkness, than in the radiant sunset of earlier. I didn't shift away from him. Somehow it seemed better to answer from within the protective circle of his arm across my shoulders.

'I had a bit of a falling out with him on the 'phone this morning,' I admitted. It seemed a lifetime ago. 'I told him we were going searching for whatever Howard Carter's map was leading to in the hills behind the Valley.'

'And he didn't approve?'

'He accused me of living out at Lara Croft fantasy.'

There was a smile in Adam's voice as he remarked, 'What a pair of wannabes we are! You Lara Croft, me Indiana Jones; between us we're a right couple of dreamers, aren't we?'

'With a shared love of Egypt.' I murmured against his shoulder.

'Which Dan doesn't approve of?' he asked again.

I sighed. 'I'm not sure it's so much that he doesn't approve. I think it's more that he simply doesn't understand my affinity with it. He doesn't feel the magic and the mystery of Egypt the way I do. The whole awesome, time-defying wonder of it leaves him cold. He was ok at first when I said I was staying behind, but this morning he told me I was running headlong into a hornet's nest, and pretty much ordered me to come home.'

'And you refused?' he asked very softly.

'I lost my temper and hung up the phone on him,' I admitted, a bit sheepishly. 'I need to sort it out with him. I don't want bad feeling between us. And it's not his fault I've fallen in lo...' I stopped short, as he'd done earlier. I think I'd been about to say I'd fallen in love with the crazy, exhilarating, intoxicating adventure we were on. But I couldn't be sure. 'I think I owe him an apology,' I added quickly, and a bit lamely. 'I know he was just talking out concern for me. He was frightened a snake would bite me; or I'd break my silly neck falling into a tomb shaft. I think that was how he put it.'

Adam shifted his position, so he could turn towards me, and look full in my face in the starlight. He rested one hand on each of my shoulders. 'Merry, are you absolutely sure you're happy doing this? Dan may be right, you know. We may be running headlong into a hornet's nest. And I'd never forgive myself if a snake bit you, or you fell into a tomb shaft. Forget all that stuff I said earlier about having the adventure of a lifetime. None of it's worth a damn if it puts you in danger.'

I looked at his handsome face, shadowed in the darkness, his eyes gleaming, full of passion and intensity. How I stopped myself kissing him I will never know. 'Do you think we're in danger?' I asked.

His warm hands gripped my shoulders a shade tighter. I think he registered the "we". 'I can't rule it out,' he said harshly. 'And I might not be able to protect you. There's a fair-to-middling chance we could get caught and spend the rest of our lives behind bars. I can't promise the men's prison's anywhere near the women's; so I might not be able to quote ancient texts to you after all.'

I smiled at him, adoring his humour, and the very real anxiety I read in his eyes.

'It's a risk I'm willing to take,' I assured him. 'Lara Croft and Indiana Jones never let a few trifling concerns like snakes, tomb shafts and the long arm of the law stop them; so I don't see why we should.'

A slow smile spread across his features. 'Meredith Pink,' he said with soft sincerity, 'you are a delight and a marvel. I am positively nuts about you.'

'Thank you,' I said politely, and tucked myself back under his arm to hide the broad smile plastered across my face.

We waited a full hour after darkness before daring to move, submitting ourselves to the engulfing silence. Ahmed had assured us the night patrols rarely strayed beyond the entrance gateway in the central Valley. Hatshepsut's tomb was way beyond it at the end of its long eastern branch from the Valley stem. But even so, we moved with the stealth of cats, hearts in our mouths as we crept from our hideaway into the Valley proper.

We didn't dare use a torch, but retraced our steps from earlier in the starlight, until we stood at the entrance to KV20. Adam squeezed my hand, then stepped forward to test the metal grille. With a slight protest of unused hinges, it swung open.

'Nice one, Ahmed,' he breathed, and I could hear the grin in his voice.

Excitement zipped along my nerve endings, and I crept forward to join him. It was as black as pitch inside the tomb entrance, and impossibly hot. We moved forward about ten paces along the first corridor before we dared switch on the torch.

We'd studied the tomb layout on the Internet before coming. It was a series of five long corridors, descending into the bedrock beneath the Deir el-Bahri cliffs. The corridors curved to the east, south, then west again, making a long thin semi-circle leading to the burial chamber, which we knew to be inaccessible.

'Here's where we start praying Carter knew enough about the flood dangers to steer clear of the burial chamber with his treasure.' Adam whispered.

'So, we're looking for something Queen Ahmes related, yes? Somehow I doubt it's going to be a beautifully painted watercolour in a lovely golden frame hung up on the wall somewhere.'

He chuckled. 'Here, take the other torch. Watch your step. The floor's uneven. Just keep your eyes peeled for anything that looks like loose brickwork.'

Our concentration was absolute. We inched forward, pretty much back-to-back. Adam scoured one wall, while I swung my torch minutely over every square millimetre of the other. I had to keep stopping to brush sweat out of my eyes. My tee shirt was sticking damply to me in the same way Adam's shirt clung wetly to his back.

'This had better be worth it,' I muttered. 'How Carter stuck it out, with bat poo to contend with as well, is beyond me.'

'So, consider yourself lucky for small mercies,' Adam smiled grimly. 'Like I said, it makes a good place to hide something you don't want found in a hurry.'

We pressed on again, deeper and deeper into the tunnel of tomb-rock. Soon a sort of dogged endurance replaced our earlier excitement. 'I stopped having fun about an hour ago,' I said miserably, as we neared another curve in the rock. I pulled my water from my rucksack and took a long swig. It was disgusting. Like drinking hot water from a bath tap. But at least it was wet, if not refreshing. It was as I had my head tilted back, with the bottle to my lips, I looked up and saw it, etched in the shadows above my bouncing torchlight. The water bottle dropped out of my sweat-slicked hands and hit the rock at my feet, splashing warm water up my legs. 'Adam! Look!'

He swung round so fast we nearly collided.

'Up there! Look! On the ceiling!'

He swung his torch beam in an arc up to the stone roof above us. There, scratched onto the rock face was the familiar sight of a female face in profile, with a feathered headdress and a vulture head rising from her brow. It was tiny, perhaps ten centimetres square, but unmistakeable.

'But Carter's letter said the object was bricked in the wall,' Adam objected fiercely. 'How the hell am I supposed to reach her up there?'

'Maybe it's not behind her,' I suggested 'Maybe she's looking at it, you know, kind of keeping watch. Look! Those rocks up there above your head look a bit loose, don't you think? The ones she's staring at?'

Suddenly the heat didn't seem so unbearable. The portion of wall I was pointing at was above Adam's height, but within stretching range. He stood on tiptoe, reached up and tugged at the jagged edge of a rock. It shifted; then pulled free in his hand, showering him in a deluge of dust. He spat it out, and wiped his face, smearing dusty tracks across his cheeks.

'Pah, revolting! A lungful of dust and bat poo! I'll remember to keep my mouth closed next time. Pass me my water, will you?' But his voice vibrated with excitement, a notch higher than usual, and gave the lie to his complaining.

Gradually, he pulled one small rock after another from the wall until he'd opened up a space about the size of a laptop. He gazed at me for a moment with his heart and soul in his eyes, and reached into the hole. 'There's something here! But I can't dislodge it! I need to make the hole bigger.'

Which seriously undermined my theory it was the tiny gold statue from the gilded shrine he was about to pull out.

He pulled a few more rocks out of the wall, handing them to me, so I could line them up on the floor at our feet. 'Ok, that should do it,' he grunted, and reached in again. Whatever it was, it needed both hands. He lifted himself up on tiptoes again, reaching forward with both arms, his hands disappearing into the black hole he'd opened out in the wall.

I shone the torch at the opening, and watched spellbound as he pulled a large flat box from the wall. It was about the size of a large briefcase. Closer inspection revealed it was, in fact, a briefcase, well, more accurately a small leather suitcase. Adam lowered it carefully to the floor, and we both knelt down with it, almost reverently, as if in prayer. It had old-fashioned metal clasps, and an expensive look about it; for all that it was dusty and a bit scuffed. I had no doubt whatsoever we were looking at what would now be considered a museum piece from the early twentieth century.

'Open it,' I begged. 'Oh my God, Adam, this is unbelievable.'

Knowing we were about to come face-to-face with a relic from Tutankhamun's tomb, perhaps something touched by him, was unspeakable. It was an object few people had touched for well over three thousand years. Howard Carter himself had put it here; the great archaeologist who'd first stepped across that great chasm of time and brought the ancient world crashing forward into the modern one. This combination of knowledge flooded over me like a tidal wave. It was all I could do to stay upright, on my knees, without passing out.

And that's when I noticed the knife. It was pointing directly below Adam's earlobe.

Chapter 16

My first thought was Ahmed. Never trust a tomb robber; the dirty, double-dealing, double-crossing, duplicitous, law-breaking, treacherous, snake-in-the-grass, rotten-toothed excuse for a so-called policeman that he was. He'd used both Adam and me, playing with us like pawns on a chessboard. He'd set Adam up to tail me when he thought I'd discovered something in Howard Carter's house. Damn his tomb-robbing instincts and his tourist policeman's ability to be on the spot when anything interesting happened. Once he realised Adam was no longer playing informer, the way he'd set him up to do, he'd switched tactics, deciding to simply wait it out until we worked it out, and led him to the pot of gold at the end of the rainbow. And now, since this afternoon's little drama, he'd pretended to be one of the gang, gleefully opening the tomb for us just like a big fat spider luring two unsuspecting flies into its web; of all the low-down, sneaky, underhanded, cowardly, downright objectionable ways to do business; and to be so hale and hearty with it. De tdree muskadeers, my foot! He might not be planning to arrest us. But he certainly planned to rob us.

And that's when I noticed the hand holding the knife wasn't Ahmed's. It couldn't be. It was a white man's hand. And it was shaking slightly.

Adam saw the horror on my face, and swung round. His expression changed from shock when he saw the knife to disbelief when he saw who was holding it. 'Ted?'

'Good evening Adam, Merry, please forgive the intrusion.'

I gaped at him. 'You're asking forgiveness when you're pointing a knife at us?'

And that's when I saw the knife pointing at him. It was a horribly large knife, digging square into the middle of the professor's back, held by a rather evil looking man emerging from the dark shadows dressed in a black galabeya and turban.

'Who the hell is he?' I demanded. Adam was still speechless, rigid with shock.

'He, I regret to say, is my son-in-law. His name is Youssef Said.'

'Why is he pointing a knife at you? And, perhaps more to the point, why are you pointing a knife at Adam?' If there was any pun in the way I framed these desperate questions, it was entirely unintentional.

Ted let out a long sigh, and his hand shook a bit more. This was not a reassuring sight, when the razor-sharp blade of his knife was so perilously close to Adam's neck. 'My daughter married him a little over a year ago. We didn't know his true character then. Believe me, he can be charming when he sets out to be, although his English is not good. But Jessica and I both speak Arabic, so this was no impediment.'

I looked at the deadly-looking knife Youssef was holding against Ted's back and found the claim to charm a bit hard to swallow. As if to prove the point on the Arabic, Youssef snarled something totally incomprehensible and took a menacing step forward.

The professor replied in the same language, but in a soothing tone of voice, which drew a short response, and things returned to something resembling a freeze-frame.

'What did he say?' I asked.

Adam found his voice. 'He told Ted to get on with it. And Ted said if they're going to rob us blind we at least deserve an explanation. What you have to understand about the Arabs is they're a rather formal race, so our new friend acquiesced, but told him to be quick.'

Ted took up his tale. 'Things were very unsettled in Cairo at the time of the revolution. Youssef was hurt in the violence in Tahrir Square and lost his job. My daughter asked if they could come to live with me. I think Youssef was already showing his true colours, and she hoped for my support in calming him. Suffice it to say, this last year has not been the easiest. It was a welcome escape to be invited to Mena House on the day you both came to Cairo.'

'None of which explains the knife,' I said uncompromisingly. 'Sorry, make that knives.'

Ted sighed, and looked deeply uncomfortable; as well he might with a huge blade pricking his back. 'It started when I deciphered the hieroglyphics you gave me. I just knew there was more to the story than you were telling me. You both had this air of suppressed excitement about you. You told me they came from a breakage in Howard Carter's house. It started me thinking. It struck me they read rather like cryptic crossword clues. So I set about solving them. I arrived at Wadjit or Nekhbet, Ipet-Sout, Nebkheperure, Tel el-Amarna, Egypt and Ra. I saw these words might spell out the word WINTER. A few days later, you phoned me from the Winter Palace hotel with more hieroglyphs. I felt it had to be more than coincidence. I deciphered the numbers you emailed me. In the middle of the night I had a brainstorm and saw they were years, all of which bore some historical significance.'

'He's a professor of Egyptology,' Adam muttered in my direction. 'Trust him to make it sound easy when we nearly drove ourselves nuts trying to figure it out.'

'My mistake was talking to Jessica about it. I was sure you must be onto something and I hoped, in time, you'd tell me what it was. Youssef overheard us, and demanded to be told what we were so excited about. I'm sorry to say my son-in-law is not a fine man. I now believe, in fact, he may be a criminal. He threatened us with violence until we told him what we'd been discussing. My daughter is now held captive in his brother's house in Cairo. She will not be set free until Youssef returns. For the last twenty-four hours we've been here following you. We observed your trip into the hills this morning, and knew you'd found something.'

I remembered that overwhelming feeling of eyes drilling woodpecker holes in my back. 'It wasn't the Gods,' I murmured to Adam. 'It was the black devil himself over there.'

'And we followed you here tonight,' Ted finished. 'Youssef's plan is simple. He will relieve you of whatever you have discovered. What he will do then I cannot say. But I hope for my daughter's sake it is nothing too rash.'

I looked at the knife again, and wondered just how much more rash it could get.

The charming Youssef barked out another gush of guttural Arabic.

'What did he say?'

'Unsurprisingly, he wants us to open the suitcase,' Adam muttered disgustedly.

The speechless reverence with which we'd contemplated the suitcase a few minutes ago gave way to an equally speechless dread. Adam and I gazed into each other's eyes in the torchlight searching desperately for options. But with a knife still millimetres away from Adam's neck, options seemed in short supply.

Another snarl emanated from behind Ted.

'I'm sorry about this Merry, but while Adam opens the case, Youssef suggests I should point the knife at you.' He fitted the action to the words and I felt the blade brush against my hair. One small slip was all it would take to dispatch me, with blood gushing from my throat. If I'd felt like passing out a few moments ago, now I'd never felt less so. My connection to life was suddenly on a precious, fragile, gossamer thread. It could be severed in a millisecond on the say-so of some Arabic nutcase. The instinct for self-preservation kicked into overdrive. A powerful rush of energy surged through me. My body jerked, and I think I had some crazy intention of grabbing the knife from Ted and turning it on Youssef.

Adam's voice forestalled me. He'd turned a narrow-eyed look on Ted. His words throbbed with a kind of leashed in fury. 'I understand about your daughter, Ted' he said tautly. 'But if that thug orders you to hurt so much as a single hair on Merry's head, so help me I'll kill you both.'

Looking at him, I didn't doubt it. It's a weird thing to say with knife to your throat, but I felt curiously better. 'Perhaps you should open the case,' I whispered.

Adam looked up into my eyes. 'Merry, if we get out of here alive,' he said softly, 'will you please remind me to kiss you? It's something I want to do very badly right now. No, let's be honest, it's something I've wanted to do very badly almost from the day I met you. Your boyfriend will just have to understand. I can't speak for Lara Croft, but Indiana Jones always gets to kiss the girl. It seems to me very unfair to have come this far, and to feel about you the way I do, without that privilege. We were prepared to take our chances with snakes, tomb shafts and the long arm of the law. But being stabbed in the back my some unknown assassin wasn't part of the plan. So, if we're lucky enough to escape, I just want to put you on notice that kissing you is something I intend to do with all possible haste.'

Impossible to put into words the luminous joy he sent cartwheeling inside me. 'I'll remind you,' I said vehemently.

It was no easy task to work the metal clasps free of their locks. Unsurprising, I suppose. If Carter stowed the case here in 1932, it had been bricked in the wall gathering dust for eighty years. But finally the little latches lifted. I levelled the beam of my torch on the case; glad to see it didn't wobble too much, from either joy or terror. Adam looked up once into my eyes; then concentrated on prising open the lid.

The tomb was a breathless enough place already. But as he lifted the lid, four sets of lungs stopped working as we collectively held our breath. The torch beam rested on a silk cloth lain carefully across the contents of the case. Adam reached out and pulled the silk aside. Underneath were rolls, or more accurately, scrolls of yellowed parchment.

'Papyrus,' Adam breathed, in a voice vibrating with wonderment. 'I dared to hope when I felt how light the case was. Oh my God, Merry, I was right!'

I stared at the scrolls and tried to get my brain to function. 'But ... but they didn't find any papyrus in Tutankhamun's tomb.'

'No,' Adam murmured on a note of sanctity. 'Exactly.'

And I realised the stupidity of what I'd said.

Adam's breath was coming rapidly now and he spoke in hushed, excited tones. 'I wondered, when Carter said Carnarvon had taken it back to England to study. I felt it had to be something with either inscriptions carved onto it, or else something written. And, when he said he delayed clearing certain items to the last possible moment, I thought it was equally suggestive. The last objects removed from the tomb were the two life-size guardian statues that stood either side of the walled up entrance to the burial chamber. Scholars have long thought if papyrus was stored anywhere, it might have been inside the wooden kilts of the sentinel statues. But, of course, none was ever found.'

'Because Carter and Carnarvon had already removed it,' I said on a note of enlightenment, 'and Almina wouldn't give it back.'

He lifted a glowing gaze to mine. 'Not until after he'd cleared the tomb, and it was too late to account for it; oh my God, poor Carter. He's quoted as saying that more fervently than anything he longed to discover papyrus which might cast additional light on the king who, "among all his objects, was still not more than a shadow". He knew full well he'd discovered papyrus. But Carnarvon had taken it out of the country, and failed to bring it back with him. No wonder they quarrelled. Carter must have been livid. Poor man!'

Impossible though it may sound, I think in the awed wonder of the moment, we'd all but forgotten the company we were in. We were reminded of it forcibly when Youssef issued another volley of Arabic. Adam and Ted exchanged a pained look.

'What did he say?'

'He wants to know where the gold is.' Adam said darkly, and looked at Ted. 'Is there any way at all you can down-play this to him, so we stand some chance of getting out of here with our skins and this suitcase all intact?'

Ted was staring into the case with the kind of expression I imagine the shepherds in Bethlehem might have worn when the Angels of the Lord appeared. 'If I've followed everything you've just been whispering to each other, you're saying that papyrus came from Tutankhamun's tomb?'

'It's a long story, but yes.'

'Good Lord Adam, that's beyond imagining,' he breathed weakly. 'It's a prize Egyptologists can only dream about. Imagine the knowledge... Imagine the learning...'

His eyes sparked with a scholarly fever, and I could see the effort of will he was exerting not to drop to his knees to pay homage.

'So, just say something to get that black-robed ruffian off our backs, can you?' Adam said tightly. 'Tell him we're all bitterly disappointed. There's no gold. So can we please pack up and go home?'

Ted wrenched his gaze away from the scrolls, drew in a deep shaky breath, and started to speak Arabic in steady, measured tones. I watched Youssef's face, slightly in shadow, just out of range of the torchlight. Fury swept across it, then he let out a bark of bitter laughter. He fumbled with something in the pocket of his robe, and pulled out a small box. Jabbing a finger towards Adam, he growled out what I can only imagine was a curse and lit a match against the blade of his knife, moving to toss it into the suitcase.

'No!' The sound tore from Adam's throat, anguish sweeping across his face. 'Carter trusted us with that, you bastard!'

We all moved at once. Adam, Ted and I acted on a single thought, to protect the papyrus. Ted and I both flung ourselves forward to slam the lid down on the suitcase. Adam leapt past us and hurled himself bodily against Youssef. The match dropped to the stone floor. It sparked at went out. Ted landed on top of me. My torch skidded away beyond reach, sending a beam of light into the blackness of the tomb corridor. Ted dropped his knife. I grabbed it, wrested myself from underneath him and spun towards Adam. 'Ted, get the torch!' I yelled.

Adam had his hand clamped around Youssef's wrist, trying to force the knife away from the side of his face. There was already a deep gash in his upper arm, dripping blood, where he'd launched himself at the Arab. They were locked in a deadly struggle, evenly matched in strength, bitterly wrestling the breath from each other.

Youssef didn't see me coming. I gripped the bone handle of Ted's knife with all my strength and jabbed the blade into Youssef's hand. He let out a howl, and his knife clattered to the floor. Adam brought his fist in a swift uppercut under the Arab's chin, knocking him backwards into the stone tomb wall. Youssef wheeled back, whacked his head against the rock and subsided onto the floor, groaning.

Adam snatched up the knife, held it to Youssef's chest, and prodded him with his foot. Youssef groaned again. 'He's down, but he's not out,' Adam muttered.

'Now what do we do?'

'Have we got anything we can tie him up with?'

'Here, use my shirt,' Ted volunteered from behind us. He was sitting perched on top of the suitcase pointing the beam of torchlight at his son-in-law's inert frame. He put the torch down, shrugged out his of shirt, and resumed his position, sitting there in his cotton trousers and a neat white vest. He looked faintly comical. But I had no doubt whatever he'd protect that papyrus with his life.

I used Ted's knife to tear long rents in the cotton, then pulled it apart with my hands. I glanced uncertainly from the nasty gash in Adam's upper arm, to the despicable creature at my feet, but decided we really should immobilise him as much as possible.

In the torchlight, I rolled him forward and did the best I could to tie his hands together behind his back. Mission accomplished, I turned my attention to Adam, winding a length from Ted's shirt around his bloody arm and securing it in a tight knot.

Another groan alerted us Youssef was coming to. He rolled over, opened his eyes, hawked loudly, and spat.

'I really should have gagged him,' I muttered. 'I didn't think of that.'

He turned a leering look on me and uttered a string of Arabic obscenities. I didn't need to understand the words to get the general gist.

'Lucky for you, mate, the lady doesn't speak the lingo,' Adam advised him. 'Otherwise I might have to take you apart for what you just said.'

'I'm sorry to say it, Ted,' I remarked. 'But I'm struggling to understand what your daughter saw in him.'

'Don't apologise, my dear. It's a sentiment I share. If it weren't for her, I'd quite happily leave him here to rot. But, as it is, I'm sad to say I need him to release her.'

A sudden sense of the enormity of our situation crashed over me. Here we were in possession of possibly the most earth-shattering relic to emerge from antiquity. We were holed up deep in a stifling subterranean tomb shaft. It was the middle of the night. Guards patrolled the Valley beyond the entrance to the tomb. We were surely up to our eyeballs in trouble. But our most pressing concern was no longer how to extricate ourselves from the situation without a long prison sentence, or how to introduce the papyrus to an unsuspecting world. It was what to do with the double-dyed devil eyeing us with brazen hostility from the floor. How to stop him blowing the lid sky high on us, while we set about rescuing some damsel in distress we'd never even met!

It was at this point in proceedings we spotted the torchlight bouncing out of the pitch darkness of the tomb corridor towards us.

'Ahmed,' Adam and I breathed in unison, and a little spark of hope flared. Perhaps help was at hand after all. I had no idea whether Egyptian tourist police carried handcuffs, although I certainly hoped so. But I knew they carried guns. Perhaps he could march Ted and Youssef back to Cairo, the latter at gunpoint, for the heroic release of the captive damsel. Better still, he might be able to find some trumped up charge on which to toss Youssef the clanger, and throw away the key. I knew this didn't guarantee the villainous Arab wouldn't blow the gaff on us from his cell. But it still seemed the only chance Adam and I might have to be left in peace with our task of creating a convincing story to tell the world.

But the face emerging from the darkness behind the torchlight wasn't Ahmed's.

'Dan?' I squeaked. Of all the day's bombshells, this was the most explosive. I couldn't have been more shocked if a stick of dynamite had blown up in my face. My poor, overwrought brain simply couldn't compute him standing there, larger than life and twice as, well, not ugly exactly, but certainly fierce-looking. I blinked a few times, as if to clear my head of an apparition. But when I looked again he was still there; here, I should say, in Hatshepsut's tomb; not safely back in England where I'd swear he'd definitely been when I'd spoken to him this morning. It was no hallucination. He sliced into my gaping disbelief with a few pithy words, aimed at garnering the few essential facts.

'Bloody Hell, Meredith! What the hell are you playing at? Who's that? And why's he pointing a knife at you?'

It's not often I find myself at a loss for words. This was one of those moments. My gaze swung stupidly from Dan, to Adam's startled face, and back again and I spluttered something incoherent. Getting more of a grip, I coughed to clear the blockage in my throat, and choked out, 'This is Adam, and he's not pointing the knife at me, he's pointing it at him!'

Perhaps, under different circumstances, and feeling a trifle less stupefied, I might have taken a moment to enjoy the look on Dan's face when he registered Adam properly, comparing him against the stereotype he'd been carrying around in his head and realising his mistake. His gaze shifted from Adam to the Arab sprawled on the floor. He took in the dapper little gentleman perched on a suitcase in his vest. And finally his unblinking stare came back to drill holes in me.

'I knew it might be bad,' he bit out. 'I had visions of finding you in hospital with broken bones, or having to shell out a fortune to bail you out of police custody. But I don't think anything quite prepared me for this.' It was clearly not meant as a compliment.

I was starting to regain some of my critical faculties. 'Dan, what are you doing here?'

'You wanted a grand gesture so here it is.'

'What?' I gaped inelegantly.

'After you hung up on me this morning I phoned work and told them I needed some unpaid leave to deal with a domestic emergency.'

As grand gestures went, he didn't make it sound very romantic.

'I drove straight to the airport. You frightened the living daylights out of me! All that talk about tomb shafts and wandering around the hills in forty degree heat among snakes and scorpions and heaven knows what. And then you accused me of basically signing us up for lifetime membership of the cocoa and slippers brigade. Well, I decided something needed to be done. So, here I am; and if it's heroics you want, it looks to me like I've arrived just in the nick of time!'

I didn't quite know what to make of this speech; delivered, as it was, as if he was some kind of wounded soldier taking up arms to defend of his damaged masculine pride. My poor, overtaxed brain was still struggling to grapple with his sudden appearance, here in Hatshepsut's tomb, right at the opportune moment. I'd never suspected Dan capable of magic, but I was starting to wonder. Right now just about anything seemed possible. 'But how did you know where to find me?' I croaked.

'When you weren't at the hotel, I went straight to the cop shop. I bumped into that same police chappie I hooked up with to rescue you last time. Mohammed, was it?'

'Ahmed,' I corrected automatically, still too dazed to take it all in. It seemed too much of a coincidence to be true. But, as I'd noted before, Dan, in the flesh, was definitely not a product of my overstrung imagination. So, I guess flukes do happen.

'Yes, well, anyway, as I was going in, he was coming out. I understand he's in on the act. And very cloak and dagger he was too, dragging me along some cliff path to show me here, rather than coming through the main gates. Fine way for an officer of the law to behave!'

'Where is he now?' I asked, trying to force my befuddled brain back to life.

'He's gone to create some kind of diversion with the guards on the gate. I imagine he pictures himself as a glorified red herring to get you out of here unspotted.'

What none of us noticed while this exchange was taking place was Youssef slowly pulling himself to his feet. He saw his chance for escape in the unexpected distraction of Dan's arrival and all the garbled back-and-forth interrogation; and grabbed it.

Springing forward, he shoved me into Adam, knocking us both off our feet, and bounded into the darkness towards the tomb entrance.

His action sliced through my shocked inertia like a hot knife through butter. My dull wits blazed back to life. 'Don't let him get away!' Adam, Ted and I all yelled in unison.

Something in the urgency of this triple command registered. After only a second's hesitation, Dan swung round and gave chase. Adam jumped up and dashed after him, taking the big knife with him. I grabbed my torch from Ted and took off in pursuit with the torch in one hand, Ted's smaller knife in the other; leaving the poor man sitting on the suitcase in the pitch dark.

I hadn't realised quite how far inside the tomb we'd come. It was an uphill sprint through the long rock-carved corridors, over the jagged, uneven stone floor with the torch bouncing off the walls around me. I stumbled twice, just about saved myself from twisting my ankle, and hobbled onwards.

As I emerged from the tomb entrance into the warm night air, I heard a warning shout, then a sound like ripping fabric. There was a sharp cry, then a dull thud and a cracking sound a bit like a muffled gunshot.

I frantically scanned the darkness, waving the torch in wide sweeping arcs. I crept forward; then spun round at the sound of loose shale sliding down the cliff-face behind me.

Adam and Dan skidded down the hillside, bringing a small avalanche of stone chippings with them. I let out the breath I hadn't realised I was holding in a cry of relief. They were both looking grimly at something just beyond my line of sight behind the tomb entrance. 'What happened?' I demanded.

'I see everytding,' said a familiar voice off to my left. 'It was Wadjit, de cobra goddess. As dis man climbed up de cliff-face, she reared up in frontd of him. I see dis witd my own eyes! She did notd bite. Itd was justd a warning. But dis man, he took frightd. His footd itd caughtd in his galabeya. He tripped, and he fell.'

'He's right,' Dan puffed, wheezing slightly from exertion. 'I was nearly onto him; then something made him freeze. I saw him take a step back. His foot got caught in that robe thing they wear. I shouted out, but it was too late. He tumbled headlong off the cliff.'

We all gathered round the inert body of Youssef at the foot of the cliff. His head was bent at an improbable angle.

'Dis man, he is dead,' Ahmed said sadly. 'He has broked his neck.'

'Oh great!' I said rudely. 'So now we've got a dead body to contend with, just to add a bit of spice to proceedings. As if things weren't already stressful enough!'

A slight shuffling sound at the tomb entrance alerted us to Ted's arrival. He emerged clasping the suitcase against his chest. It looked to me to have a pretty decent handle. That he chose to hug it instead spoke volumes about his feelings for the precious cargo inside. It dawned on me then it would take a stronger person than me to part the professor from the papyrus.

He picked his way across to stony Valley floor to see what we were looking at. 'Oh,' he said. 'Poor Jessica. By which I mean to say, what a relief! But how will I release her now?'

Adam explained in a few short sentences for Dan and Ahmed's benefit who Ted and Youssef were, what they were doing here, and the predicament Ted's daughter found herself in. I listened to it all in a kind of transfixed disbelief; still not quite sure how events had spiralled quite so far out of control. The couple of hours I'd spent with Adam hidden up under the overhanging cliffs above the Valley at sunset seemed a lifetime ago.

'I will fix itd.' Ahmed announced. 'I will go to Cairo, and I will free her from dis bada mana who keeps her prisoner.'

'We need to get out of here,' Adam said pressingly. 'But what are we going to do about him?'

'I will fix itd,' Ahmed announced again. 'I will say I caughtd him trying to break into a tomb, and I gave chase. De rest of de story can be de true one. You, all, go now, yes?'

I suddenly realised we hadn't planned a getaway. Assuming it would just be me and Adam, I guess we'd just thought to creep back along the cliff path and make our way back by either Deir el-Bahri or Deir el-Medina. We hadn't accounted for carrying a suitcase with us, however light. Nor had we anticipated the company of our uninvited guests. It was an unusual time for a stroll over the hills. Adam's arm was oozing blood. Ted was in his vest. We were all sweat-stained and dusty. And the suitcase, being almost antique, was hardly unremarkable. Should we be stopped, it seemed hugely unlikely we'd be allowed to proceed without some searching questions being asked.

We all looked rather blankly at each other while Ahmed swung the metal grille back across the tomb entrance and locked it in place. At some stage, the rocks we'd removed from the corridor wall would be discovered. I could only hope it would be some considerable time in the future.

'You stdill dere?' Ahmed asked, turning back from the gate. And then I think he saw our quandary. 'Take de car,' he said, handing Dan the key. 'You know where I parked itd, yes? On de odder side of de hill?'

Dan nodded, 'I think so, if you set us on the right path.'

Ahmed urged us forward. 'I will fix itd here wid de guards, and wid dis body. Go now. I see you later.'

'We'll go to my flat,' Adam called back over his shoulder, and we started scrambling up the starlit rock path. 'We'll meet you there.'

Adam dropped back to help the professor up the slope.

Dan huffed up next to me. 'Are you ok, Pinkie?'

I still wasn't quite sure how I felt about Dan's unexpected arrival. Deep down, a guilty, niggling little voice was asking if it might just get in the way of the kiss Adam had promised me. 'I will be, when we've got that suitcase safely stowed somewhere,' I said matter-of-factly, deciding to stick to the most pressing matter in hand.

'Was that it then? Was that what all those clues were leading to?'

I nodded.

'Anything worth finding?'

I stopped and turned round. Adam had his arm around Ted's shoulders, gently steadying him. There was no way the professor could see his feet with the suitcase still clutched against his chest like that. My gaze rested briefly on the case, my mind's eye seeing the papyrus scrolls inside. Who could say what secrets from Tutankhamun's world it might reveal?

But it was Adam's face my eyes were drawn irresistibly back to.

Adam looked up, met my eyes and smiled softly.

'Yes' I murmured. 'Definitely something worth finding.'

THE END

Printed in Great Britain
by Amazon.co.uk, Ltd.,
Marston Gate.